"Van Gieson may be the next Sue Grafton."
—*Booknews* from The Poisoned Pen

"Van Gieson writes with a poet's flair for imagery."
—*The New York Times*

"Van Gieson's Southwest is breathtaking. . . . Smart, involving, informative. The author's best to date."
—*Kirkus Reviews*

"[Neil Hamel is] tough, funny and independent, a solid addition to the sleuth pantheon."
—*Boston Globe*

By Judith Van Gieson

The WOLF PATH

JUDITH VAN GIESON

HarperPaperbacks
A Division of HarperCollins*Publishers*

FOR EAMON DOLAN

HarperPaperbacks   *A Division of* HarperCollins*Publishers*
10 East 53rd Street, New York, N.Y. 10022

A hardcover edition of this book was published in 1992 by HarperCollins*Publishers*.

Cover illustration by Jeff Walker

First HarperPaperbacks printing: September 1993

Printed in the United States of America

HarperPaperbacks and colophon are trademarks of HarperCollins*Publishers*

10 9 8 7 6 5 4 3 2

ACKNOWLEDGMENTS

I am grateful to the New Mexico ranchers and biologists who were so willing to share their time and points of view and who might prefer to remain anonymous; attorney Alan M. Uris, my legal advisor; Kevin Lancaster and Romulus and Remus at the New Mexico Supreme Court Law Library; wildlife experts Stephen Bodio and Daniel Malcolm; New Mexico experts Art Judd and Tasha Mackler; my trusted readers Dick Cluster and Irene Marcuse; wolf advocate Dan Moore; Nick Allison, my eagle-eyed copy editor; Alfredo Lujan for checking my New Mexico Spanish; Claire and Richard Zieger and Lincoln Hansel for keeping me abreast of wolf news; and Dora Atkinson for putting me up (and putting up with me) in Santa Fe. Any errors in this book are the author's own.

A special thanks to Pamela Brown and Shaman for introducing me and so many others to wolves and for starting me on the wolf path.

1

It was 104 where I live, in the Duke City, Albuquerque. Heat vapor flattened the hulking gray mountains and made them shimmer. Cars heated up on the interstate, boiled over and fell off. Outside my office a thistle bloomed with poisonous purple vigor. Inside, the swamp cooler wheezed and tried to create the ambiance of a Carlsbad Cavern. The skirts of my secretary, Anna, were rising daily. The clothes of my partner, Brink, wrinkled. When the temperature reached 105 I expected Anna to show up in shorts, and Brink not to show up at all. We sat in the Hamel and Harrison Building, our frame stucco law office on Lead, drinking iced coffee for breakfast—it was too hot for huevos rancheros, too hot for green chiles, too hot for Red Zinger tea, too hot for law, too hot for order, too hot for people.

"Jeez, getta look at this," said Anna, skimming the *Journal*'s front page. "Someone saw God in a flour tortilla."

"Happens every summer," I said.

"And it got so hot in Phoenix yesterday," she continued, "they had to close the airport. The planes couldn't get off the ground."

"How hot is that?"

"A hundred twenty-two."

"Shit."

"Once it's over a hundred what difference does it make anyway?" Brink's fuzzy caterpillar eyebrows humped—they do that when he asks a question. "It's only a matter of a percent, just a degree."

"Yeah? And what's the difference between life and death, reason and insanity, happiness and drugs?" I asked him. "Just a degree."

"Oh, I forgot to tell you," said Anna. "You had a call yesterday from March Augusta."

"Yesterday?"

"You'd already gone home."

"Right." I got up, went into my office, closed the door, lit a cigarette and opened the window where we've installed wrought-iron bars to keep us in and them out. Swampy hot air mingled with desert hot air, but thinking about March had a cooling effect. The last time I had seen him was in November in Fire Pond, Montana. Snow was on the ground and it had gotten cold, but not as cold as it would get. March was a former client, an environmentalist who had been accused of murdering a poacher. He has a great voice, a Western voice, a voice with a lot of space and time in it.

"Neil Hamel," he said, when I got him on the phone. "How the hell are you?"

"Pretty good. I hope it's cooler up there."

"One-oh-two in Fire Pond yesterday."

"A hundred and two in Montana?"

"Makes you wonder about global warming, doesn't it?"

"I do my part. I never use hair spray and I don't drive an air-conditioned car, either."

"I have some good news. Katharine is pregnant."

"How nice."

"And we're getting married."

"Married? Well. Congratulations." You had to expect that sort of thing from men you were attracted to: they got married and they had kids. Happens all the time. They're in motion when you're standing still. Well, whenever I get a twinge of marriage envy, I remember what another Katharine, Katharine Hepburn, said: "If you want to sacrifice the admiration of many men for the criticism of one, go ahead, get married."

"How's *your* friend?" he asked.

"The Kid? He's fine."

"Good. The reason I'm calling, Neil, actually, is to ask your help for a friend of mine, a guy I knew years ago in California. He was pretty radical in those days and the federal government had a file on him a foot thick. He's straightened out now, gotten interested in wolves, and he has an educational program where he travels around the country with Sirius, a young timber wolf. There's a plan in New Mexico to try to reintroduce the lobo, the Mexican gray wolf, near Soledad. Juan's going to be down there next week giving his program."

"Juan? Is he Hispanic?"

March laughed, a good sound, muffled by a thick red beard that I remembered well. "No, but he calls himself Juan Sololobo. Like I said, he's from California. Did you know, by the way, that Sirius is the Wolf Star, the brightest star in the sky?"

"No."

"The Pawnees thought the wolf came out of the spirit world in the southeastern sky every night and crossed the Milky Way, only they called it the Wolf Path."

It was the kind of thing March would know. He'd told me once that Venus was bright enough to be visible during the day but that most of us had lost the ability to see it.

He got back to his business. "Juan has to have a permit to keep a wild animal in every state he visits. Sometimes officials hassle him over this, particularly if they are antiwolf. If they decide the permit is incorrectly filled out, they could confiscate Sirius. It's happened before with other wolves and Juan's a bit paranoid. I was wondering if you would mind going down there to help him out with the permit and just be around if he has any trouble. There's a lot of antiwolf sentiment in Soledad."

"I don't suppose he's the kind of guy who goes looking for trouble?"

"He'd probably say that trouble went looking for him."

Well, if there were no people like that there'd be no work for people like me.

"I told him what a good job you did representing me," March added.

"Thanks."

"Don't mention it."

"What exactly did this Sololobo do in his radical days, anyway? Kidnap heiresses?"

"Robbed a couple of banks. People who robbed banks back then were radical, remember? Now they're the presidents and CEOs."

"And guess who's paying for it? How does Sololobo know the federal government has a file on him?"

"One of his ex-wives got it through the Freedom of Information Act. So, will you go?"

"Well ..." I said.

"Don't worry about the money; Juan can afford it. He figures lawyers' fees into the cost of doing business."

"Well ..." I said it again.

"Have you got something else on?"

I flipped through my calendar—divorce, divorce, real estate closing, divorce. "Not much."

"Well?"

"March, it's 104 here, it was 122 in Phoenix yesterday. Soledad is practically in Mexico. It will be an oven." For once in my life I didn't feel like going anywhere.

"Neil, you're not gonna let a little bit of heat scare you off, are you?"

"I didn't say that."

"Good. Then you'll go?"

"I didn't say that either."

"Give me one good reason why you won't do it."

I had a reason, but a *good* reason? "Oh, all right," I said. "I'll go."

"Great. Juan's first wife, Jayne Brown, has a ranch near Soledad—that's J-a-y-n-e, by the way. Juan's going to be staying there and there's plenty of room for you, too."

I took a look at my clock, which told me I had a closing to go to five minutes ago. "Nice talking to you, March."

"You, too, Neil. Juan will be in touch about when and where to meet him, but you'll let me know how it all works out, won't you?"

"Yeah," I said.

The Kid and I spent the evening on my deck at La Vista Luxury Apartment Complex watching cumulonimbus building up over the Sandias and sipping Jell-O shots. Jell-O shots are a summertime favorite in the Duke City, a mixture of Jell-O and an appropriately flavored liquor: orange Jell-O and Cointreau (or Cuantro, as it's spelled around here), lemon with vodka, lime with triple sec and tequila (a.k.a. Margarita shots). It's a way of having your Cuervo Gold and eating it, too. They're dessert and cocktails together, forget about the dinner. I served them in wineglasses and we sucked them down. As the day came to a close, the clouds darkened, the cicadas screamed, the beat went on, a primitive, insistent undercurrent that was omnipresent in this summer of $15,000 car stereos that pulverized the pavement. It was music that I didn't listen to so I didn't hear lyrics, only beat, not a heartbeat, just a beat, a deep, dark, summertime beat.

"Kid, how many people can there be out there with $15,000 car stereos?" I asked him, since he was an auto mechanic and knew about these things.

The Kid shrugged. "When they're that loud, Chiquita, it doesn't take very many."

That was true. We live in a time in which virility is measured by the things boys are able to buy or steal: the boom of a bass, the power of an amp, the speed of a car, the caliber of a gun, the air in a shoe. Music had become a weapon. Maybe it had always been a weapon, but technology had ratcheted up the escalation, as I recently heard a general say. Technology had made one man's pleasure or power trip or stereo everybody else's pain. It made me think of Jell-O and a simpler place.

"Kid," I said, "remember March, the guy I defended in Montana?"

"Yeah, I remember."

"He called me today." The Kid waited. I told him the news. "He's getting married and they're expecting a baby." The Kid nodded as if to imply that was good for them. "He has a friend he wants me to represent who educates people about wolves. The friend is going to be in Soledad with a wolf next week giving his program and March is expecting some problems about a permit."

"Is *he* going to be there?"

"Who? March?"

"Yeah."

"No. Just the friend and his ex-wife."

"Soledad is very hear the border, Chiquita," the Kid said.

I cut him another shot of Cuervo green, plopped it in his glass. "You've been there?"

He ignored the question, which he tends to when his past comes up. "The wolves that lived down there are the Mexican wolves, the lobos," he said. "They are smaller than the wolf of the north. There are not many left. I hear them sometimes in the Sierra Madres when I was a boy." What he was doing in the Sierra Madres as a boy I didn't know. As far as I did know the Kid grew up in Mexico City, one of numerous offspring of a Chilean father and an Argentine mother, political exiles who disappeared from their country before their country disappeared them. Any extra money he had went back to Mexico still. The Kid threw his head back, faced the sky and howled, a long, eerie cry that was one of the loneliest sounds I'd ever heard. A dog across the arroyo answered back, a dog in La Vista answered him—and this was supposed to be a pet-free complex.

"They have lobos here, you know, in the Rio Grande Zoo," the Kid said when he'd finished howling. "They had four pups in the spring. You want to go there Sunday to see them?"

"To the zoo? On a Sunday?" Zoos reminded me of my childhood and were not among my favorite places.

"Why not?" he said.

We stayed outside a little longer and watched the storm build. It appeared from where we sat to be moving slowly, a formation of rain marching from high country to low, from Rio Arriba County to Otero, from the Sangre de Cristos to the Soledads, from I-25 to I-10. The lightning came first and fingered the Sandias, stabs of light, white, gold, violet bolts hitting the mountain peaks in an electric dance. In a good summer storm—and this was one—the bolts connect in the atmosphere with horizontal flashes. One powerful surge circled the sky. Once the thunder kicked in, it made car speakers seem irrelevant, puny, monaural. The thunder pounded, the rain came fast and hard. The ground doesn't absorb rain in this part of the world; it repels it. In fifteen minutes Civic Plaza would be ankle deep in water, the diversion channels built to control flash flooding would be full and churning and some drunk would likely fall in. The rain crossed Tramway, marched down Wyoming. When it hit Montgomery we went inside, closed the windows and got into bed. The cruising cars rolled up their windows or went home, the thunder and lightning headed south, but the rain lingered. The Kid went right to sleep—he always does—and there was nothing to listen to but the sound of much-needed rain. It felt like a night when bad dreams might not get through the rain, when I wouldn't be reaching for guns in the nightstand or fighting off nightmares of killers like I had been all summer. I went to sleep too.

The Kid and I don't get out together often. We don't have a social life and a circle of like-minded friends. Usually when we're together—and that had been every night lately—it's dinner at my place, then bed. On the nights the Kid worked late playing the accordion, it was just bed. As I'm used to seeing him up close in my living room, deck or bedroom, I forget what he looks like from a distance to the rest of the world. He's tall, long-legged, skinny as a street dog, with thick black curls. *El greñas*, the mophead, they say where he comes from. In the winter he fades but in summer his skin has a warm glow and his hair becomes electric. He was holding it in place with a red José Cuervo bandana that he'd folded into a *cholo* roll. As we walked through the zoo a whole lot of women turned to watch him go. It was enough to make me wonder what I looked like. Had the Kid changed, I asked myself, or did he have some magnetism I'd never noticed before? There was something quick and determined in his walk, the way he held his head, some quality of alertness that attracted attention.

Even without staring women I've never been crazy about zoos. They remind me of grammar school with no recess, marriage with no possibility of divorce, a life sentence in a padded cage. I don't like being on the inside looking out or the outside looking in. I didn't much like childhood either. Zoos are tough when it's 70 degrees, worse when it's 102, but that's exactly what it happened to be when the Kid and I got there Sunday on a vapor lock of a day, a day when your car had to sit and let the gas fumes settle for a half-hour before it would even think about starting up again. The heat made me want to shear the fur from the llamas, remove the polar bears from their chlorinated pool and get them to an arctic floe, go home and crank up the air conditioner.

The Kid led me through a latticework passageway that the sun had burned into a maze of patterned illusion, past the booths selling Kodak, popcorn and pink cotton candy that looked like fiberglass insulation with sugar, on to the place where the lobos lived. We stood on a rise and watched them through a window in their fence. From a nearby cage some South American condors, black vultures with a long wingspan, humped their wings and watched us watching them. The lobos had a large enclosure, bounded by a high coyote fence and shaded by cottonwoods. They were native New Mexicans until they were eliminated from this state. The heat didn't bother them. They were shedding their fur in large clumps and they paced the enclosure relentlessly, wearing vegetation to dust. They looked like medium-sized dogs, with white markings around their faces and dogs' long noses, but they didn't act doglike; there was something uncompromisingly wild in their pacing and their yellow eyes.

"*Mira*," the Kid said. "*El lobato.*"

He pointed toward a mound in the center of the pen, where a pup tugged at an adult caregiver. In a wolf pack only the alpha pair breeds, I knew, but all the wolves participate in raising the young. Three lobos were pacing, the adult and pup stood on the mound, more were resting at the back of the pen in the shade of the cottonwoods, but I couldn't tell how many. They had a way of slipping in and out of vision even when they were standing still.

"You are lucky," the Kid said. "People don't get to see the *niños* very much."

"You've been here before?" I asked.

"Sure," he said. "I like to watch the lobos." Apparently he didn't mind revisiting childhood, but maybe he hadn't had one.

A sign beside the pen told the sad history of the lobo, a widespread and efficient predator in the Southwest for 20,000 years, wiped out in only decades by our federal government. Once New Mexico became a ranching state that was the end of the lobo. By the 1950s they'd been shot, dynamited, poisoned into oblivion. The last known New Mexican survivor was trapped and killed in 1965. The Endangered Species Act was passed in 1973, requiring the government to undo the harm it had done. The lobo was listed in 1976 and in 1982 a recovery plan was approved, but by then the only lobos left were in old Mexico. A few were trapped and brought back here to start a captive breeding program, and now there were a total of thirty known lobos in existence, making them one of the rarest mammals in the world. It would be foolhardy to keep such a limited population in one place, so when pups were old enough to take from their mother, they were transported to other zoos.

I recalled something the sign didn't say. A few years ago a

shipment of pups had been stolen en route from the Rio Grande Zoo to Texas. Now when lobo pups traveled they were escorted by armed guards.

"Do you remember when the pups were stolen?" I asked the Kid.

"I remember," he said.

"Did they ever find out who did it?"

"No. It was somebody in a truck wearing a motorcycle jacket with a black *vizór* over the face like—how you say it, Darth Vader?—and a gun."

"It was a hunting rifle."

"They were not the only ones stolen. More pups were taken in Arizona. Did you know that?"

"No. Who do *you* think did it?"

"Who knows, Chiquita?" the Kid shrugged. "People in this country are crazy."

"They're not in Mexico?"

"They're crazy there, too, but people have more here and they can make more trouble."

"Maybe it was a hunter. The kind of guy who would raise pups to adulthood, set them free and charge his friends $5,000 to come over and shoot them."

"It could be a rancher," the Kid said. "They kill lobos."

"Or someone, maybe, into breeding exotic pets."

"Or one of your environmental people who wanted to free them. If that happened, it's better they take them to Mexico. Lobos are safer there."

"Why?" I asked. "They kill animals in Mexico, too, don't they?"

"Not where the lobos live. That's where the Norteños are and everybody else is afraid to go."

"Who are they?"

"*Narcotraficantes.*"

"Drug dealers don't kill wolves?"

The Kid shook his head. "No. The Norteños are simpatico with lobos; they are outlaws, too."

A little boy about eight years old wearing mirrored sunglasses, holding a cone of cotton candy and looking more like somebody's plump and pampered darling than an outlaw, walked up to the adjacent window, poked a sticky finger through and pointed it at the wolves. "Bang, bang," he said, "you're dead."

2

I saw a TV commercial recently in which an automaker invited me to have a long and meaningful relationship with a car. I'd had a long relationship with an orange Rabbit and what it meant to me was clogged fuel filters, dead carburetors, breakdowns on lonely roads, breakdowns in traffic. As the Kid says, when they get old it's one thing after another. After my friend Lonnie Darmer died, her parents gave me a chance to buy her yellow Nissan and I took it. So far it had been reliable, although a bit heavy with bumper stickers for my taste. I'm not sure it's wise for an attorney to be making so many statements at once: STOP THE UGLY BUILDING, DON'T BUY EXXON, WHIP WIPP, BETTER ACTIVE TODAY THAN RADIOACTIVE TOMORROW, NEW MEXICO NATIVE—that one wasn't even true; I had grown up in Ithaca, New York. I ended up in this state when I went to UNM law school. One day I planned to scrape all the messages off. I also planned to check the tire pressure, wash the car every week and get the oil changed regularly, too.

To get to Soledad I headed south on I-25, the lonesome highway, where you have to drive fifty miles to find gas or food and the billboards show their bare backsides because there's nothing beyond here to advertise. The Rio Grande Valley was a green snake, the land above it was desert; animals inhabited the higher elevations. Clouds made falcon shadows on the mesas, gray mountains loped wolflike to Mexico. There's a 328,000-acre land grant courtesy of a king of Spain here that doesn't appear to have any life on it. It's the kind of land that takes a hundred acres to feed one cow, bare as the moon, but did it get that way before the cattle started grazing on it or after? Some people say that this was once fertile grassland and modern management reduced it to dust, but those are fighting words in ranch country.

I hadn't put the Nissan through its paces yet and it didn't seem to be worth a cop's time to patrol such a deserted stretch of highway, so I took a quick look around and when I didn't see anybody watching I put the pedal to the metal and the rubber to the road: 80, 85, 90. At 95 I lost my nerve. The engine was willing, but the fragile metal body shimmied and bucked.

I slowed down to a conservative 75 and tuned in to Christy Hubbard, the DJ from Socorro. "Now *you* have a nice day," she said, emphasizing the "you" like they do around here. Christy stayed with me from Belen to Soledad, two hundred hot miles, three long hours. Linda Ronstadt was not in the market for a boy who wanted to love only her and James Taylor was sweet baby James again. They stuck with what they liked down here and why not? Nothing else changed; why should the music?

I passed by Socorro, Truth or Consequences and not much else until I came to an eighty-mile string of man-made lakes that seemed unnaturally blue, maybe because there wasn't any green around them, just moon-colored stone. I've heard that people come here on Sundays from miles around to watch the water flow. I got off the interstate at 218 and headed south to Soledad. This was ranching country, the land of 50,000-acre spreads. The few visible houses were surrounded by the bones of yard cars and all the mechanical appliances their owners had ever known. Every ten miles or so I came to a sign that said HARPER'S HEREFORDS or CHAROLAIS, THE FRITZ AND HELEN EWALD RANCH, and a dusty road pointed toward infinity, not a place you'd want to live alone. I passed some of Fritz and Helen's Charolais, big spooky white cattle, precious as Brahmans in India. In New Mexico cattle have rights, too, including the right to roam unfettered. If you want to keep your neighbor's cattle off your property legally, *you* have to put up a fence. After thirty miles of empty highway a couple of long-distance motorcyclists passed me from the opposite direction. They had stuffed animals tied onto their handlebars and wore black helmets and visors pulled down over their faces, Darth Vader visors, like the Kid said. CAUTION WATCH FOR WATER, a roadside sign read, but the dip it guarded looked like it hadn't been wet in a century. COURTESY PAYS, said another, only there was no one to be courteous to.

The road began to climb so subtly that I didn't notice until my ears popped. The soil got redder, the yucca taller, the black volcanic rock of the malpais began to appear. It was August and the tarantulas, known to some as wolf spiders, were on the march. Big fuzzy black and brown creatures, crawling all over the hot highway, they reared up as I approached and took a swing. In the purple distance I began to see the Soledad Mountains that connect with the Sierra Madres at the border. When I reached I-10 I turned west. The Soledads took on definition as I got closer, an exposed spine: rocky, barren, jagged as broken bone. The view was so spectacular that I was glad I had eyes to see it, and so empty that I began to wish for something to fill it up.

When Soledad appeared I was ready. First came the front

sides of the billboards. Jesus was Lord over Soledad, Tom and Patricia Cook had been married for fifteen happy years, 25,000 friendly people welcomed me, motel rooms were only $14.95 a night and American owned, every one. The city was on the west side of Soledad Pass, and, as I crossed over, I saw it spreading its tentacles of McDonald's and Burger King. I'd worked up a big thirst on the highway so I got off at the first exit I saw, got on a secondary road and stopped at the Galaxy Deli. Soledad is only twenty miles from White Sands Missile Range and under the influence.

In spite of its zingy name, the Galaxy Deli was dimly lit and quiet. I poked around in the cooler, picked out a Papaya Punch and took it to the counter behind which a Hispanic man with a long and deeply lined face sat. He wore dark glasses and a long-sleeved khaki shirt. His elbows were on the counter and his chin rested in his hand. He was so still that at first I thought he was sleeping. As I approached, though, he cocked his head and seemed to be sizing me up with antennae that I couldn't see, hearing things about me, maybe, that even I didn't know. He had the preternatural acuteness of the long-term blind, but I wasn't sure he'd want me to notice.

"*Buenas tardes,*" I said.

"*Buenas tardes.*"

"Your Papaya Punches are cheaper here, only fifty cents." I laid the juice down on the counter, handed him a dollar bill. He put it in the cash register and counted out two quarters.

"Where are you from?" he asked. He had a slow, careful voice and a trusting manner. He'd have to be trusting in his position—a blind man handling money. It probably brought out the best in some people, the worst in others. I hoped that if anyone screwed him he just averaged it into the cost of doing business or staying alive, because there's that certain percentage of people who will put it to you no matter how you behave or what you do, whether you trust them, whether you don't.

"I'm from Albuquerque," I said.

"That's a long way away. What brings you to Soledad?"

"I'm a lawyer and a client of mine is giving a program about wolves at the high school."

"They're talking about bringing the wolves back, aren't they?" he asked.

"Yes," I said.

He tilted his head as if he were looking far, far away and motioned me closer. "They've already come back," he whispered. "I can hear things that other people don't and I hear the wolves at night at El Puerto. It's a lonely, lonely sound."

Juan Sololobo had already sent me a copy of the permit in question. I'd looked it over and it seemed in order to me, but you couldn't blame a person with his history for being uneasy. Instead of marching to the Vietnam War he'd gone AWOL, he had told me when I called to say I'd represent him. He got into robbing banks to support his antiwar activities and did time for it. He probably had that extra chromosome buzz common to cons and ex-cons that immediately raises the hair on the back of law enforcement officials' necks, the way a wolf raises the hackles on certain other people's. The way he told it, two outlaws (he and the wolf) had banded together and were trying to find a peaceful and law-abiding way to promote their cause. They hadn't always been successful, he admitted. Wolves brought out the beast in men. Other wolves of his had been set loose, confiscated, poisoned, shot and tranquilized to death.

"How did you get involved with wolves, anyway?" I asked him.

"It started years ago in California," he said, "when my first wife, Jayne, brought a wolf pup home. She was trying to make a pet out of it, but I could see that wasn't going to work so I began educating myself about wolves and then I started breeding them—that's legal as long as you keep them penned up. When I got penned up myself Jayne went on breeding 'em, but she split soon after I got out of jail. I kept the wolves and eventually I started giving the program. Siri is a descendent of Lupe, that original pup. Jayne lives in Soledad now. You'll meet her; Siri and I are going to be staying at her place. You ever been married?"

"Once."

"It's a bitch, ain't it? I get along fine with 'em before I'm married to 'em and after it's over, but when you got that legal arrangement, it gets tough."

It was one way I made a living, severing those legal arrangements—it *was* tough. "How many times have you been married?" I asked him.

"Four." Four marriages were bad enough, but four divorces? Who would want to put oneself or anybody else through that? "I'll always have a soft spot for the first," he said, "someday you may, too."

"Not a chance."

"Jayne was only seventeen when I married her. God, she was beautiful, always knew her own mind, too, even then. I'm kind of sorry we never had a kid. Maybe things would have turned out different if we had."

"What keeps you going?" Was I talking about marriage, wolves or life when I asked that question? I wasn't sure, but he was, because wolves were his real marriage and his life.

"You have to believe in something," he said, "and the wolf is bigger than me ... or them. He's a magnificent animal who deserves better than man has been giving him. Wait till you see the response I get from those kids down there, you'll understand."

Juan Sololobo's program was held in the Soledad High School Auditorium for a group of Upward Bound students who had been sentenced to summer school. I arrived just as the program was about to begin. The auditorium was full of restless teenagers who were there because they were disadvantaged in some way (it was a requirement for getting into the program)—by poverty, maybe, diet, heredity or parental neglect, but not by energy. They'd been blessed when it came to that. They wore jeans and T-shirts and had a lot of hair—they weren't impoverished when it came to hair either. They laughed, they joked, they chewed gum and they weren't for one instant still. Juan was ten minutes late, which gave them a lot of time to get restless.

Finally he entered the auditorium holding a leash that Sirius was pulling. This was my first glimpse of Juan Sololobo and he looked moderately tough, which was about as I had expected. He was medium height for a man, around 5'10". His arms, totally visible because he wore a Levi's jacket with the sleeves ripped off, were well muscled. "He's got cords," one girl behind me giggled to another. "Cordy," her friend replied. Juan's hair was moderately long and moderately gray and it curled around the edges. His stomach probably wasn't as flat as it used to be, but he still looked okay in jeans. His eyes were pale blue and alert but they had a baffled expression, as if he weren't sure how he'd ended up being pulled around an auditorium by a wolf.

"Be cool," Juan said to the room. "Like all wolves, Sirius is very intelligent and psychic. He can feel your energy, so stay cool and calm. If one person in here doesn't like him, or scares him, he will sense it and want to leave. He may come up to you and say hello. If he does, keep your hands calm and gentle, put them out and let him sniff."

He began walking around the room with Sirius, who was as wired as the teenagers. Sirius was only two years old, Juan said, and he liked to play. He was big, a lot bigger than the zoo lobos, and had thick gray fur. His eyes were yellow, slightly slanted and intense. Sirius pulled Juan around the auditorium, walking right up to the kids, sniffing them and climbing across the writing arms of their chairs if he felt like it.

The kids tried to be blasé, but when a full-fledged wolf sniffs your hand and looks you in the eye, it makes an impression. This, after all, was the premier predator, an animal that could run for twenty miles without a break, cover a hundred miles in a day, take out a moose. As Sirius cased the room with every sense alert, he gave the impression that he was operating in a higher physical and sensory gear, that his kind of energy and awareness was knowledge and there were things he knew that we never would or could. After he'd checked us and the room out, Juan led him up to the stage where first wife Jayne, a California blond, was standing. She was about as tall as Juan and wore jeans too. She had long legs, a slender body and breasts that were firm as unripe mangos, the kind of body that after twenty-five takes workouts, silicone and liposuction to maintain. Her eyes were blue, her features even, her teeth perfect, and her long blond hair tumbled over her shoulders. It was smooth, silky, well-taken-care-of hair, but the style should have been abandoned by now. There's a time when Alice in Wonderland hair makes a woman look younger, and then there's a time when it makes her look like she's trying to look younger, and then there's a time when it makes her look old. Jayne was still striking, but too chiseled to be pretty. When her smiles faded, hard lines lingered. Her kind of looks must have been a meal ticket once had she chosen to cash it in, and why wouldn't she? Good looks are like a trust fund established at birth with one catch: if you spent the interest, you'd have to start living on the principal, and if you spent the principal, you'd have to start living—like the rest of us— on your wits.

The wolf bounded across the stage and climbed on Jayne like an old friend. He was big enough to put his paws on her shoulders and wrap a large mouth around her head. Jayne smiled and gave him a hug, which, given his furriness, must have been an irresistible impulse.

"Don't worry, folks," Juan said. "That's just his way of saying hello."

When Sirius climbed off Jayne, she knelt down, picked him up and draped him over her shoulders like a large fur piece. The wolf went limp enough to let her do it. "Now this," said Jayne, "is the only way to wear fur."

"A wolf is a friend," Juan lectured, "not a pet. Unlike a dog, he doesn't care about pleasing you, me or anybody else. You leave them alone in the house and they will pull down everything that moves and pile it up in the middle of the floor. Jayne knows that because she's tried. You can't house-break a wolf either."

Jayne put Sirius down on the stage. As if on cue, he peed and a pungent smell circled the room. The kids giggled as the scent went by.

Juan and Jayne worked well together on this level anyway, and they presented a program that corrected a lot of misin-formation about the wolf. One sign of its effectiveness was that the Upward Bound teens remained still. When the talk-ing was over Juan showed a film with beautiful scenes of wolves in the wild punctuated by heartbreaking scenes of the harm man had done.

At the end of the movie, he stood on the stage with his

hands on his hips. His wary eyes circled the auditorium, but he didn't seem to find what he was looking for. "I hope that movie gave you something to think about," he said. "I won't be a bit surprised if I get hassled after the program by the local sheriff who, I hear, is not crazy about wolves. If anybody wants to stick around and be a witness, your help would be appreciated. Now ... any questions?"

A pale, skinny boy wearing a baseball cap turned backwards and a black Anthrax T-shirt that advertised either a rock group or a livestock disease leapt to his feet so quickly that it looked as if he'd sat through the rest of the program just to get to this. "I got a question," he said. "I want to know why *she* ..." he pointed to Jayne, "won't let anybody go to the falls no more."

Jayne gave the boy a hard smile. "The ranch is still my private property."

The boy was not impressed by smiles, good looks or property rights either. "We've been swimming there since we were kids and the people that owned the place before you never cared about private property."

"Well, I do," Jayne shrugged.

"You got something to hide?" the boy asked.

The bright color in Jayne's cheeks didn't come from blush on. "I have nothing to hide but if I want to keep people off my land I've got the right. The deed has my name on it, nobody else's."

Another boy stood up beside the first one, wearing a similar Anthrax-and-jeans uniform. He had wheat-colored bangs that flopped in his eyes. "It's the only place to swim for fifty miles. We're not members of some country club, you know."

Jayne's charm—like her lip gloss—was slick, bright and starting to wear off. "Get under a hose for all I care. Your rights end where my property begins," she snapped, "and no one gets on my ranch without my permission. You got it?

No one." It may have been an acceptable point of view in California, where every undeveloped piece of land was protected like the gold mine it was expected to become, but Soledad was a long way from California and a long way from gold.

Juan raised his hands. "Hey, folks, come on, lighten up. Siri's picking up on the bad vibes." Sirius had, in fact, begun pacing anxiously. "I'll tell you what, let's all have a good howl to calm everybody down." Juan threw his head back and let out a long, expressive "aaahoooo."

"Aaahoooo," the kids chimed in, louder and louder, entering into the spirit, except for the Anthrax boys who turned tail and walked out.

"Aaahoooo," said I. It beat primal screaming or being yelled at in a crowded motel ballroom by some ESThole. Someday a New Age entrepreneur would probably make a bundle traveling across the country giving howling workshops.

Sirius was not impressed. All howling meant to him was that he didn't have to perform any more, the program was over. He padded to the door and waited to be let out.

"That went well," I said to Juan as we walked across the parking lot toward the battered van that he and Sirius traveled the country in. "I didn't notice anybody in the audience who looked like they were getting ready to arrest you." Jayne followed behind us, holding the wolf's leash and talking to him all the while. A group of Upward Bound students followed her. One of them reached out and patted Sirius.

"He's so soft," the girl said.

"Now remember," Juan answered. "He's your friend, but he's not a pet."

"He's a great guy," Jayne said, "but awfully quiet. Is he always that quiet, Juan?"

"Pretty much," Juan said to her and then to me, "It's not over till I'm out of Soledad. Believe it. The police are too smart to take Sirius away in front of a bunch of school kids. That's why I don't arrive until the program starts and I don't advertise where I am staying, either."

Victim mind? Paranoia? Caution? Wisdom? I hadn't decided yet. Paranoids have real enemies, too, but a sure sign of losing touch is attributing superior intelligence to them. I don't often give small-town law enforcement officials a lot of points for brains; stubbornness maybe, brains no.

When we reached the van, Juan opened up the side door and Sirius leapt in. The back of the van was his home, and chain link separated him from the driver and passenger seats. Juan turned on the engine and the air conditioner. It was too hot to be sitting in a car in a fur coat.

"You'll be staying at the ranch, won't you?" Jayne asked me. "Good. I've got some local people coming over later who Juan wants to educate about wolves." She threw up her hands. "Me, I think it's impossible to change minds around here, but Juan insists on trying."

"You won't know if you *don't* try," Juan said.

"Yeah, well, you don't know these people as well as I do. I've got my truck so why don't you follow me on back to the ranch."

"Okay," I said, but as I turned toward the Nissan, a police car drove up, parked and disgorged the local sheriff.

"Here it comes," said Juan, shaking a weary head. "I knew it."

"Bastard," whispered Jayne.

The sheriff was wearing a cowboy hat, cowboy boots and Ray-Ban aviator sunglasses. There was a lot of him and the exertion of pulling the bulk from one hot place to another was producing sweat—in buckets.

"That's a wolf you've got in there, isn't it?" he said, indicating the van. "You need a permit to bring a wild animal into Soledad County."

I handed it to him. "Here it is."

"And who might you be?" he asked.

"Neil Hamel," I replied. "Juan's lawyer. The permit is in order."

"Um," said the sheriff, replacing his Ray-Bans with a pair of reading glasses and taking the time to study the fine print, the punctuation and the spaces between the lines, too.

"Maybe there's a place for *him* in our program," joked one of the Upward Bound kids.

"Do you think he's smart enough?" whispered another.

The sheriff eyed the kid over the top of his glasses, then went back to his reading. "It's completed all right," he said begrudgingly, "but how do I know that this here wolf"—he looked toward the van—"is the same as this wolf?" he rattled the papers in his hand. "I think I'm going to have to bring him in and have the vet look him over to be sure."

"That wolf belongs to me. You've got no right to bring him anywhere," Juan said.

"It would be an illegal seizure," said I.

"If you don't cooperate I'll have to call the vet in to tranquilize him."

"Tranquilize him?" Juan said. "You mean kill him, don't you? You watch, kids, if he tranquilizes Siri, the next time we see him he'll be dead. 'Too bad we miscalculated the dose,' they'll say. That's the way they work and they've done it before."

The kids hung around the door of the van. "Lighten up, dude," one of them said.

The sheriff sputtered, Jayne looked at her watch, a car flew across the parking lot, spinning gravel as the driver braked to a stop and hopped out. He ran toward us, the cameras hanging from his neck flapping, tape recorder in hand.

"Tom Charleton, *Soledad Times*," the reporter said, pushing the record button.

"I should have known *you'd* show up," grumbled the sheriff.

"It's about time," said Jayne, but she smiled as she said it, the confident smile of someone whose plan had worked. You had to wonder why people so skilled at getting the press and the public for free were wasting their money on a lawyer.

"If you take that wolf I'll be taking photographs of you doing it. If you have it tranquilized, I'll have to photograph that, too," Tom Charleton said.

"Now Sheriff, do you want to see a picture of yourself in the paper tomorrow, taking away the animal who has been an inspiration to these kids who are trying so hard to improve their lives?" Juan said.

"That animal's a troublemaker and a killer," replied the sheriff. "The wolf's no inspiration for nobody except to make more trouble for law-abiding citizens. You keep that animal locked up, you hear. He gets loose and you're going to be answering for it."

"Yessir," one of the students giggled. But it was hard to tell which student. The sheriff tried but he couldn't do it, so he turned on his heel and walked away.

"Thanks, kids, and you, too, Tom," Jayne said.

"It's news," said Tom. "I'd like to come out to the ranch tomorrow and get some pictures of you and the wolf," he said to Jayne.

"No problem," said Jayne. "Call me."

"Aaahoooo," one of the kids started to howl, and another picked it up until they were all howling. Sirius did not answer.

3

Jayne's ranch was close enough to town for her to get in every day if she wanted to and she had a big 4 x 4 truck to do it in. It had the tires and springs necessary to cushion the ranch-road blows. She led the way down her dusty road, Juan and Sirius followed in the van and I followed them. She took the bumps a hell of a lot easier than the elephantine van or the pint-sized Nissan, which had toy tires and no shock absorbers that I noticed. Every rock in the road made a lasting impression on my butt. Jayne sped away while we crawled over the top of one rut, down a valley, up the next. She was putting miles between us, but no one was in any danger of getting lost; the road didn't go anywhere else and the cloud of dust she stirred up would be visible from the next county.

The road was only three miles long, but it felt like a hard thirty. The ranch buildings were a mirage. I could see them (when Jayne's dust storm didn't cloud the view) but it was hard to believe I would ever reach them. It had probably been a completely isolated spot at one time and on two sides it still was; the spiky Soledad Mountains were on the east, the south was ranch desert that rolled across the horizon.

The highway over the pass was probably the northern boundary and the sprawl of suburban Soledad marked the west. To a Californian urban sprawl meant real estate investment and I had to wonder if that was why Jayne had bought the place—the proximity to development. As we got closer it began to look like a desert paradise, the kind of place that Conservation Committees lusted after and that should never be broken up. The house and outbuildings were nestled in close to the mountains. There must have been some water near the house because there were trees shading it, not big trees, but trees. A pen held a bunch of horses and they collected at the near end of it under the trees. Jayne waited while Juan and I parked our vehicles and got out. The air was pure and still, the hundred-mile view went beyond Soledad into the next county. The birds in the chamisa sang a happy song.

"You've found paradise this time, babe," Juan said.

"You know what paradise means to me, don't you?" she smiled and rested her hand, briefly, on his arm. "I can ride every day."

Up close you could see that paradise needed home improvements; the barns lacked paint, adobe slid off the walls of the house. Houses require maintenance, adobes more than most. If you didn't pay attention, a couple of good hailstorms could pelt your walls off, and this was the season for it. This place was a kind of desert paradise, like Juan had said, but it wasn't a place I'd want to live in alone (and I like living alone); too much solitude (I don't consider horses good company), too much work. I didn't know much time Jayne spent in solitude, but I could see she hadn't been doing the work.

Jayne went inside to get ready for the meeting. Juan led Siri over to the tennis court and I followed him. The court, which was hidden from the house by a shed and some trees, was as neglected as the rest of the property. The sagging net was ripped, the all-weather surface had cracked and weeds were poking through. It's a tough weed that can break through pavement and survive without water. The chain-link fence was still intact, however, which made the court good enough for Juan's purposes.

"I always look for a tennis court when I get to a new town," he explained. "It's a great place for Siri to run around and it's about the only place you'll find in most towns that's got walls high enough to hold him. A wolf can jump an eight-foot fence from a standstill." He led Sirius onto the court and shut the gate and the two of them began to play. Juan threw a tennis ball and Sirius chased it. The ball bounced, the wolf pounced like a stiff-legged dog and, like a lot of dogs, although he wanted Juan to throw it again he didn't want to give the ball back. The love Juan had for Sirius was palpable, but it was tough love. He treated the wolf with discipline and respect; he didn't baby him. I leaned my shoulder against the fence and thought about what makes a wild animal so irresistible. A large part of it has to be their furriness. I wondered if it was some deeply buried genetic memory of a time way back when we were furry (or at least hairy), too. When I see fur like that I want to touch it and then I want to bury myself in it.

Off in the distance a dust devil made its way up the road and at the center of the swirling storm was a truck, which became visible once it parked and the dust settled down. It wasn't much of a truck, your basic brown model that had humped a bunch of bad roads. The bed was closed in like a camper. A man stepped out and wandered over to visit. He looked like a cowboy in jeans, boots, a Western shirt—a cowboy with ulcers. He had the sour expression that goes with an acidic stomach. His hair was gray and thin, and he looked to be middle to late fifties, a few years older than Sololobo, about the same height, although more tense and wiry. His skin, which was probably naturally white, was suntanned, deeply lined and weathered. His neck was scaly as an old turtle's. That's the way Anglo skin gets in the Southwest when people don't use sunscreen. His cheek twitched sporadically as if a cricket had gotten under his skin and was itching to get back out. His right hand, scarred and crippled, hung limp at his side.

He offered his left hand to me. "Norman Alexander," he said.

I took it. "Neil Hamel."

"Let's see, you're probably not a rancher so you must be a biologist or an environmentalist."

"Lawyer," I said.

"I suppose they've become as necessary at environmental meetings as everyone else."

"S'pose so."

Juan had walked up to the other side of the fence from where we stood. Sirius chased the tennis ball. I was curious to see how he would introduce himself. "Juan Sololobo," he said, reeling off the name without a trace of embarrassment.

Norman Alexander looked at the wolf. "How old is he?" he asked. "Two?"

"That's right," said Juan.

"They're still quite playful at that age. Where did you get him?"

A suspicious glaze was slipping over Juan's pale eyes. "You're not with the government, are you?"

Norman's cheek jumped. "Not anymore, and even if I were still employed I wouldn't be working for the branch that would bother you. I was a U.S. Fish and Wildlife biologist in Alaska before I retired, and I did a lot of research on wolves. Do you think Jayne would have invited me here if I intended to arrest you?"

"I didn't know that Jayne *had* invited you," Juan said, but he was visibly relieved, relieved enough to open the gate, come outside and shake Norman Alexander's hand. "I've been breeding wolves at my place in California off and on for about twenty years. I try to breed for sociability. This program wouldn't work if I had a wolf who didn't like people."

"I'd get him a companion, if I were you, maybe a dog," said Norman Alexander. In the court the wolf was ignoring us and playing with the ball.

"He's got one, a malamute, but that dog, Io, got into a fight right before we left and he's been laid up. He's been a good buddy to Siri." Juan had brought a chain with him which he used to pull the gate shut. He fastened it with a padlock. "See you later, pal," he said to the wolf. We began walking toward the house. "What's your part in this meeting?" he asked Norman Alexander.

"Scientist," Alexander said.

We walked through the courtyard and into the house. The courtyard had a forgotten ambiance and was as overgrown as you can get in the desert. The gate that led outside hung permanently loose and open. Terra-cotta pots under the portal were filled with weeds. The house itself felt worn out by history. Jayne seemed to be letting time march through the house—in the front door, out the back.

I followed Juan and Norm into the living room, which was large enough for dances and weddings and had a fireplace so big you could walk into it if you wanted to. There was plenty of space for a grand piano and several groups of furniture, but they weren't here. The space was filled with floating flecks of dust. There was a large credenza along one wall with shelves where Jayne appeared to keep her valuable papers. The credenza was made out of ancient, elaborately carved dark wood—the kind of piece that some conquistador had hauled over here from the old country, that belonged in a museum or a Texas lawyer's office. Jayne didn't have the desk to go with it, however, only a card table and some metal chairs. She'd set the card table up for the meeting with a pot of coffee, sugar, cream, cookies, honey and herb teas. The only other furniture in the room was a sofa with lariat-swinging cowboys etched into the wood and two chairs to match. They were collectors' pieces, too, but of a different kind, the L.A. kind, the kind people love for their funk, furniture that belonged in the den, not the living room, or not this living room, anyway.

This room had once been graceful and elegant, I thought, the floors polished and decorated with Oriental rugs. A chain with a bare light bulb that hung from the ceiling looked like it had once balanced a chandelier. Faded pink velvet drapes hung over the casement windows. They reached from ceiling to floor, which made them too heavy to billow, but the windows were open and the velvet did shift position every now and then. The living room walls had probably been museum white once but were darkened by soot except for evenly spaced rectangles where paintings had hung, valuable paintings I imagined, because the one that remained was by an artist I consider the most valuable of all, Frida Kahlo. It made me wonder what Jayne's last husband had been. A gentleman rancher? A drug dealer with good taste? Money (wherever it comes from) enables you to hang somebody else's misery on the wall and suffering was something Frida knew all about.

The painting was smaller than you might have expected from Frida Kahlo, who has a larger than life (and death) presence. It was lit by its own little lamp and it glowed with fierce determination. Frida stared at me intensely, eyes hedged by a thicket of barbed-wire eyebrows. A monkey balanced on her shoulder and a banner waved underneath her with the words ARBOL DE LA ESPERANZA, MANTENTE FIRME. Tree of hope, keep firm. It looked like someone had sold off just about everything of value in the house except this painting, which was probably worth more than the rest of the stuff put together and not just monetarily either.

Juan noticed me standing in front of Frida. "You like that picture?" he asked.

"Yeah."

He shook his head in disbelief. "So does Jayne. What do people like about it anyway?"

I thought for a moment and remembered something the Kid once said about me. "She had balls."

"Jayne says its spirit is that if you're treading on thin ice then you might as well dance."

"That, too." Frida, after all, had had numerous affairs with Trotsky and various others in between bouts of rotten health and unimaginable pain.

"Me, I like to see women smiling," Juan said.

"You're not one of those guys who stops women on the street and says 'smile,' are you?"

"When they look unhappy I do," he said.

Juan pointed the way down the hall to the guest room. The house was shaped like an L. The living room was at one end of it, my bedroom at the other, the walled courtyard in between. The guest room was spare as a nun's cell. It was old and neglected, unlike my place which was neglected and new. This floor was bare, mine was yellow shag. This furniture was old and wood, mine was new and laminated. The room probably had its own ghosts but at least it didn't yet have mine. The window was open; I closed it. I travel light and it took only a few minutes to unpack.

When I got back to the living room three more guests had arrived. Jayne introduced me first to Bob Bartel, a biologist who worked for the U.S. Fish and Wildlife Service in the Soledad area. He was fortyish, well over six feet tall and lanky, with the soft brown eyes of a gentle dog. He wore a short-sleeved pale green polyester shirt, darker green polyester Levi's, a belt with a silver Indian buckle, a bolo. It could have been a uniform, except for the buckle. "Howdy," he said to me.

"Howdy," I replied.

Bartel stood beside a couple whom Jayne introduced as Don and Perla Phillips, owners of the neighboring ranch. "I betcha 'neighbor' doesn't mean here what it does where you're from," Don Phillips said affably.

"You're probably right," I answered, thinking of my neighbors at La Vista whom I never saw but sometimes heard pounding each other into the wall we shared. The only way you'd hear a neighbor out here would be if they called you on the telephone, the only way you'd see them was if they drove up the road.

"Where *are* you from?" asked Perla.

"Albuquerque," I replied. She had the grace not to ask why anybody would want to live there. She was affable, too. Perla was about 5'2" and a little on the plump side. He was medium tall, stocky and strong. They were both rosy-cheeked blonds with fine hair who looked like they ate beef and drank milk.

"Jayne's our nearest neighbor and her house is fifteen miles away as the crow flies," Don said, "a lot further than that by road."

Jayne looked at her watch. "Where is Buddy Ohles anyway?" she said.

"Can't we start without him?" Juan asked.

Jayne shrugged. "He's the ADC representative; he'll want to be heard." She was acting like a conductor who needed to have all her players in place before she could begin the performance.

The ADC or Animal Damage Control, I knew, is a branch of the Agriculture Department. It is known to some as All the Dead Critters because one of its functions is killing animals that are bothering ranchers. Unlike many federal employees, ADC hunters are known for the enthusiasm they bring to their work.

"Mark my words, as soon as you start Buddy will show up," Bob Bartel said.

Jayne looked at her watch again and stood up. "Well, as you all know, the Endangered Species Act requires the federal government to reintroduce species like the lobo, the Mexican gray wolf, that have become extinct in the U.S. The government has come up with a plan ..."

"I hope they printed it on smooth paper," spoke a voice from the doorway of the living room.

Don Phillips grinned. "Once you start talking about wolf reintroduction, you can count on Buddy."

"Damn right," said Buddy. He was a ferret of a fellow, about 5'8", with sharp features and bright little eyes, dressed in camouflage hunting gear and boots, a foot soldier in the war against wildlife.

Jayne ignored him and continued. "The only site that has been offered so far is the White Sands Missile Range. In spite of the testing that goes on there, it is actually not a bad habitat for the wolf. They've got thirty-two hundred square miles, there are plenty of elk and other suitable prey, cattle grazing isn't allowed, there is limited human access."

"The problem is the wolf's not gonna stay on the missile range," Buddy said. "Would you?"

Jayne stared him down and kept on going. "With all due respect to Norm Alexander, Juan has probably spent as much time with wolves as anyone and probably knows as much about the wolf as anyone," she smiled at Norm and then at Juan. Her smiles seemed softer in the evening light than they had in the afternoon. I wondered if she'd put pink bulbs in her lamps. Dusk wasn't kind to Southwestern women, but this was a very dark dusk; a summer storm was moving in. I could already hear the distant thunder. "There has been a lot of misinformation about wolves. Since Juan is in Soledad giving his program at the high school anyway, he'd like to share some of his knowledge with us."

Buddy had moved up closer to Jayne. It's hard to keep a man who's been licensed to kill by the federal government in the back row. "There's only one thing you need to know, a wolf's gotta eat to live and a wolf don't know the difference between a fast elk and a slow elk. That's a cow," he said to those of us who weren't ranchers. "A wolf don't know the difference between the White Sands Missile Range and Don Phillips's ranch. Now if Don here calls me up and tells me that one of those lobos has wandered down his way and is killing his stock, why I'm gonna have to shoot him, endangered species or no, that's the law."

"Is it, Neil?" asked Jayne.

"Yes and no," I replied. "If the lobo is released as part of an experimental population, it is the law. If they come back on their own, it's not. An endangered species that isn't considered an experimental population can't legally be shot for killing livestock without a federal permit. It makes it difficult, if not impossible." I'd been doing my homework.

"You a lawyer?" Buddy Ohles asked.

"Yes."

"Goddamn. You can't even go to the bathroom anymore without a lawyer wanting money to tell you how to do it."

I'm used to hearing my profession maligned, it happens all the time, but by someone who kills wildlife for a living?

The meeting was slipping away from Jayne and she tried to grab it back. "Some of the environmental groups intend to put money aside to compensate ranchers for losses."

Don Phillips stood, hitched up his jeans, smiled slowly and said, "I reckon I can speak to that." He was perfectly at ease, but you'd have to expect that from a rancher. They're well known for their PR skills. Anyone who has seen them in action knows better than to underestimate their effectiveness. They're well organized, too. Ranchers turn out for meetings, shuffle their boots, hold their hats in their hands and get what they want. Their percentage of the population is declining—only 4 percent now—but you wouldn't know it from the impact they have. The mystique endures. "You know my great-granddaddy came to Soledad Country in 1885 and we've been ranching here ever since then," Don said. A rancher can use the word "granddaddy" and get away with it. "A wolf's got a range of up to a thousand square miles. They're good travelers and can cover one hundred miles in a day. They're not gonna stay on White Sands, and I've got the statistics to prove it on my computer, if anybody's interested."

Juan Sololobo reached for his coffee cup, and I noticed that he had L-O-V-E tattooed on the fingers of one hand between the knuckle and the first joint and W-O-L-F tattooed in the same place on the other. He was guzzling coffee like it was beer. People who drink too much coffee often used to drink too much something else, one rush replaces another. Caffeine is a more socially acceptable addiction, but chugging it didn't do anything to erase the impression that Juan was a man with errant chromosomes. He was still wearing his Levi's jacket with the sleeves cut off and his hard-muscled arms exposed, which didn't help either. The outlaw persona was probably more effective with Upward Bound students than with ranchers. He was about to speak but Bob Bartel beat him to it.

"Those statistics don't relate to the lobo," Bartel said. "We've never really had the opportunity to study the lobo in the wild."

Don Phillips continued. "Bloodlines are very important to us. I've got cows that are worth $20,000 and we inseminate them with bulls worth a million. Those cows contain genetics that are not reproducible and have taken us fifty years to achieve."

"Now how are you going to compensate a rancher for a loss like that?" barked Buddy Ohles. "Those cattle are an investment in the future. You gonna compensate for the offspring and the offspring's offspring?"

Perla Phillips had her say. "You know, the wolves were removed once before because they were a problem. If the city people had to live out here with young children like we do, they wouldn't be so eager to bring them back."

"There has never been a documented case of an unprovoked wolf attack against a human being in America," Juan said. "The wolf's got millions of years of genetic coding not to kill humans and it's spent a lot of those years learning to fear 'em, too. It's not gonna start killing now. What animal would want to eat a human anyway? They're the dirtiest, smelliest critter around."

Perla ignored him. "Once those things start roaming around you never know what's gonna happen. Man's got the responsibility to manage the resources God gave us. It says so in Genesis 1:26."

It was getting to be too much for Juan. "You know, the Indians lived in harmony with the wolves and all living creatures until your granddaddies came here with their goddamn bibles."

"You don't believe in the bible? I bet you don't believe in God or the devil either," said Perla.

"I believe in the interrelatedness of all living things," said Juan.

I believed in looking out the window. Wrangling was lawyer's work, but on this trip I'd been hired to take care of a permit, not to settle unsettleable disputes. I tuned out Buddy Ohles's invective, Don Phillips's self-serving propaganda, Perla's preaching, Juan Sololobo's defense and thought about God and the weather. It's no secret that man creates God in his own image. Since the symbol of power in America is a late-middle-aged white man you'd have to expect God to be, too. That's the kind of God who knows all the answers, gives all the orders, expects them to be obeyed and pulls out the thunder and lightning and high-tech weapons when they're not. As for the weather, it happened to be getting a lot darker outside than it ought to be at this time of day and year. Given the kind of fuss the prevailing winds were making, they had to be whipping the road into dust devils, crashing against the Soledads, turning back on themselves like riptides and making a whirlpool around the house. The house seemed agreeable—a place that was accustomed to being trashed by the elements. The occupants were at each other's throats. It made you wonder what purpose could possibly be served by bringing together such disparate points of view about anything, especially the wolf. There didn't seem to be any meeting ground when it came to wolves. Either you loved them or you hated them, either you believed in the devil or you didn't, either you faced your own internal mess or you projected it onto something else and declared war. The wolf was a handy target for man's darkness—it had been for millenniums—but getting rid of them hadn't gotten rid of the darkness.

The windows were open to the restless wind and the velvet drapes shifted arthritically like an old lady trying to get comfortable. A flash of lightning x-rayed the tree outside the window, overexposing its forked limbs. Thunder rumbled. I wondered idly whether this was going to be a rainstorm or hail. Either one is a force to be reckoned with. Rain pelts with a sharp sting, reactivates waterfalls and gets the diversion channels churning, stops cars dead in the road where those CAUTION WATCH FOR WATER signs are located. Hail comes in the size of a pebble or a golf ball. Hail turns heat to hypothermia. Hail flattens gardens, dents cars, causes automobile dealers to sell whole lots cheap. It's fun to watch, if you're inside and don't have a garden or a new car.

Lost in my weather reverie, I was as startled as everyone else when a loud howl came from just outside a velvet-draped casement window. "Aaahoooo," it went, sounding to me like the wolf was at the window. In the circumstances I should have feared more for the wolf than for myself, but I couldn't stop the lizard that clawed up my spine.

"What the ..." Juan said as he jumped out of his chair.

The curtains parted and something shaggy and human-sized stepped into the room. It stood on two legs, wore a carefully crafted papier-mâché mask with pointed ears and yellow eyes, and had a piece of ratty gray fur with a long tail hanging down its back. It made a shadow on the wall much larger than human-sized. The ghost of a Pawnee scout? A Navajo skinwalker? The bogeyman? A sheep in wolf's clothing? It shook its shoulders and the fur shimmied, revealing a pair of Reebok running shoes.

"Charlie Clark," Bob Bartel chuckled, "I'd know you anywhere."

4

Charlie Clark took off the wolf mask, tucked it under his elbow and grinned at us. Once the mask was off, his hair sprung loose. Another mophead, he had hair as curly as the Kid's, but lighter and finer. He looked about the same age, making him mid-twenties, but he seemed younger than that in spirit. The Kid has an old soul—the price you pay for growing up in Mexico. The price you pay for growing up in the U.S.A. may be a soul that is permanently imprinted sixteen. The wolf boy's gray eyes shone brightly behind his granny glasses and he seemed quite pleased with the effect he was having. "Howdy, folks," Charlie said. Perla Phillips, who didn't look the least bit pleased, got up and left the room.

"And now I suppose we gotta listen to the opinion of the goddamn Sahara Club," grumbled Buddy Ohles, "who don't give a damn about our national defense or our mission. Don't give a damn about economics, jobs or anything else that matters to real people."

"Wrong again, Buddy. I'm with Wolf Alliance."

"Why don't you just wag your tail and go on back where

you came from?" Buddy asked. "We don't need your people down here no more than we need wolves."

"I'm a native New Mexican," Charlie replied, "got no other place to go back to."

"Goddamn environ-meddlers. You know the wolves ain't gonna be hanging around White Sands on Sundays waiting for city people to come by and take pictures of 'em. If people want to look at 'em they can go to zoos. That's where they belong. They never were smart enough to survive in the wild anyway."

"The reason they didn't survive in the wild is because you guys did everything but nuke 'em. You would have done that, too, if you'd had the weapons," said Charlie.

"Well, the coyote survived, didn't it?" asked Buddy. *Coyote* is a two-syllable word in Soledad, pronounced *ki-oat*.

"With no help from the ADC. You guys killed 86,000 of 'em last year."

"And we performed a real service to the citizens of this country, too."

"Right. What you got for your trouble is a smarter coyote whose litters get bigger every year to compensate for the losses. You keep this up and the coyote will get so smart, it will pick up your guns and fire back. Ranchers could practice some husbandry techniques: guard dogs, better fencing, night herding, night corralling. They can't go on turning livestock loose forever and expect the rest of us to pay for the losses."

Buddy squinted his eyes and looked close at Charlie Clark. "You got that pale, unhealthy look of a veterinarian. I bet you wear leather shoes, though, don't you?"

"I'm wearing running shoes, Buddy, see?"

"Why don't you run on home?"

Bob Bartel chuckled to himself while this dialogue went on. Norman Alexander looked at his watch. Juan Sololobo stared with dazed disbelief, shifting his coffee cup from one tattooed hand to the other. He was used to being the center of attention and this meeting had taken a turn he hadn't anticipated, although he may have been relieved to see someone else taking the heat. Hail began to fall, bouncing hard as it hit the roof and the ground like golf balls from heaven.

"Shut the windows," Jayne demanded of someone, anyone.

Juan got up, bumped into the coffee table and sent a cup of coffee tumbling to the floor.

"Shit," said Jayne.

"Sorry," mumbled Juan, bending over to pick up the coffee cup.

Don Phillips got to the windows first and wrestled them shut, but not before some hail bounced in. I went over, picked an ice ball off the floor and cradled it in my hand. It took a powerful high-altitude storm to produce something as big and cold as that when it had been a hundred hot degrees a few minutes ago. It was tempting to run outside and cool off, but the hail was hard and would hurt like the ice balls little boys threw at little girls where I grew up. I watched it fall and in a few minutes the ground was white. As soon as it stopped the kids around here (who may have never seen snow) would probably figure out how to put socks on for mittens and start throwing it. Perla Phillips came back into the room, went to her husband's side and whispered in his ear. Don listened carefully and put his arm around her.

Jayne and Juan came up beside me at the window. "I'm worried about Sirius," she said.

"You ought to know by now that you can't baby a wild animal," Juan answered in a weary I've-been-through-this-a-thousand-times-before voice. "Wolves live outside in the Arctic; they're tough. They curl up in a snowstorm, sleep through it, and when it's over they stand up and shake the snow off."

"But those wolves are used to it; Siri isn't and there's no shelter on the tennis court. We should bring him in the house."

"No we shouldn't," Juan growled. "Wolves don't belong in houses." Someone needed to remind this couple that they didn't have to bicker; they were no longer married.

"You could put him in the van," Jayne said.

"No, I can't do that either. He's not going to like being cooped up in the van listening to the sound of hail pelting the roof. That kind of racket would terrify him."

"I want to go out and see how he's doing."

"You can't go out in this."

Jayne watched the hail and the minute it stopped she pulled on a pair of boots and went outside to check on the wolf.

Norman Alexander and Bob Bartel sat on the sofa talking about radio collars. Charlie Clark brushed aside his wolf skin, sat down next to them and made himself an herb tea.

"An activity-monitored collar can tell you within hours if an animal has died," Alexander said. "We had good luck finding them by plane."

"Why don't you insert radioactive disks in their bellies," asked Charlie Clark, "so their shit glows in the dark and you can track it by satellite?"

"Just another way to waste the taxpayers' money, if you ask me," said Don Phillips.

Charlie Clark wouldn't let that go by. Charlie Clark didn't seem like the kind of guy to let anything go by, a born agitator. "You welfare ranchers should talk about wasting the taxpayers' money. You lease your grazing land from the federal government for a quarter of what you'd pay for private land. Every $1.00 you generate costs the taxpayers $1.25."

Don Phillips smiled as if he'd heard that one before and given his answer before, too. "Well, you know that land we lease was pretty sorry land. That's why the BLM took it over in the first place. I don't know that there's anybody interested in it but us. We've been good caretakers."

Bob Bartel, who was in the unfortunate position of having to please everybody, brought the conversation back to wolves. "If we have to radio-collar them and insert radioactive disks in their bellies and if we have to spend money then we'll do it. Under the Endangered Species Act the government has an obligation to try to return the wolf, but we want to do it in a way that will do the least harm."

"It's not going to work here," Norman Alexander said, a firm look replacing his usual sour expression. "It's not going to work anywhere, because there is insufficient heterozygosity in the breeding population."

"That's a matter of opinion," said Charlie.

"I happen to think my opinion is better than yours." Spoken by a person who was male, pale and a scientist besides, a man who was used to having the last word.

Dismissed by Charlie Clark who was also male and pale but thirty years younger. "I don't," he said.

"Well, I know something about breeding and I'm with Norman on that one," said Don Phillips.

Juan Sololobo, who had been standing by the window listening to all this, spoke up. "Well, now you've all said how wolf reintroduction is going to affect you. All I ask is that you think for a minute about how it will affect the wolf. It's a magnificent, intelligent, powerful being that was here long before we were and has every right to be here still. Everyplace wolf reintroduction is mentioned is going to find some reason not to want it, but if those thirty lobos in captivity are not released somewhere soon they're gonna get too tame to go back. And there will be no more wild lobo, only some old zoo animal. Think about that for a minute. The end of a magnificent species that once freely roamed this earth. I can't think of anything sadder. All it would take is just a little bit of adjustment, a little change in your attitude—nothing major—and the lobo could live here, too."

"All right!" said Charlie Clark.

No one else said anything. Now that the storm was over there was nothing to keep them anymore. They all stood up and were preparing to leave when the door burst open and Jayne ran in. Her face was flushed, her hair was wild and her hands were shaking. "Oh, God, this is a disaster," she cried, "a goddamn fucking disaster. Sirius is gone."

It was Juan's worst nightmare come true. He stood still and got so pale you could practically watch the blood draining out of him. He pressed his hands to his forehead for an instant and then he said, "He can't be gone. I locked him in; he can't be gone. Not here, not on Jaynie's property."

But he was. We all went outside and stood beside the tennis court shivering and wondering what to do. It looked like someone had snipped through the chain with a wire cutter. The gate was open, the chain was dangling free, the still-locked padlock had fallen to the ground. The tennis court was empty except for a layer of hail and a yellow tennis ball stuck between the links of the fence. Hail holds no tracks, animal or human, and once it melted there wouldn't be any tracks on the ground either.

Juan, who was too distraught to think clearly, ran around calling out "Siri," but like he'd said, Sirius was a wolf, not a pet, and there was no answer. Norman Alexander and Bob Bartel analyzed what a wolf in that situation would do. Run away, was their opinion. Buddy Ohles analyzed how he would track him. Don Phillips worried about his cattle, Charlie Clark worried about the wolf.

I thought about means, motive and opportunity. A wire

cutter wasn't hard to come by—it could be purchased in any hardware store—and it could this very minute be sitting in any one of a number of vehicles parked in the driveway. But I wasn't a cop and I didn't have the right to look. I put motive aside for a moment and moved on to opportunity, to who had arrived late: Buddy Ohles and Charlie Clark. Who had left the room: Perla Phillips and Jayne Brown.

Jayne went inside and dialed 911 and was told that Sheriff Ohweiler would come by in the morning. It got dark soon and everybody went home. Those of us who remained at the ranch had a restless night. Juan and Jayne stayed outside and howled for Siri. Around midnight I went to the guest room, took my old friend Cuervo Gold from my bag and had a hit. Then I got into bed and tried to sleep even though I know that sleep—like sex—isn't something you can try for. You have to just let go and let it happen, but wakefulness was a vise that had been squeezing me between its fingers. It wasn't the howling or worrying about Sirius that kept me from sleeping, although I couldn't help listening for the difference in pitch that might indicate the response of a real wolf. Howling was better than the sounds I was used to: pounding stereos, screaming cicadas, air conditioner hum, sounds operating on a frequency that pushed at the limits of the sanity envelope.

It was the expectation of a bad dream that had been keeping me awake, but after a while the desert air (which always cools down at night) and the howling had a soothing effect. I fell into a real sleep, and I didn't dream about people who smiled as they killed, either. It hadn't hurt at all to put some distance between me and Albuquerque. I dreamed the dreams I used to have, dreams of the opposite. In the desert I dream of rain forests and waterfalls. In the city I dream of space. When I'm alone I dream of the Kid, when I'm with the

Kid I dream of being alone. I woke up once during the night layered in black velvet. It was dead quiet, the kind of quiet that sucks sound in and swallows it up. Expecting the Kid to be lying next to me guarding my dreams like he had been lately, I reached out for his shoulder but it wasn't there. I felt quickly all over the bed and found nothing but an unslept-on pillow and then I remembered I was in Soledad alone. That was why it was so quiet. I listened to the silence wondering what had woken me, relieved it wasn't my bad dream, although it might have been someone else's.

The quiet was broken by a sob that came from the adjacent bedroom, followed shortly by another. The sobs were harsh, irregular, painful, wrenched straight from the gut, the sobs of someone who didn't know how to cry, a man. A good cry has a steady flow, but he was fighting it, not letting the tears come and go. That's the kind of cry that gets rid of nothing, that would leave him feeling like shit in the morning and left me feeling like a voyeur now.

"Oh, Jaynie, Jaynie, Jaynie," Juan Sololobo cried, "if I lose this wolf, too, it'll kill me."

"Shh," she said and began to comfort him in the way she wanted to or knew how. When I heard the bed creaking softly and rhythmically, I turned my back and pulled a pillow over my head. Sex could be an expression of many things, I thought. One, which I hadn't really considered before, was comfort.

"I hope *you* got some sleep anyway," Juan said over breakfast—a bowl of granola and a banana.

"More than I've had since spring," I replied. Jayne hadn't gotten up yet but Juan had and he sat across from me at the kitchen table. He picked up the skim milk carton, sniffed to make sure the milk hadn't gone sour and poured it over his granola. He looked terrible. His skin sagged like unset concrete, shadows hung under his eyes. I could imagine how he felt, too, physically and emotionally—losing a beloved animal ranks way up there on the life sucks list. A crying hangover may have been news to him, but I doubt if there's any female in America who gets as far as high school without knowing how it feels the morning after: ragged nerves, a stuffed-up head, dry, puffy eyes, emotions that are drained like life had pulled the plug. Juan had gotten up before anyone, made a pot of coffee and was already on his third cup. He'd been outside and circled the house a couple of times, too, he told me, and seen no sign of the wolf.

By the time I got to my coffee I needed a cigarette. "Do you mind?" I asked Juan, pulling my Marlboros out.

He shook his head no, hesitated for a minute, then said, "Let me try one."

I lit it for him, then lit my own and took a couple of deep wake-up drags. The minute he inhaled he started to cough and continued to cough until I punched him on the back. He ground the cigarette out. "Ugh," he said. "I haven't had one of those things in years. Thought it would help. Maybe there's nothing that will help."

I wasn't averse to a shot of Cuervo Gold in my morning coffee myself and I had the bottle in my room, but I didn't suggest it. If he was, as I suspected, a recovering alcoholic, that would be the worst thing to do. I watched him gulp down some more coffee.

"Do you sleep alone in Albuquerque?" he asked me.

"Not lately."

"Living with someone?"

"Not exactly."

"Not living with someone but not living alone either. Now that's an interesting state of affairs."

"It must be something like being married but not being married, being divorced but not being divorced, if you know what I mean."

"Yeah, I know what you mean. I never could get all those different states straight. I can't love 'em just because I'm married to 'em or hate 'em because I'm not. I sure hate sleeping alone though. I know that. Maybe it's time to just settle down and stick with one."

"This wouldn't be a bad place to do it."

"It's a beautiful spot all right, but there's one thing wrong with it."

"What's that?"

"It's in Soledad." His thoughts returned to the wolf. A few minutes' diversion is about the best you can hope for when something bad happens. Thoughts always return to the hurting place, like a tongue feeling for a missing tooth. "They're gonna kill him," he said. "They'll be all over those mountains today looking to kill him."

"They don't have the right to unless he attacks their livestock. Would he do that?"

"I'd say no—he's never killed anything in his life—but they'll say yes. They'll find a dead carcass somewhere too decomposed to tell what got it and blame the kill on Siri. Shoot, shovel and shut up, that's the way they operate."

"Is there any chance he'll just come back here?"

"A chance," he said and laid his hands on the table, staring at L-O-V-E and W-O-L-F. "Would you mind sticking around while I talk to the sheriff? He's due here any minute."

I was his lawyer, after all. "I don't mind," I said. "Who do you think did it?"

"Buddy Ohles," he replied. "Who else? He's got a bad case of trigger itch."

5

Jayne joined us eventually, sniffing loudly as she entered the room to let me know she'd smelled my smoke. She walked up behind Juan, leaned over him and let her long blond hair tumble down and dangle into his empty cup. She had the aura of a well-stroked cat or a woman who's just had sex with someone who knows her well. There's an excitement that comes from sleeping with a stranger, a satisfaction that comes from sleeping with someone who knows what you like. They'd spent a lot of time together once, but not recently, so they were probably having it both ways with the added spice of risk thrown in. They must have known the chances of making this last were not great. Since my own sex life had taken a hike, I'd begun speculating about everyone else's.

Juan reached up with his L-O-V-E hand and held Jayne's. She smiled lazily, making me feel like a voyeur, no, an audience, because *voyeur* implies that Jayne didn't want to be watched and she seemed to be enjoying it. She disengaged her hand, turned away, arched her back, stretched her arms up to the ceiling, to the side, to the floor. She was wearing short shorts, a T-shirt and running shoes. Her body was California fit, her breasts silicone perky. If you ask me the fit body craze is as tyrannical as bound feet, girdles and corsets used to be—another way to make you feel that what you are naturally isn't good enough.

"Jayne runs every morning," Juan said, shaking his head in a mixture of admiration and disbelief.

"Care to join me, Neil?" she asked, bending over and looking up at me through her hair while her palm lay flat on the floor.

"No thanks." I was already pondering my next cigarette.

"I thought women lawyers ran," Jayne said, standing up, flinging her hair over her shoulders and bending backwards.

"That's women detectives," I said. "Women lawyers drink."

By the time Jayne returned from her run she'd lost the happy cat look. Maybe because Sheriff Ohweiler had shown up and was sitting at the kitchen table. It was only ten o'clock in the morning but both of them were sweating profusely already. His was staining the crevices of his khaki uniform; hers evaporated from her skin. She didn't bother to shower, just poured herself a glass of OJ and sat down at the kitchen table.

Juan, Ohweiler and I had already been outside and examined the chain and the broken link. It would appear to any objective observer that someone had taken a pair of wire cutters and cut through the chain. Objectivity, however, was not Ohweiler's middle name.

"You know that's a powerful animal," he said. "If it pushed against the gate, it could have stressed the weak link and split it right open."

"It was a clean break, Sheriff," I said. "A weak link would have just opened up. Somebody cut it."

"And he didn't push against the gate either," Juan replied.

"How do you know that?" Ohweiler asked. "You were inside, weren't you?"

"Siri is my wolf; I know."

"Well, I'll take this in for evidence." Ohweiler had proceeded to remove the chain and padlock, put them in a plastic bag and lock them up in the trunk of his car.

When Jayne arrived he was berating Juan for his so-called careless manner of securing a vicious animal. Juan's L-O-V-E and W-O-L-F hands gripped the table. He was getting pretty stressed himself, although I didn't think he was likely to break. "Sirius isn't vicious," he said. "There are kids all over the country who can tell you that."

"He locked the door with a quarter-inch chain and a padlock. I saw him do it," I said. "That's not exactly careless, either."

"We're going to be testing that lock and chain for fingerprints," Ohweiler said, "and signs of stress."

"You'll find mine on there," Jayne said, "because I touched it when I went out to check on Siri."

"Mine, too," said Juan.

"Um," said the sheriff. "You never should have left that wolf alone in a place that isn't visible from the house in a town that's not known for loving wolves. If you ask me it was pretty damn careless to bring a wolf into Soledad in the first place, pretty damn careless."

"That tennis court happens to be on private property, Sheriff," Jayne said. "Seems to me I've got the right to have a wolf locked up on my property if I want to, especially a wolf that's got a permit."

"You got the right if you can keep it on your property, but chances are that wolf ain't on your property, chances are that wolf is going after somebody's pet or cattle. Don Phillips found a dead calf on his ranch this morning and something killed it. Bob Bartel's out there inspecting it right now."

"Didn't take you guys long, did it?" said Jayne. "Calves die all the time and you and Don Phillips know it. It could have been a coyote, could have been a dog, could have been a mountain lion, could have been natural causes."

"What about finding out who set the wolf free?" I asked. "Isn't that why you were called over here?"

"It's under investigation, ma'am, but right now I'm charging your client with not securing a vicious animal under Section 77-1-10A."

"Bullshit," said Juan, who pounded the table so hard his coffee spilled out of its half-filled cup.

"Juan's wolf gets set free or stolen from my property and you charge *him* with not securing a vicious animal?" Jayne shook her head in disgust but not amazement. Apparently that was the way the law worked in Soledad County.

"Municipal Court meets tomorrow, 9 A.M.," Ohweiler said to me. "Your client can be arraigned then."

It was a pretty speedy arraignment for a suspect who wasn't being held, but it meant I wouldn't have to make a special trip back to Soledad for a routine procedure so I said okay.

Ohweiler wrote out a desk appearance ticket and handed it to me. He pulled his bulk up out of the chair, put on his Ray-Bans and his cowboy hat and went out the door.

"Not securing a vicious animal?" Juan asked me. "What the hell kind of a crime is that?"

"A misdemeanor," I said. "The maximum penalty is a year in jail or a $1,000 fine. If you plead guilty and say you're sorry, the judge will probably fine you $100 and that will be the end of it."

"Sorry for what?" said Juan. "Siri isn't a vicious animal to begin with and he wasn't insecurely kept either. Why should I have to pay a fine?"

"You want to go to trial?" I asked.

"Can I?"

"If you want one, you have the right to a trial." But who would do that when they could just pay a $100 fine? Juan Sololobo.

"Okay," he said. "Let's go for it."

"Are you out of your mind?" Jayne asked. "You know how they can fuck you over in a courtroom."

"A trial is going to cost a lot of time and money and there's no guarantee you'll win," I said.

"But I'm right," Juan said. "Any jury's gonna see that Siri's not vicious and that the last thing I would ever do is be careless with him." Juan had more confidence in his ability to sway a jury than Jayne or I did. She threw up her hands and went to the shower. Maybe the reality of being in a courtroom tomorrow would change his mind. I hoped so. In the meantime we had some things to discuss.

"The subject of your past record is going to come up at the arraignment," I warned him. "It's all on computer. Maybe we should go over it once more just to be sure I've got the whole story."

"When I was Bill Wiley I went AWOL from the marines, but, hell, they were probably glad to get rid of me. Then we got into antiwar activities, robbed some banks. All the money went into the movement. We didn't keep a penny of it for ourselves. I was convicted in federal court of driving the getaway car for a bank robbery, was sentenced to seven and did five long years."

"That's it?"

"Yeah, that's it," he said.

The municipal courthouse was a medium-sized, user-friendly stone building, not imposing enough to dissuade Juan from wanting a jury trial. When we got there a bunch of Upward Bound kids were hanging around outside waiting for him.

They'd been tipped off by someone. "Kids," Juan shook his head. "They're the best secret weapon in the world." But these kids weren't exactly secretive. They followed us inside, howled, cheered, booed and made such pests of themselves that the judge threatened to clear the courtroom. Juan was arraigned under Section 77-1-10A, it being unlawful for any person to keep an animal known to be vicious and liable to attack or injure human beings unless such animal is securely kept to prevent injury to any person. "Not guilty," Juan said loud and clear.

I saw some faces I recognized in the courtroom—the girls who had commented on Juan's cordy muscles, the boys who had made fun of the sheriff—and some faces I didn't. The two boys in the Anthrax-and-jeans uniforms who had bitched at Jayne were not in attendance, I noticed. Bob Bartel was.

After Juan had been arraigned I scheduled a date for a full hearing with the clerk. Juan hung around outside the courthouse and told wolf stories to the kids, an irresistible audience for him. I caught up to Bob Bartel as he descended the courthouse steps two at a time. "Have you got a minute?" I asked him.

"Sure thing," he said, although he kept right on walking. Unlike those of most Soledad residents his boots had cleats, not cowboy heels. This man walked for a living.

"What brought you to Juan's arraignment?" I asked him.

He smiled with his canine brown eyes. "I like going to court. In fact, I always kind of thought I'd enjoy practicing law for a living." We reached the bottom of the steps and he started striding down the street.

"Really? I always thought I'd enjoy practicing walking for a living." He laughed. "Is there any place we could sit down?" I asked.

"You bet." He turned a corner and led me behind the

courthouse to where a couple of picnic tables sat under an ancient cottonwood, the kind of place lawyers come to eat their lunch. But not to clean up after themselves, judging from the trash that had been left behind. Bartel brushed the benches off and we sat down. "I'm the research biologist for the FWS in charge of wolf recovery," he said. "I need to keep an eye on public opinion and your client has sure been stirring it up. He's made friends with the kids in Soledad, I see. That'll help."

"Ohweiler said you examined the dead calf."

"Yup."

"Well, what do you think?" I asked him. "Did Sirius kill it? When my client goes on trial the dead calf could be presented as proof of Siri's viciousness."

Apparently Bartel was one of those rare people who stopped and thought before he spoke. And then he thought some more. He was, after all, an employee of the federal government whose words could be used against him. "Whew, that was a long pause, a short dog with long paws." He smiled. "Sorry. The truth is it can be very hard to tell what killed an animal unless someone actually witnesses the kill. We've got mountain lions, coyotes and feral dogs in Soledad County and they're all capable of killing cattle. Even domestic dogs will pack up and kill livestock. You can't always tell by examining the corpse, either. This kill was fresh and I could see bite marks. They were smaller than I would have expected from such a large wolf, more the size of a coyote or a medium-sized dog, I'd say. But I don't have the wolf available for comparison either and there *was* a witness."

"Who?"

"Perla Phillips. She was out riding and she saw 'a big furry thing' running away from the kill site."

"'A big furry thing'?"

"That's what she said."

"Couldn't that be a coyote or a dog?"

"Could," he said. "But Perla claims it turned its head and looked back the way a wolf would but a coyote or a dog wouldn't."

"And how does she know what a wolf would or wouldn't do? Has she ever seen one?"

"You'd have to ask her, I guess. She has seen a lot of dogs and coyotes, I can tell you that. I wouldn't underestimate Perla. She had four brothers and she grew up learning to ride and shoot as well as any man. If she'd stuck to riding instead of raising kids, she'd be getting her name in the Cowgirl Hall of Fame by now."

I reached down to scratch my leg. "I wouldn't do that if I were you," Bartel said, looking at a tarantula crawling up my pants so carefully that I hadn't consciously known it was there. It was big and covered with thick black and brown fur. I watched it raise a hairy leg and inch upward.

"It's a beauty, isn't it?" asked Bartel.

It had an ugliness so strange and fierce that I supposed you could call it beauty. I had no idea where tarantulas ranked on the list of desert creatures that sting, bite, strike and poison, but I felt more curiosity than fear as I watched it crawl. My fear impulse, however, isn't as reliable as it ought to be. Bob Bartel stood up, took a handkerchief from his pocket, placed it over the spider, picked it up—very gently— and placed it several feet away on the ground. The tarantula was furious and swung at him. Bartel chuckled. "They can bite pretty good, but you'd survive. It could make you dance, though," he smiled. "Tarantulas are called wolf spiders in Europe and there's a folk belief that a bite from one will make you dance like crazy. We have wasps in the Southwest who capture these guys and feed them to their young. They're called tarantula hawks and they're big as hummingbirds. Nature works in strange ways." He shook his head and hitched up his polyester pants.

"So do humans."

"They're nature, too," he said, "even though sometimes they'd like to forget it." He put his foot on the picnic bench, rested his elbow on his knee. "Look at that spider. Now why would anybody want to kill something as beautiful as that? But they'll kill every one they can around here. Run 'em down on the road in their cars, stomp on them with their boots. They go up and down the arroyos shooting turtles, snakes, anything they can fix in the sight of their hunting rifles. They learn to shoot by practicing on live animals and it's legal as long as they're nongame animals and they're not on anybody's protected list." He shook his head. "Those are the boys I grew up with and I can tell you they're not happy to see me coming out on the side of the wolf."

"Why are you doing it?" I asked.

"Because it's my job?" His mouth smiled at the query, but his eyes did not. "I'm a biologist. That means you go to school, school and more school and after you graduate you go to work for the federal government. I'm the one who gets out in the field and does the studies, but the guys who make the decisions are the politicians in suits and ties."

Not being the kind of person to let anyone else make my decisions for me, especially someone in a suit and tie, I asked, "Suppose you don't like the decision?"

"Well, if you're like me and your goal is to make it into the middle class and take care of your wife and kids, then you do what they say, go home and forget about it. Every now and then we get lucky. Government biologists were responsible for bringing the red wolf back to North Carolina, you know. Not all environmentalists wear big beards and flannel shirts and make provocative statements. Some of us are raging, raving moderates. The American public should be very proud of what's happened in North Carolina. We start- ed there because wolves had been gone so long the hard-core opposition had died off. We've gotten good cooperation from

local citizens, including hunters, and the wolves are repro-
ducing well. I was there when they were released from their
cages and it was something to see. The wolves hesitated
when they got to the door. Even animals get used to their
cages and it was a strange and hostile world they were looking at. The wolves looked all around, thought it over and
kept right on going. Curiosity is a big motivator for animal
behavior. You might even say it is a form of intelligence."

He stopped for a minute, embarrassed to find that he'd
been making a speech. It took him a while to get started, but
once he'd gotten warmed up he was a verbal marathoner.
"I'm sorry. You had a question back there, didn't you? Oh
yeah, why am I coming out on the side of the wolf? Because
it's right," he said. "Because the wild is where they belong,
because wolf recovery would complete the link that was
there before man came along, because it was wolf predation
that made the ungulate herd so fast and sleek, because a
wolf is at the top of the food chain and the health of the wolf
is an indication of the health of the whole ecosystem,
because the habitat at White Sands can support them.
Because one thing I'd like to hear before I die is the howl of a
wolf in the Sierra Oscura."

The black box he was carrying beeped and he pulled out
the antenna and spoke to it. "Bartel," he answered; the radio
squawked back. It sounded like static to me, but made sense
to him. "Be right there," he said.

"Don Phillips found another calf kill on the ranch," he
told me. "I've got to go on out there and take a look. It's
been nice talkin' to you." He had that subtly flirtatious
manner of men in the rural West. There's always an undercurrent with guys like that that they're a man and you're a
woman and that's something that ought to be celebrated.

"My pleasure," I said.

6

When I got back to the courthouse Juan Sololobo was still standing on the steps doing what he loved best—talking to the world's greatest secret weapon. I had nothing to do that afternoon and I didn't have to be back in Albuquerque till morning, so I decided to go out to the Phillips ranch myself. If anybody wants to call curiosity a form of intelligence, it's all right with me. But mine isn't a lawyer's interest in closed-door negotiation and settlement. I have the curiosity of an investigator who wants to get out there and see who's lying, who isn't. Some lawyers pay investigators to go out and do this kind of work for them. Not me—although I was willing to leave the examination of dead cattle to Bob Bartel. It was cowgirl Perla Phillips that I was curious about, a less than objective observer when it came to wolves. She had God on her side and when He steps in common sense can take a hike. If my client was going to be tried for not securing a vicious animal, the dead calf could well be introduced as evidence of Siri's viciousness. I needed to know whether Sirius had really killed it. Perla had also left Jayne's living room the night the chain was cut and Siri set free. Maybe she'd freed him looking for the opportunity to kill him. Since trouble had a way of following Juan Sololobo, I left him talking on the courthouse steps and went the way I prefer to go—alone.

It was miles of bumpy road to the Phillips ranch. I looked at the desert and wondered if there was any locoweed out there driving the Phillips cattle berserk. Cattle liked it, I knew, because it was the first plant to turn green in the spring, but by this time of year it was probably as brown and dried out as everything else and the cattle that had started eating it then would be long dead. When it comes to addictive substances cattle are as dumb as humans. Once they start on locoweed they don't give up until they get depressed and uncoordinated and their organs stop functioning. The plant can be sprayed with chemicals, but it costs $10 to $15 an acre and when you have 20,000 acres it adds up. It's a hard life being a rancher, but what life isn't? And ranchers have a lot going for them: they don't have to face an office and a partner five days a week; they have the big sky, the wide open spaces, no neighbors and a greater sense than most of us of being in control of their destiny.

The Phillips ranch road led eventually to a bunch of end-of-the-road buildings. They were on the frontier; there was nothing beyond here but sky, desert and Mexico, where the wolves and the drug dealers roamed. The buildings were nestled under trees like they were at Jayne's place, only there were more buildings here. It was, after all, a working ranch and there were a couple of small houses and trailers for the help. The ranch house had a portal in front and a horse was saddled up and waiting outside. Perla sat on the porch with two plump, fair-haired toddlers pushing trucks around her feet. She watched me curiously as I parked the Nissan and walked over.

"I'm Neil Hamel," I said. "Juan Sololobo's lawyer.

We met at Jayne's the other night."

"Juan Sololobo," Perla shook her head, "now where did he get a name like that?"

"Gave it to himself, I guess."

"What kind of a name is Neil Hamel?"

Was I going to have to explain once again that I was named after my uncle who was in the Tenth Mountain Division? "American," I said.

"Is that right?" The toddlers pushed a truck back and forth between her boots. "I'm getting ready to go riding," Perla nodded toward the waiting horse. "Chili's been getting lazy. He needs a workout. Esperanza, one of the ranch hands' wives, is coming over to put the kids down for their nap. You ride?"

"No. I've never been that crazy about horses myself." And only a few minutes ago I was claiming to be American.

"Is that right?" Perla said again. "Me, I try to get out every day. My family lost our ranch to the White Sands Missile Range and I grew up in town. It's a real pleasure to be able to ride when I want to."

"It must be lonely out here, if you're used to town," I said. The words filled a conversational void, and they sounded like it.

"I'm too busy to get lonely."

A small Hispanic woman with a long black braid came around the corner of the house, a recent arrival from Mexico, I figured, by the way she wrapped herself tight in her rebozo, stayed near the side of the house and kept her eyes on the dusty ground.

"*Hola*, Esperanza," Perla said.

"*Hola*," Esperanza replied.

"*Buenos días*," I said.

"*Buenos días*." Esperanza's feet were bare, but it didn't much matter, because the skin on the bottom of them looked as tough as the tires people sole huaraches with where she came from. She walked over to the toddlers, picked the youngest one up and snuggled his blond head under her chin. Mexican arms are empty unless they have a kid to hold. Perla was ready to ride, Esperanza was ready to cuddle; it was time for me to state my purpose.

"Juan Sololobo was arraigned this morning on charges of not securing a vicious animal," I said.

"He never should have brought that thing into Soledad County," Perla shook her head. "Never. Wolves are nothing but trouble." The child who was in Esperanza's arms dropped his truck and the other one made a quick grab across the ground to take it. "Waah," the truckless one cried. "See," Perla asked, "how kids move quick and make noises like that? They look like baby animals on the ground and a wolf thinks they're dinner."

"A wolf wouldn't come near your house," I said.

"Who knows what those things will do? I've seen a coyote take a calf and I've seen the cow's bags all torn and bloody, I've seen her cryin'. It's not the kind of thing you'd want to see again."

"Wolves are much shyer than coyotes. They're known to stay as far away from people as possible and there's never been a documented case of an unprovoked wolf attack on a human being in North America, either." Juan would have been proud of his lawyer.

"I'd sure hate to have *my* kids be the first, wouldn't you?"

I didn't have any kids, but I didn't tell Perla Phillips that since childless women were probably as un-American in this world as wolves. "I was wondering if you might have seen or heard anything unusual that night at Jayne's when somebody set the wolf free."

"No."

"Maybe when you left the room ..."

"I went to the bathroom," she said. "I didn't see or hear a thing. I got my period and Don and I were pretty disappointed. We want to have a big family; next we're hoping for a girl."

"Bob Bartel says you're sure the animal you saw near the calf was a wolf. How did you know?"

"Granddaddy Phillips saw plenty of wolves in his day and he told me that only a wolf will turn its head and look back like that critter did."

Esperanza picked the other child up and headed inside. She had one towhead in each arm now, which made her appear even darker and tinier. Toddlers' big heads always make them seem larger than they are.

Perla was watching something over my shoulder and I began hearing it, the thundering sound of hooves pounding the ground, a sound anyone who spent her childhood watching Western movies would instantly recognize. I turned and saw a cloud of dust approaching fast. The cloud reined to a stop when it reached the portal and the dust settled to reveal Buddy Ohles in camouflage hunting gear sitting on top of a sweating horse. He had a rifle sticking out of his saddle scabbard. "Where's Don?" he called in a highly excited voice while the horse did a nervous reined-in-place dance.

"Halfway to the border looking at another calf kill." Perla remained calm. She didn't seem to get excited about much. "Why?"

"I trapped the wolf," Buddy crowed. "He came back to feed on the calf and I caught him not twenty feet from the carcass. He's a big, gray bastard. I want to get Don up there." My presence had made barely a blip on his mental antennae; he had more important things on his mind.

"Bob Bartel is with him," Perla said, verbally underlining Bartel and glancing pointedly in my direction. "I'll get them on the radio."

"Okay," Buddy answered, but some of the excitement had gone out of his voice. Bob Bartel's introduction had put the damper on.

Buddy's dust devil turned and galloped off and Perla went inside, leaving me all alone with Chili. I took a good look at him, big brown thing. He looked back with placid eyes that said he didn't get excited about much either. Buddy Ohles was going after an entrapped wolf—Sirius—with a loaded gun, hoping, no doubt, to get there before Bob Bartel did. Was I the kind of person who could sit on Perla's porch and let that happen? The best way to follow was the way he'd gone, on horseback.

It wouldn't be my first time on a horse. I'd been a red-blooded girl growing up in America. I'd never had blue or even white ribbons hanging all over my bedroom, but I had briefly had a horse infatuation. I fell off, fell out of love and moved on to boys while my peers were still learning to post and trot. I should have known then and there that my infatuations weren't going to resemble anyone else's.

"How 'bout it, Chili?" I said. "You want to take me for a ride?"

Chili swung his tail, swatted a fly. I remembered how to mount a horse: grab onto the saddle, stick the left foot in the stirrup, swing the right leg over the back, but my right leg didn't want to swing—it got halfway up and stuck on the saddle. I yanked it over, pushed my foot into the stirrup. I remembered a riding instructor from back then saying, "Heels down, ball of foot on stirrup." Was that English or Western? These stirrups had been set for Perla, who was 5'2", and I had to crook my knees way up to squeeze into them. My heels fell where they fell. I also remembered the riding instructor saying, "Straighten your back, stick out your chest." "The horse can't see my chest," said I. "I can," the instructor replied. Another reason I gave up riding.

I remembered what came next: pull on the reins, but not hard enough to hurt the horse's sensitive mouth; give him a kick, just hard enough to let him know you mean it; click your tongue. "Click, click," I poked Chili with the heel of my running shoe. Chili shook his head, swung his tail at a fly, gave some thought to dinner. Running shoes didn't impress him; he was used to heels, spurs, leather. "*Vamos, caballo*," I said, but Chili *no comprende Español* either. "Move it." I kicked again harder and he loped off in one of those moves somewhere between a walk and a run that I'd never been able to get the rhythm of. Chili's hooves left the ground, my thighs slapped the saddle. Chili came down, I bounced up. My knees were too high up and near his neck to get any kind of a grip. Posting hadn't been my forte; I couldn't follow the leader in ballroom dancing either. My butt ached with every step, my thighs would get rubbed raw if we continued like this. Buddy Ohles was disappearing in the dust. "Get your ass in gear, Chili." I kicked harder and, I'll admit it, yanked on the bit. He got the message this time and began to run. I hunkered down, bent over his neck, and hoped like hell he wouldn't get a cactus spine in his leg or step in a hole. Now I recalled what it felt like to have a thousand pounds of galloping horseflesh between my legs with no control over it, something like the feeling I used to have on a rental horse rushing back to the stable. Only the ante had been raised; I was bigger and stronger now, but so was the horse. This was how I'd hit the dust before, thrown by a pissed-off and hungry horse. But you wouldn't expect a rancher to put up with a totally obstinate beast, and once Chili got into the spirit, he didn't seem to mind having someone on his back. He seemed to enjoy running after Buddy's horse. I'd gotten an adrenaline rush and we were going too fast to feel fear anyway. I just held on, watched the ground and let Chili have his way. We caught up to Buddy just as he had dismounted and was tying his horse to a bush.

I swung my leg over the saddle, dropped to the ground and tied Chili up, too. He'd barely broken a sweat, unlike Buddy's tired and panting horse. Perla kept him in shape. "What are you doing here?" Buddy asked with the cutting edge of suspicion in his voice.

"What are *you* doing here?" I answered. "Aren't wolves Bob Bartel's job?"

"Anything that kills livestock is *my* job." He pulled the rifle out of its scabbard and began walking toward a boulder with a large shadow, not long yet but deep and dark, the kind of shadow that appears flat on the surface but if you looked into it hard enough you'd see life flapping and crawling. A squawking raven flew overhead.

A shiver rippled through Chili's muscles, and he whinnied and danced in place. I patted his shoulder. "Hang on, boy," I said. "I'll be right back."

There was a cactus beside the boulder, the kind with spines that leap out and stab as you walk by. Keeping my distance, I circled around it and followed Buddy to the far side of the boulder where the calf carcass lay baking in the decomposing sun, ribs sticking up and exposed, body eaten hollow, head swollen. Like Perla Phillips had said, it was not a pretty sight. Near it lay Sirius, his foot caught in the steel jaws of a leg-hold trap, his eyes wide, yellow and frightened. He remained strangely quiet and watched us with wary intelligence. He was part pet and, although being trapped probably terrified him, he'd be expecting us to help.

"You know, even if the wolf was eating on the carcass, that doesn't prove he killed it," I said.

"Does to me." For a minute it seemed like Buddy was macho posturing to impress me and the wolf. But when he aimed his rifle both Siri and I knew he meant to kill. Siri pulled his ears back. The gray fur stood up around his neck.

He bared his canines and growled low in his throat. It was a fierce and intimidating display. Any other animal would have put its tail between its legs and fled, but Buddy was the one animal that had nothing to fear, the animal whose weapons were its thumb and its brain. With his brain he had created hard, stiff, projectile weapons of destruction—guns. The leverage of his thumb made it possible to build and fire them. Those two weapons had made man all but invincible in the wild.

"Bob Bartel's gonna be here any minute and he'll be wanting to stop me, but I ain't gonna let him do it," Buddy said. "Gonna be puttin' you out of your misery, old boy." He peered through the sight seeking his target: the heart, the head, the brain, the liver. Siri cried and struggled against the trap.

I couldn't say I thought about what I did. Images fly, thoughts crawl. I saw the wolf's frightened eyes, his paw trapped in a metal grip, blood, a bullet blasting gray fur to bits. But I didn't see Buddy shooting a woman—me. I got there without knowing I was doing it and found myself standing between Buddy and Siri staring down the dark end of a long rifle with Buddy focusing on me through the sight. "Get out of my way," he said, but I didn't move. "Goddamn, wolf lover, I got a job to do. Get out of my way."

I had that sense of crystalline clarity, unnatural calmness and purpose that hits people at the moments when they ought to be scared to death. It's a feeling some have been known to get high on. "No," I said.

Buddy circled to his right; I stepped in front of him. He circled left; I followed. He stopped and stared at me with narrow eyes, while his jaw worked a wad of tobacco in his cheek. I could see him considering—not the pain a bullet or the butt of a rifle would cause me, but the inconvenience it would cause him. Bartel and Don Phillips would be arriving soon and there he'd be with the gun smoking in his hand. It would take some explaining, more than Buddy was capable of. He thought it over, chewed, spat a stream of tobacco juice near his boot. "Goddamn wolf lovers," he said, putting his rifle down and kicking the ground. "Goddamn."

7

Buddy paced back and forth muttering to himself, and I stood between him and the wolf. Siri's ruffled fur settled down and his ears moved back into place. He stopped growling, kept on watching. I wanted to approach him, but I didn't dare. I didn't want to get any closer to Buddy Ohles. His anger had boiled over and was oozing out of him in drops of sweat. Although Siri's leg was caught in the trap's grip, he wasn't bleeding and didn't seem to be in pain. Not that I could have done anything about it if he were.

Bob Bartel and Don Phillips arrived eventually in Bartel's government-green truck. Siri's ears picked up when he heard them coming (long before I did). While the men got out of the truck and walked over as fast as Don's cowboy boots would allow, I thought about what had made me step between a gun and a wolf. Bravery? Stupidity? Who knows what anybody will do when challenged or why they do it? Since reason had not been involved, I settled on instinct. It was instinct that sent the wolf in this direction once it was set free, instinct that led it to kill and/or eat the calf, instinct that made me want to protect it. Instinct maybe that made Buddy want to kill it, except that he was the only one who'd planned what he did.

"What's this, a New Mexican standoff?" said Bartel, looking from Buddy to me to the wolf.

Buddy spat a brown tobacco goober at the ground. "That wolf killed the calf and came back to finish it up. My job is to kill it and then some goddamn wolf lover gets in my way."

"My job is to come up with a recovery plan for the lobo and if you kill that wolf, you're gonna be getting in my way," Bartel replied.

Don Phillips stuck his thumbs in his jeans and spoke up. "And how many losses do I have to take because some damn fool doesn't have better sense than to try to keep a wolf for a pet or because environmentalists get a notion to bring back a predator? Once a wolf starts working on your livestock it's not gonna quit. That calf there could have been my next champion bull."

"No one's proven to my satisfaction that this wolf killed this calf," Bartel replied. "It came here to feed on it, sure, but wolves are carrion eaters. If that wolf *didn't* kill this calf, shooting it isn't going to do your livestock any good, now is it? We'll have a dead wolf, a bunch of angry citizens on my back and an animal out there that will kill again."

Buddy danced in place like a tied-up horse. "You grew up here," he bitched at Bartel. "You had country values before you became a wolf lover."

"I'm a wildlife biologist employed by the federal government, Buddy. With all due respect, that means I represent some ten-year-old kid in Illinois who wants to have a wilderness experience just as much as I do ranchers."

"You want watching wolves kill cattle or cougars kill sheep to be part of some kid's wilderness experience?" Buddy asked.

"You know how I feel about your killing that cougar." Bartel spoke quietly, but his lips got tight and he seemed as close to anger as he was likely to get. His displays were subtle.

Anger and displays came easily enough to Buddy. "That sucker wasn't doing what it was put here to do—eat deer. It was killing sheep. I don't know why everybody made such a goddamn fruckus about my killing a cougar anyway."

"It was an FWS lion, Buddy, we were the ones who radio-collared it, we were the ones who were studying it."

"That radio collar didn't keep it from killing sheep, did it? So now your job is to keep me from doin' my job? What are you gonna to do next, put a collar on me?"

The thought of Buddy wearing one of those monitored bracelets that kept criminals close to home didn't sound so bad to me. It would keep him from causing any more fruckuses, fracases or ruckuses either.

Buddy kicked the dirt. "Damn waste of the taxpayers' money if you ask me."

"Keeps us both employed, though, don't it?" Bartel said. "I do it for the Interior Department, you undo it for Agriculture. Now why don't you boys go on back to work and let me take care of this situation. Don't you worry about this wolf none, Donald; I'll see that he won't be bothering your cattle anymore."

"You do that, Robert," Phillips said.

"That's Perla's horse out there, isn't it?" Bartel asked.

"Yup," Phillips answered.

"Can you ride it back home? I'll take Neil in the truck with me."

"You betcha."

They left, Don with a rolling cowboy walk, Buddy scrambling to keep up, trailing long-legged shadows behind them.

"Takes an unusual person to step between a gun and a

wolf," Bartel said to me when they were gone. "Lot of men wouldn't have done that. Bet you didn't think Buddy'd shoot a woman, though, did you?"

"I didn't think, period."

"Buddy gets riled easily, always has, but I wouldn't be too hard on him. He's got a job to perform, too, and he gets a bellyful of complaining from ranchers. Maybe you've heard the saying up there in Albuquerque that you should never judge a man till you've walked a mile in his boots?"

"Yup."

"Well, down here we say you should never judge a man till you've held his weapon in your hands."

"His ... weapon? You mean his six-shooter? His repeater?"

Bartel smiled. "His gun? His hunting rifle?"

"Still sounds like a euphemism to me."

Bartel had a nice, easy laugh; everything about him was nice and spare and lean and easy. "I mean that thing he puts bullets in and shoots animals with. It changes a person to be looking through the sights of a gun, and the more powerful the gun the more it changes the person. You never know how you'll react until you've held one yourself. That's one reason I don't carry guns anymore. Well, let's see what we can do for this guy." He walked slowly up to the wolf with his hands out, his eyes averted, talking all the while. His body language showed respect, but not fear. His voice was soft and gentle. "Hey, fella," he said. "You just take it easy now. I'm sure not gonna hurt you."

The wolf watched warily, but it let Bartel approach. He seemed to be one of those people who could tame birds and talk fear from the wild. His gentle manner, his voice, just his presence had an effect more soothing than drugs. "You're wedged in there pretty good, aren't you?" he said. "Well, just hang on. I'll be right back, and we'll get you fixed up in no time."

He went to his truck and came back around the boulder with his arm at his side. With a gesture so quick and fluid I hardly saw it, he lifted a gun and fired it at Siri. Before I could protest he said, "Don't worry, it's just a tranquilizer." Sirius started, his eyes widened and he struggled groggily against the effects of the drug. So much for trusting humans. Not having a whole lot of trust myself, I couldn't help wondering if this would turn out to be one of those "accidental" overdoses of tranquilizers that would kill the wolf. Should I have stepped in front of Bob Bartel, too? I'll admit that I'm not always the best judge of men and killing Siri would be one way to keep Don Phillips happy.

As if he had read my suspicious mind Bartel said, "Don't worry; that'll only put him out for a little while, till I can get him to the zoo and have the vet there take a look at his leg. Norm Alexander always claimed he didn't need tranquilizers, that he could calm a wolf just by talking, and you know what happened to him?"

"No."

"He got bit. He'll never get back full use of that hand either. His fingers work pretty good but his thumb is useless and without a thumb you can't do much. A wolf can cause a lot of damage if it wants to. They can kill a human easily, but even when they've been provoked, they don't. They only fight hard enough to prove their point. But dogs—dogs kill people all the time, yet everybody who's afraid of the wolf has a dog. You tell me."

He waited several minutes for the tranquilizer to take full effect and when he was sure Siri was knocked out he stepped on the trap, released it, bent down and examined the foot. "He'll be okay," he said. "Nothing's broken here." He picked Siri up by the loose fur on the back of his neck. "It's called piloerection when that neck fur stands up in anger or in fear," he told me. He draped Siri around his own neck like a fur piece. The wolf hung limp as a boa, but he was breathing softly and regularly. I could see that. Bartel carried Siri to the pickup and laid him gently in the back. The truck had a government seal on the door and two large antennas on the roof that he noticed me looking at.

"Those are Yagi antennas," Bartel said. "They're what we use to track our radio collars." He got behind the wheel and I climbed into the cab next to him, which was filled with equipment apparently used in radio tracking, including a compass, headphones and a receiver. "If you don't mind I'd appreciate it if you'd keep an eye on the wolf. It's gonna be a bumpy ride."

"Sure," I said.

"Your car at Perla's?" he asked.

"Yup."

"She know you took her horse?"

"She does now."

"You know Perla and Don are good folk. Not the big bad welfare ranchers you folks up north would like to believe. Perla's family's ranch was taken by the federal government in the thirties to make White Sands and they were never compensated for it. She's gonna feel doubly scorned to see the wolf put on land that once belonged to her family."

"She mentioned that."

"It's not something you'd ever forget if it happened to you. Ranchers are just people trying to stay alive, reproduce and make a living just like you and me."

"I can't speak for you, but *I'm* not trying to reproduce," I said.

"You sure? Copulation biology can sneak up on you," he smiled. "The wolf is operating from the same biological drives as we are: to eat and reproduce. It's just an animal, but a wild animal. It's not a pet. I don't like to see people trying to turn it into a dog. A wolf's never gonna follow you around and ask for your approval or a pat on the head. A wolf's a hell of a lot smarter, more efficient and stronger than any dog will ever be. It's a powerful predator, but that doesn't make it the devil or the bogeyman either. It's just an animal." He turned his head around and looked at the drugged fur ball in the back of his truck. "But it's a beauty, isn't it?"

"Yes," I said.

We bumped along the Phillips ranch roads. They say the return trip always seems faster that the going out, but I could have sworn we were going at a slower pace than I had on Chili. Bartel had a wolf to watch out for. When we reached the Nissan, he said, "I'm going to take the wolf to the Soledad Zoo and he'll be kept there until the charges against Juan and the cattle kill issue are settled. I ought to be the one to tell Juan that, if you don't mind. If you get back to Jayne's before I do, I'd appreciate it if you wouldn't say anything."

"No problem." I had something I wanted to ask him before he got away. "What happened with Buddy and the cougar?"

"We'd radio-collared some mountain lions at White Sands and were doing studies on 'em. When we radio-collar an animal we give the frequency to other government agencies in the neighborhood. The idea is that we can keep an eye on each other's collars. The lion wandered off the range and started going after a rancher's sheep. Without notifying us Buddy took it upon himself to use our frequency to track and kill it. He got the lion, gave us back the collar."

"That's a rotten thing to do."

"We called it unethical," Bartel said. "But if I ever catch Buddy doing a thing like that again I'm going to see that he loses his job."

I stopped at the Galaxy Deli on my way back to the ranch to kill time and quench my thirst, and stood still inside the doorway for a minute while my eyes made the adjustment from too much light to too little. The blind man at the counter was quiet as a predator, listening, using invisible antennae to size me up. It's unnerving to think you can reveal your identity in the dark just by standing still. Once my eyes had adjusted enough so I could pick out details in the shadows, I saw that he had turned in my direction with a curious expression on his long face. "Hi," I said, telling him before he had a chance to tell me. "I'm Neil Hamel, the lawyer from Albuquerque. I stopped by here a few days ago. Remember?"

"Ernesto Sandoval. *Buenas tardes*," he said.

"*Buenas tardes*."

He thought for a moment. "You like the Papaya Punches, is that right?"

"You have a good memory."

"They're over there in the cooler."

"*Gracias*."

"*Por nada*."

I picked out my drink, came back to the counter and gave him fifty cents, which clinked as he dropped it in the drawer.

"Heard any more wolves?" I asked him.

"Last night, but it was only one, near El Puerto. They say it is the moon that the wolves howl at, but they come out anyway, even when there is no moon. He howled because he was lonely. 'I'm looking for a mate,' he said. I could hear him. Do you have a mate?" he asked me.

"Not exactly. And you?"

"Oh, yes, Yolanda, and she's an excellent woman, too. I couldn't live one day without her."

I hung around the beginning of Jayne's road waiting for Bob Bartel. I had no desire to get to Jayne's first knowing Juan's good news and bad but not being able to tell. It was too hot to sit in an nonmoving, non-air-conditioned car, so I got out, leaned against the trunk, fanned my shirt and drank my Papaya Punch wishing I had six more. It was drier than dust out here. A hawk circled over the Soledads' spine, brown birds sang in the chamisa. Even in the desert, drab birds sing a happy song. I closed my eyes and listened to the sounds of the other world, the parallel universe that only occasionally intersects with ours. A wolf howling in the Soledads would be part of that world. I opened my eyes and saw a juniper not far from the road with bark as scaly as alligator hide. The forks in its branches were shaped like jagged lightning. Some cactusy type of plant with long, skinny arms had yellow blossoms for fingertips. A spiny yucca was getting ready to bloom. It was late afternoon but still as dusk. Did that mean a storm was coming? It was too early for me to tell, but maybe the cactus knew. Desert vegetation always seems unnaturally still, anyway, like it's waiting, watching, reaching deep for water. In the distance the hawk hovered over a break in the spine. I stared at that spot and saw a road coming out of it, an old road, almost grown over with mesquite and rabbitbrush, but the scar it had made on the desert's skin remained. *La puerta*, feminine, means door, I knew, but *el puerto*, masculine, means the mountain pass, the place you could cross from east of the Soledad peaks to west. I wondered if that was the *puerto* Ernesto had talked about. I looked away for a minute to be sure I hadn't imagined it, but when I looked back it was still there, just a trace, the memory of a road, winding down the mountain and across Jayne's property.

8

A cloud of dust let me know that Bob Bartel's pickup was coming. I got back into the Nissan and rolled up the window in anticipation. I didn't have one of those windshield screens that has a picture of sunglasses on one side of it and says NEED HELP CALL POLICE on the other. The car had gotten so hot that you needed a glove to get it into first gear. Bartel slowed down when he approached, smiled and waved, but didn't stop. He probably didn't want to give his dust devil time to catch up to him. I sat in the hot car waiting for the dust to settle, wondering which was worse, eating road dust or getting crisped in your automobile. Every summer people forget how hot a car can get, leave a pet inside, come back to find the animal dead from heatstroke and end up hating themselves for their stupidity and carelessness. As soon as Bartel's dust began to settle, I rolled down the window a few inches and followed him to Jayne's.

Juan Sololobo was sitting under the portal when we arrived. He wore jeans and his trademark Levi's jacket with the sleeves cut off. His own cloud—a black one—hung over him. He was drinking something from a dark blue glass. As I had been staying at the ranch, my return was expected. But there was no reason for Bartel to come here unless he had news (good or bad) and a wave of expressions surged across Sololobo's face when he saw him, ending in a kind of hopeful grin. "You found Siri?" he yelled the minute Bartel stepped from the truck.

"Yes," Bartel said for the good news.

"Where? Is he all right? Is he alive?" Juan put his glass down, left the shade of the portal and hurried over to us.

"He's all right. Buddy Ohles set a trap and caught him near the calf carcass."

"A trap? That bastard. Did he break his leg, too?"

"There were no teeth in the trap; it looks like the leg will be all right," Bartel said. "You ought to give thanks to your lawyer here; she made sure Buddy Ohles didn't hurt your wolf."

It wasn't the kind of thing you could bill a client for. I got a big hug instead from Juan's sweaty arms, and felt like I'd been licked by a dog with a large and sloppy tongue.

"I had to tranquilize him to get him out of the trap," Bartel moved on to the worse news.

"You *tranquilized* him?" Juan was a bowlful of emotion and it was starting to quiver.

"Take it easy, Juan," I said, "Siri's all right. I saw the whole thing."

"If he's all right, then why isn't he here?"

"I took him to the Soledad Zoo for a thorough examination," Bartel said.

Juan's watery interior wobbled back toward equilibrium. "Okay. Well, then, when do I get him back?"

"I can't give him back to you until the charges of not securing a wild animal are settled and until we establish whether he killed the calf."

Juan turned toward me and his angry establishment-baiting past bubbled to the surface. "Why don't you do something? You're my lawyer," he demanded. When all else fails, blame your lawyer, who, no matter how far out of the mainstream, will always appear establishment to someone.

It wasn't the first time I wished I were nobody's lawyer, especially with the kind of clients I get. My job was to represent his best interests. It was in his best interest to shut up but I couldn't think of any way to tell him that without getting wet.

"Just give Siri back to me. I'll take him out of Soledad County and we'll *never* come back. That's a promise," Juan pleaded. His words were submissive but his voice was loud and his posture aggressive. His arms got bigger, his Levi's jacket smaller. He moved in close, violating Bartel's space.

Bartel stood his ground. "I can't do that," he replied.

The liquid wobbled precariously at the lip of Juan's bowl, broke its surface tension and slopped over. "Goddamn it, Siri is my wolf," he yelled. "You gotta give him back to me now, man, you gotta." He grabbed Bartel, placed his L-O-V-E and W-O-L-F fingers near the throat and began to shake. The physical attack caught Bartel by surprise; he'd probably expected only verbal abuse. He didn't respond at first and stared at Juan with startled eyes. I wondered if I'd have to step into the middle of another fruckus, but there wasn't any room between these two.

Bartel grabbed Juan's forearms with his wiry fingers and the two of them clutched each other and danced around like boxers who couldn't get unstuck until the moment Bartel tripped and lost his balance. As he struggled to regain it he relinquished his grip on Juan's arms. Juan got his hands around Bartel's throat. Bartel began to gag, his eyes bugged out.

"Let go of him, Juan," I demanded.

Jayne ran out of the house wearing a pink warmup suit,

her blond hair flying, her face made up, her eyes bright. "Stop it, Billie," she cried, reverting to an earlier name in the excitement. She wrapped her arms around Juan's muscular back and pulled at him. "C'mon baby," she coaxed, "it'll be all right. I'll take care of you."

Pouring off the excess emotion had left some room in Juan for reason. I saw it flash quick as lightning in his pale eyes. "Oh, man, I'm sorry," he said, releasing Bartel. "You were just doin' your job, I know. Everybody's got to do their job. I lost control and I'm sorry."

"C'mon, baby, let's go inside." Jayne kept her arms around Juan and led him toward the door. I couldn't help wondering how much she had witnessed before she came running out and whether she'd taken the time to put her makeup on first and/or waited till she was really needed.

Bob Bartel brushed at the spot on his throat where Sololobo's big hands had held him. "Whew," he said.

"I'm sorry," said I. I didn't much enjoy having to apologize for an out-of-control client.

"Not your fault," Bartel replied.

"You all right?" I asked.

He shook everything to see if it still worked. "Looks like it." He smiled the rueful smile that got him through the wolf-loving, animal-protecting day. "Guess it means I'm doin' my job anyway," he said. "Now that everybody in Soledad County is ready to kill me."

Juan felt sorry all over again at dinnertime and he apologized some more by cooking chicken burritos with onions and red peppers. He went to the trouble to char the peppers on top of the stove and peel the blackened skin off. They taste better that way, but it was more effort than I'd be willing to make. While Juan cooked, I remembered that an almost new bottle of Cuervo Gold was waiting in the duffle bag in my room.

After a day like this I was ready for it, but I let sleeping bottles lie, as this appeared to be a nondrinking household. Not even a cooking sherry in the cupboard. Maybe Jayne was too fit to drink herself, maybe she was trying to keep temptation away from Juan.

Whatever anger he was still carrying around, he didn't dump it in the food. The burritos were a little tame for my taste but not bad. We ate in silence. When dinner was over Jayne wrapped her arm around Juan's and leaned her head on his shoulder.

"Maybe they'll let me go to the zoo and visit him anyway," Juan said.

"Maybe," said Jayne.

I had nothing to add and I turned in after dinner, thinking if I got up early I could make it back to Albuquerque by noon. When I got to the guest room, I reached into my duffle bag and felt around for my old friend. My hand came up empty, felt some more until my fingers settled around the top of a bottle that was not where I remembered having left it. I pulled it out and came up near empty again. An almost full fifth of Cuervo Gold was gone. So that had been the liquid in Juan's glass and the fluid sloshing around inside him as well. The big questions were—had he drunk *all* of it and what had inspired him to look here?

I didn't ask. Juan was still in apology mode when I got to the kitchen the next morning, dressed, packed and ready to go. He was drinking coffee and frying up huevos rancheros. He flipped the eggs over, turned around and gave me a shame-faced, I'm-sorry look, but I wasn't in the mood for apologies or forgiveness. All I wanted was a cup of coffee and to hit the road. "No eggs for me, thanks, just coffee."

"You sure? I make the best huevos rancheros in California."

We weren't in California but I didn't feel like telling him that either. Maybe Juan thought I hadn't discovered the missing tequila yet or maybe my silence allowed him to pretend to himself that he hadn't even taken it. In any case, he started acting like he'd been let off the hook, smiling happily and pouring me some coffee. His moods shifted faster than tumbleweeds in an April wind.

A phone rang somewhere in the house. We heard Jayne answer it and then we heard her hang up. "Those little bastards," she said loudly as she slammed the receiver down. She came into the kitchen wearing her workout clothes and her power makeup. "That was Ohweiler," she said. "Would you believe it? The Upward Bound kids were the ones who cut Siri's chain, the two that argued with me. They parked their car down the road and snuck up here during the storm. Ohweiler stopped them for a moving violation last night, searched the car, looking for drugs, probably, and found the wire cutters. He fingerprinted them and the prints matched the ones on the chain."

Juan shook his head. "Why would kids do something like that? Kids love wolves."

"They were pissed because I wouldn't let them swim here, remember?"

"Jaynie, what difference would it make if they did swim here? They're just kids."

"Just kids? Sure, Juan. Look at all the trouble they've caused already."

Bill at night was Juan in the morning and someone else maybe by midafternoon.

"It's still my property. No one's taken it away from me yet," Jayne said, reminding Juan of the property that had been taken away from him.

He turned to his lawyer. "Can Bob Bartel give Siri back now? They can't go on charging me for not securing a vicious animal when those kids cut the chain, can they?"

They could but I didn't tell him that yet.

"Will you call him?" Juan asked me.

I looked over his shoulder at the clock on the stove. Eight o'clock, early enough for the sheriff but not for a federal employee or for me either. "When I get back to Albuquerque," I said.

It wasn't supposed to rain until afternoon, but not long after I reached I-25 it began to pour so hard drops pummeled the Nissan like pellets. The windshield wipers were working overtime trying to keep up when the one on the driver's side went into a crazy little dance, fell over and died. Visibility decreased from poor to zero and I was swimming underwater with my eyes open and the current against me. I slowed to a crawl, leaned over and peered out through the passenger's side of the windshield. After a few near-blind miles I saw a state police car pulled off on the shoulder and I pulled off behind it. It was still pouring, but at least when I stopped moving I was able to see. A cop stood beside the car wearing a Smokey the Bear hat wrapped in plastic. The rain dripped off the brim and trickled down his shoulders but it kept his face dry. A small, dark man in the back seat turned around and stared at me through the rear window with trapped, helpless eyes. An illegal alien, I figured, who had found some path across the border and was about to be sent back home again.

The trooper walked over to the Nissan and I rolled down my window a few inches. "I've got a problem," I said.

He was young, clean shaven and, except for his face, soaking wet. "Me, too," he replied. "You first."

"My windshield wiper is broken. I was wondering if you had a screwdriver or something I could fix it with."

"Well, ma'am, I'd sure like to help you, but my tools are

in the car, and, um …" He smiled an embarrassed smile, as well he might. "I saw that wetback running across the road there and I stopped to catch him. Those Mexicans are damn dumb about cars; it's lucky I didn't run him over. They're like animals, you know, you're not even aware they're livin' in your country and all of a sudden they dart out in the road and you damn near hit 'em. After I locked him up I needed to relieve myself and I, well, I, uh, locked myself out." He tapped the radio on his hip. "I've radioed for help but it's gonna be a while before anyone gets here."

"Can't your prisoner let you in?" What difference would it make if the guy escaped, I thought. He'd probably come back across the border again tomorrow, anyway.

"The back doors can't be opened from the inside and he can't get into the front. I'll just have to wait. You don't have far to Truth or Consequences. There's a gas station there where they can fix you up."

"Thanks anyway," I said.

"You betcha," he replied.

9

By the time I got to Belen the lightning was flashing in my rearview mirror. When I reached Albuquerque fifteen minutes later, I'd driven through the rain. I stopped at Baja Tacos and got myself a burrito with extra chile and a lemonade to go for lunch. I didn't need any more caffeine; one cup of Sololobo's coffee was an all-day buzz, although his burrito for dinner hadn't lit my fire. No one was at the Hamel and Harrison office eagerly awaiting my arrival; no one was there at all. The swamp cooler sang a solitary tune, the temperature was somewhere between hot and life threatening. There were signs that Anna had been at her desk recently, maybe even this morning. No signs of Brink.

Since cold drinks hadn't been cooling me down, I gave hot food a try. One of nature's laws is that the closer you are to the equator the hotter the food gets. The purpose is either to cool you off or to disguise the rancid taste of unrefrigerated meat. The meat in my burrito had no taste, it was filler. The chile was what counted. It was heat-wave-in-August, break-a-sweat chile. Who needed to work out when you had green chile to get the heart and adrenaline pumping? After that burrito my office felt cool, proving that discomfort, like everything else, is relative and that one way you can count on making things look cool is to dip into what's hot.

Once I'd finished eating and cleaned up, I called Bob Bartel. "Out in the field," a secretary said. Next on the list was March Augusta, the man who'd sent me to Soledad to begin with.

"What are you doing indoors on an August afternoon?" I asked. "I expected you to be out fly fishing or something."

"I've already been fishing," he replied, "and now I'm sitting around waiting for you. How did it go?"

"Far be it from me to say who's responsible, but trouble and Juan got together."

"Uh oh. What happened?"

I told him.

"Wait a minute," he said. "Some kids cut a chain and set Sirius free and Juan is being charged with not securing a vicious animal?"

"That's right. That's Soledad County for you. There's more. Bob Bartel, the biologist, won't give Siri back to Juan until he determines whether Siri killed the rancher's cattle."

"How is Juan taking it?"

"Great. He put his hands around Bartel's neck and shook."

"Oh, God, did he hurt him?"

"No. He was doing his best but Jayne broke it up before any harm was done. There's something I want to ask you ..."

"Shoot."

I wanted to know about Sololobo's drinking, but drinking was a touchy subject with March and me, one we'd had a go-round about before. "What kind of a guy is Juan?" I asked.

"He's exactly who he pretends to be."

Subtlety was getting me nowhere. "What I really want to know is does he have a drinking problem? He acts like a recovering alcoholic to me. He drinks coffee all day and has wild mood swings, and I suspect he was hitting the bottle before he attacked Bartel."

"Well, he used to be a mean drunk, and it got him into a lot of the trouble he was in. As far as I knew he stopped. It must have taken something major to get him started again."

An escaped wolf, a bottle around the house.

"It *would* have to happen at Jayne's place," March said. "She'll probably see this as an opportunity to bring them back together. Juan told me it was wolves that brought them together in the first place. Jayne was into exotic animals back then and was known all over California for it. It was always said that if you wanted a boa, she was the one to call."

"I don't know if I'd say Jayne wants to get back with Juan. I'm not sure I could say *what* Jayne wants."

"That's easy. Jayne wants what's good for Jayne."

"That place needs a lot of work. She could probably use a man around—or why doesn't she just sell off a few acres and use the money to fix the place up if she doesn't want a man around?"

"She can't. Her last husband put the ranch into a trust for the Conservation Committee. Technically she got the property in the divorce settlement and can live on it until she dies, but she can't sell an inch of it."

"What does she live on?"

"Who knows? Her looks?"

"She's not the ex-wife who got Juan's file through the Freedom of Information Act, is she?"

"Yes."

"You know, only the person who was actually under investigation is entitled to his or her file. Jayne wouldn't have access to what the feds have on Juan unless she was involved too."

"It wouldn't surprise me."

"What did she do? Do you know?"

"No. I met Juan after he got out of jail when he and Jayne were breaking up. He doesn't like to talk about that period of his life. I think he feels guilty about whatever happened to Jayne even though he went to jail and she didn't. You'll let me know what happens next, won't you?"

"Yeah," I said.

Montana is the land of big sky and big quiet. I envied March for that, having been aware of an undercurrent of hot summertime sounds on my end while we talked, the throb of the swamp cooler, the high-pitched scream of the cicadas. The cicadas were at it when you got up in the morning, when you ate lunch, when you went to bed at night. It was the kind of annoying sound—like a fingernail scratching a blackboard—that could drive you over the edge, if you were close to the edge. The edge wasn't exactly in sight, but I'm always aware that it's out there somewhere and probably closer than you think. My thoughts were interrupted by a booming bass that rattled the bars of my cage—the sound of fifteen grand, or more, parking on Lead. The spiders on the spider plant shimmied, a Bic pen boogalooed to the edge of the desk, rolled over and fell off. No one who was a rock-and-roll teenager in the sixties likes to think she could get to a point in life where she'd find herself screaming at someone else to turn the music down. Even if it *was* 102 and I was trying to get some work done, did I have to propel myself through the reception area and out the front door yelling, "Turn that fucking music *down*"? The beat emanated from an immaculate sixties Impala, two-tone turquoise and white with fins, wire wheels and purple biscuit velour upholstery. Fuzzy dice hung from the mirror. The driver, who was wrapped around the chain-link steering wheel, was cute, if you like the type, with a black goatee and a smirk for a smile. My secretary, Anna, was curled up next to him combing her hair. The music got lowered just enough that I could hear her say, "Jeez, what's the matter with *her*?"

"Where'd you find stereo man?" I asked once Anna had settled down at her desk and her lunch date had blasted off, crumpling the pavement behind him.

"On the corner of Montgomery and Wyoming."

"What was he doing? Dancing in the street?"

"You really want to know?"

"I asked, didn't I?"

"Okay. I wanted to meet some new guys, see, so I stopped my car, put the hood up and looked at the engine. In forty-five minutes fifteen guys stopped." Considering Anna's summertime look—short black boots; short, tight size 6 skirt; size 20 hair—that wasn't surprising.

"Good thing you weren't on East Central," I said, where the hookers hang out.

She ignored me. "It's the best way in town to meet men and there's always something wrong with my car anyway. They all look at the carburetor, the fuel filter, or the fuel pump and they tell me it's vapor lock and to wait a few minutes and it'll go away. You ought to try it sometime."

"I've already got a man who can fix *my* car, thanks."

"I'll say. Anyway a bunch of them took my number. Stevie was the best looking."

"What happened to George, the computer salesman?"

"He's boring," she replied, looking in the mirror and making a final adjustment to her moussed-in-place hairdo. One slightly out-of-place curl made me wonder if her lunch date had been more than that. If, in fact, it had been a nooner. Anna's hair didn't get mussed often. It was a slow day, one boss had been out of town, the other was out to lunch and it was summer, after all, when thoughts turn to sex, even in the middle of the day, especially in the middle of the day. I looked at Anna more closely. She didn't have the happy cat look of someone who'd had sex in the afternoon, she had the lazy cat look of someone who'd eaten too much and wouldn't be getting any work done.

"What's wrong with boring?" I said. "George showed up on time, he has a good job, he drives a Toyota with a normal radio." Just because I didn't go for boring myself didn't mean I couldn't recommend it to someone else.

"I'm only twenty; I want some excitement."

"Remember that excitement at twenty can lead to poverty and teenage dependents at thirty-five," I lectured.

"I don't see you settling down with Mr. Right and *you're* not poverty stricken," she said.

"I'm not rich either. And since when have I become a role model anyway?"

"Hey, you're the boss."

"Right," said I.

The Kid came for dinner. I made Margaritas and Chile Willies, his favorite, a mixture of blue corn tortillas, salsa and Monterey Jack cheese. I served it with a jícama and carrot salad on my coffee table. The Chile Willies were hot and gloppy, the jícama was cool and crunchy. While we ate I told him about Juan and the wolf.

"Why does this guy have to show the wolf off like some animal in the circus?" the Kid asked.

"He's trying to educate people so they'll leave the wolf in the wild alone," I answered.

"He has to make a pet out of him to do that?"

"I wouldn't say Sirius was a pet. Juan has trained him to be comfortable with people, but not to be a pet."

"Too bad he didn't get on the wolf path when he was free and go to Mexico. He'd be safer there."

"That path still exists?"

"*Sí*, only people use it now instead of wolves. Lobos are very smart and they always find the best path. Because they go so far they have to be very careful of the feet. When you cross the desert the wolf paths are the best ones to follow." The Kid paused, sipped at his Margarita, continued. "Before I came here I lived with the Norteños in the Sierra Madres. They had a wolf that somebody shot. She didn't walk good and could not take care of herself so they tied her up. They had chickens and the chickens were always disappearing. It couldn't be the wolf, they said, because the chickens were too far away from her chain, but one day I watched her. She pushed her food in her dish to the end of her chain and she left it there, went back and waited in the shadows. When the chickens came to eat the food, she came out and ate them, the feathers, the feet, everything." The Kid shook his head in admiration. "It's a beautiful animal."

It was a long speech for him and when he was done he went back to his dinner. If eating and sleeping with enthusiasm are a sign of mental health, then the Kid is a paragon. You could add working—working hard came naturally to him; he had, after all, grown up in Mexico. And if you threw in loving, well, he hadn't been bad at that either.

"They call men who cross the border alone lobos, too," he said when he'd finished eating. "Did you know that, Chiquita?"

"No."

"Wolves don't like to be alone. They will travel hundreds of miles to find another. How did you sleep in Soledad?" he asked.

"Okay."

"You didn't have that dream?"

"No."

"Not once?"

"No."

He stood up but it wasn't to go into the kitchen and help with the dishes. "I think I go home now," he said.

"Why?" I asked.

He shrugged. "The dream is gone. You can sleep alone."

"Well, yeah, I can, but that doesn't mean you have to go home." I'd been spending too much time thinking about other people's sex lives. It was time to put some energy back into my own. Was that because the dream had gone, because I'd put some distance between me and my memories of a killer or because I'd put some distance between me and the Kid? Who knew? I did know that for the first time in months I was feeling a hormonal surge. My surges have a way of expressing themselves in monosyllables. "Kid," I said, "why don't we ..."

He knew what I meant. "You want to do *that*, Chiquita?"

"Yes."

"I don't have any of those things." He meant condoms.

"That's okay. I do."

"Okay, Chiquita, *vamos*," he said.

It was a night like no other, followed by a day like most at Hamel and Harrison, full of real estate and divorce, the urge to settle down succeeded by the urge to hit the road. The swamp cooler wheezed. Bob Bartel did not call me back. Brink kept his cool by staying home. It was one of those quiet Friday afternoons when the phone doesn't ring and the mail is junk. It's a chance to catch up on your paperwork, if you're into paperwork. It was a chance for my body to catch up, too, on some missed sensations. I don't know if anyone ever takes sex for granted, but you can get more or less accustomed to it. When you've been away, however, your body kind of replays the moments and hums and glows. That's what was I doing, drawing on my yellow pad, wondering if the Kid was humming, too, when the phone rang around four.

It was Juan Sololobo and trouble had found him once again. "It's bad this time," he said. "Worse than '68."

"What are you talking about?" I asked, trying to bring my mind back to the rotten reality of the law.

"Bob Bartel," he said.

"What happened?"

"His truck went off the road last night on the west side of Soledad Pass, rolled down an embankment and burst into flames."

"Shit."

"He's dead."

"Oh, God, not Bob Bartel," I said.

"Hang on. It gets worse. The cops think it wasn't the fire or the accident that killed him. It was the bullet shot through his head. Can you guess who they want to blame it on?"

"Don't tell me."

"Me," Juan Sololobo said.

"How do you know that?"

"Ohweiler came by wanting to know where I was last night."

I'd already been to court once for Juan, which made me his attorney of record. Ohweiler had no right to question Juan without my permission and he had to know I'd never give that permission. He wasn't the brightest guy in the world, but he'd know that. He was taking advantage of Juan's ignorance of the law and/or his propensity for doing things he shouldn't. Juan should have remained silent and refused to answer questions. He should have asked for his attorney. "You didn't tell him anything, did you?"

"I told him that I was home in bed with Jayne."

"Anything else?"

"No. He pissed me off when he started talking about Bill Wiley. What right does he have to go poking around my past?"

"Juan, I'm your lawyer, remember? You're paying me to represent you. That means *you* don't talk to the police about anything ever, *I* do. Got it?"

"I *was* telling the truth."

"It doesn't matter."

Legally all Juan was required to do was give his name. Anything else would be deemed coercive and inadmissible, fruit of the poisoned tree, in court—if it got to that. But that didn't mean that Ohweiler wouldn't find some other way to use it to his advantage. Dealing with the police is bad enough. Dealing with your clients can be even worse. I took a look at my calendar, saw a weekend coming up. "I'll be back down there Monday. In the meantime you're not to say a word about this to anybody."

"All right," he said.

Next I called Sheriff Ohweiler and got into pissed-off attorney voice. "I'm Juan Sololobo's attorney of record and you have no right to question my client." I could see Ohweiler sitting at his desk in his sheriff's suit breaking a sweat. Because I had gotten tough? Or because it was 102?

"You got nothing to worry about," Ohweiler said. "You got a client that would rather lie than eat. He started lying from the minute he gave us his name. Juan Sololobo. Hah! We know he's Bill Wiley."

"What have you got on Bob Bartel's death?" I asked.

"What we got is that someone was trying to make it look like an accident, like Bob was coming home from White Sands or somewhere and fell asleep. A witness saw the truck go over the embankment at 1:30 A.M. and someone in motor-cycle gear trying to hide beside the road."

"What did the medical examiner say about the head

wound?"

"It was clean like it came from a high-powered rifle, not a handgun. Bob's wife says he never came home from work. She called me around eight lookin' for him. Wasn't much I could do in the dark but check the bars and Bartel never hung out in them."

"What reason do you have to suspect my client?"

"He had a motive. Bartel took his wolf. And he damn near killed him for it a few days ago. You saw it yourself."

I'd seen somebody get shaken up. I hadn't seen anybody get damn near killed. Other than the principals, there'd been only two witnesses: Jayne and me. Had Bartel gone to the police? I doubted it. "How do you know that?" I asked.

"Bartel told Frank Boyd, his supervisor."

"Hearsay," it came out automatically. "Inadmissible."

"Ma'am, it's hotter than Hades in here and I got an investigation to conduct. You got any more questions?"

"No," I said and hung up the phone.

10

Bill Wiley and Juan Sololobo were one—or two or as many emotions and identities as could be contained in his cordy body. I'd seen the sober Sololobo and the drunk Sololobo and I'd seen the sober side apologize for the drunk. He'd entered fully into the spirit of each, exactly who he was pretending to be at the moment he was pretending to be it. Had I seen Bill Wiley yet? I wondered.

Bob Bartel had been a simpler person, a government employee, not an outlaw, a guy who was working to stay in the middle class, give his kids an education and do right by our wildlife, a gentle man who had a sense of humor, too, who had a family and a wife who probably loved him. He'd be an easy man to love. He should have lived to be ninety, died in his sleep, spent his declining years talking to trees, taming birds and playing with his great-grandchildren. I asked myself the question that always comes up when someone dies before their time. How old had Bob Bartel been anyway? Early forties, I guessed, a few years older than me. Smarter in some ways, dumber in others. I, for example, know better than to trust my fellow man, and it was one of them that killed him. Maybe one that he trusted, probably one that he knew anyway; most murderers are known to their victims, at least in rural America.

If the murderer had been Bill Wiley/Juan Sololobo, we were in deep trouble. Me, because I'd have to defend a man who might have been under the influence of my own tequila when he committed the act. If he'd drunk all he'd stolen that first afternoon, he would have been comatose instead of angry. He must have saved some tequila, but what had he done with it? Drunk it the night Bob Bartel died? Juan was also in trouble, because I'd have to defend him and because trouble seemed to be his middle name. I decided to wait a while before I called March with the worse news.

I took a look through my desk calendar—nothing there that couldn't be handled early next week by Brink, although I'd probably have to beat up on him to get him to do it. Then there was the Kid. Getting out of town a lot was easing the transition from almost living together to not, but I would have gone anyway. That's the kind of woman/lawyer I was. Did the Kid care that we were drifting back to the way things were? Did he prefer it that way? Had he even noticed? He couldn't complain about last night anyway. If that's what separation does, who's to complain? I read in a women's magazine in a waiting room somewhere that couples who argue have the best sex. There's a certain creative tension between people who don't agree about everything, don't have the same interests and backgrounds. The Kid and I didn't always agree, didn't always disagree, but no one would ever accuse us of being locked in place by similar backgrounds. I suppose you could get to a point in life where you could do without that kind of tension, where you'd want a man who was your clone. But a lawyer? I'd been down that boring highway. I called and invited the Kid for dinner.

"You're going back to Soledad?" he asked me later.

"Yeah."

"Why?"

"Because my client is about to be accused of murder."

"Why do this April and his friends always get accused of murder?"

"Maybe it's because they care about wildlife and that can be an unpopular cause in this country."

"Did he do it?"

"He says he didn't."

"And you? What do you think?"

"I don't know yet," I said.

I went a different route this trip, getting off I-25 at San Antonio. There's a cafe in San Antonio. I was hungry, but the place had no windows and I don't go into bars alone that I can't see the inside of. I was on Route 380 heading for 54 and 70, which pass the White Sands Missile Range and Holloman Air Force Base, that great football field in the sky where our modern-day gladiators prepare for war. Driving down this lonesome highway was a tribute to Bob Bartel because the Sierra Oscura at White Sands was where he had done his study for the federal government, where he had recommended that the lobo be reintroduced and where he had hoped to hear wild wolves howling before he died. The fact that missiles were tested at White Sands didn't necessarily make it an unsuitable wolf habitat. It was a vast area, 3,200 square miles, as Jayne had said, and the largest military installation in the country. There was already plenty of wildlife in the mountains: cougars, imported African ibex, antelope, deer and a good prey base for the lobo.

The question of whether White Sands was the best place for the lobo could be moot anyway. It was the only place that had been offered. The Interior Department liked it, they said, because it was federal land, because there was limited human access and no cattle grazing was allowed, a rare occurrence in New Mexico, where cattle grazed everywhere, and state and federal officials belonged to the cult of the cow. The army didn't like it, they said, because they didn't want nonmilitary personnel on their land. Ranchers were opposed because they thought the wolves wouldn't stay put, and because the missile range was on land that had been taken from their families in the first place and they had never been compensated for the loss. The animal they hated was going to be put on land that had been stolen from them so they felt doubly scorned. Environmentalists weren't crazy about White Sands but were inclined to think it was the best (if not the only) alternative.

Route 380 was the northern boundary of the vast expanse of federal land that housed White Sands National Monument, White Sands Space Harbor (the space shuttle alternate landing site) and White Sands Missile Range. Trinity Site, where the world's first atomic bomb exploded, was here, too, in the valley of the Jornada del Muerto, the Journey of Death. To the south was the loping gray Sierra Oscura, where the deer and the antelope played, where Bob Bartel had done his studies, reimagined the lobo and done what was right.

At Carrizozo I turned south on 54 and passed the Stallion Range Center, the Small Missile Range and the Oscuro Bombing and Gunnery Range, an oxymoron. How long could a place that tested bombs and guns remain obscure? And if it wanted to remain obscure, why put a sign on it? I reached Alamogordo, the town that serviced White Sands and Holloman Air Force Base. The streets there were named Saturn Circle, Uranus Place, Neptune Court, New York City. Alamogordo had a fast food strip to rival anyone's and was the home of the Dare to Dream Space Center, a rare combination of high tech and low food. It appeared that anything could come out of the sky and land here, and a lot of things already had—space shuttles, state-of-the-art warplanes, missile debris. If UFOs want to contact us this would be a good place to do it, I thought. They spoke their language here and the aliens could always pop in for a taste of real earth fat at McDonald's.

White Sands National Monument is on the south side of Alamogordo on Route 70. Except during hunting season it's the only place the government allows public access. It's also where you find the sands that give the place its name. At sunrise and sunset they turn New Mexico mauve, but in the middle of the day they are blazing white, whiter than snow. I've driven the sixteen-mile road into the sands plunging deeper and deeper into the Arctic at the same time that it was getting hotter every minute, the kind of dislocation felt by a person who is freezing to death and starts tearing off her clothes. But even in midday in midsummer the sand remains cool enough to walk on barefoot. Footprints linger long after you're gone, until the sand drifts and covers them up. It's a place you can't get lost in until the wind blows. Then the sands whip around like snow, making dunes that build up, achieve a brief balance (the angle of repose), fall down and start drifting all over again.

A large sign beside Route 70 said the highway was often closed for missile testing and this happened to be one of those times. The idea was to protect citizens from debris that rained down from the missiles and antimissile missiles that were tested here. Waiting in the hot sun behind a line of automobiles with their engines running made me feel like I was going to the beach. The wind blew, the air smelled of exhaust and brine. There was a thump as a missile hit a drone somewhere in the part of White Sands where the deer and the antelope did not play. Three sleek gray jets in triangle formation flew low and fast across the road, roared overhead, turned in unison, gained altitude and flew away. I liked to think they were F-16 Fighting Falcons. It had to be an adrenaline rush to be a master of the air flying a Falcon on the cutting edge of the technology envelope, thinking of all the things you could zap with just a push of a finger. It was a seductive fantasy even to me and I don't play high-tech games. It was thrilling to see what modern technology could do, to watch planes that were fast and powerful and worked, as long as you didn't think too much about their deadly purpose. The military experimented with these weapons for years before firing them, as they like to say, in anger. But sooner or later weapons that are designed, built and tested are bound to be used, if only because so much thought and effort goes into them, or because billions of tax-payer dollars have been spent on them, or just because they are there. One of nature's laws is that if man studies something, he won't do it, but if he builds it and holds it in his hand, he'll use it. White Sands was a monument to one side of man's curiosity: to experimentation, tinkering, technology. I had to wonder what that kind of mind-set would do to a wolf.

11

When I got to Soledad I questioned Juan Sololobo at Jayne's kitchen table. The kitchen was where he liked to be—it's one place you can always find water in the desert. He held a large cup of coffee (three sugars) in his W-O-L-F hand. An herb tea and a yellow legal pad sat on the table in front of me, a Marlboro smoldered in a dish (no ashtrays in this house). Jayne had taken one of her horses riding, which was all right with me; I wanted Juan to myself. Jayne had a way of reappearing suddenly so I kept one ear alert for her and began my interrogation. But first there was another issue that had to be dealt with.

"You've had lawyers before," I said. "Didn't any of them ever tell you not to talk to the police?"

"Sure, but I forgot this time, sorry."

What can you do with a client who's sorry but goes on doing the wrong thing anyway? Keep him away from liquor and law enforcement, for starters. Get the case over with as soon as possible. As for his need or compulsion to do the wrong thing, I was a lawyer, not a shrink or a priest.

"What I told Ohweiler was the truth," Juan said, peering into his cup's sugary black depths.

"It doesn't matter. Don't tell the police anything, not even the truth; they'll find some way to use it against you. Sooner or later Ohweiler's likely to show up here with a search warrant. If he does, you don't say anything but hello and good-bye. Got it?"

"Got it," Juan said.

"Okay, now I need to know exactly where you were for the twenty-four hours after I left here at 8:30 on Thursday morning. Your whereabouts is important. You did, after all, threaten the guy." I picked up a pencil in my lawyer hand.

"Who knows that but you and Jayne?"

"Anybody Bartel told. His supervisor, for one."

"Probably made it seem a lot worse than it was, too."

"Where were you and what did you do?"

"It was raining so I hung around here in the morning, did some repairs for Jaynie. When the sun came out about 11:30 she went riding. I had lunch, took a walk."

"Where?"

"Not far, up to the falls, maybe three miles from the house. I got back around 4."

"Why didn't you ride?"

"I don't like to ride." A man after my own heart, although I had developed a soft spot for Chili. "I'm not like Jayne; she goes out every day. Loves to ride, always has. She's been crazy about animals—all of 'em—ever since she was a kid."

"What time did Jayne get back?"

"After I did. Around 4:30."

Juan sipped at his sugar, I wrote on my pad.

"Nobody took the truck or van anywhere?"

"Nope."

"You didn't talk to or see anybody but Jayne?" I continued.

"Nobody. I don't know anybody in Soledad."

Unfortunately, he had known Bob Bartel. "What happened after 4:30?"

"I cooked. I started a big pot of posole and around 6:30 we ate. We had that, tortillas, beans. I made a jícama salad. The posole was a little on the hot side for Jayne. Ask her. She'll tell you. We talked about old times. I took a Xanax and went to bed before 10."

"You didn't have anything to drink, did you?"

"Hell, no, drinking doesn't put *me* to sleep."

So I'd noticed.

"Listen." Juan placed his tattooed hands on the table. "I'm gonna be honest with you. I got into your tequila the day I shook up Bob Bartel."

The next question was how had he known where to look, but I didn't ask.

"It was a dumb thing to do and I am real sorry, real real sorry. It's been years since I had a drink. It was only because I was so damn upset about Siri. I love that guy."

I'd noticed that, too.

"I'm gonna pay you back, but I'll just give you the money and let you buy the stuff if you don't mind. I don't want it around the house."

"Forget it," I said. I hadn't brought any Cuervo Gold this trip so my conscience was clear. "You didn't drink all you took that day, did you?"

"No. I was disgusted with myself and Jaynie was pissed, too, so I threw the rest away, flushed it down the john in fact. She always hated my drinking. That was one of the things that broke us up."

"So you took your Xanax and slept all night?" One of those things would do it for me.

"Well, actually." Juan finished his coffee, cradled the cup in his L-O-V-E hand. "Jaynie woke me around 1. I remember seeing the time on the digital clock. She'd had a dream that turned her on and she wanted to make love. I was kind of dopey from the Xanax and it took me a while to wake up, but I got into it. Sure you don't want any coffee?"

"No."

He got up and poured himself another cup. I heard a car come down the road, a door slam and footsteps crunch the gravel. Juan heard it, too, and his ears picked up. If he'd had any hackles on the back of his neck they'd have gone into piloerection. His pale eyes got the look of a wary wolf, but that's like saying wary lawyer. What else but wary would a wolf or a lawyer or an ex-con be? There was a knock at the door that had the loud thump of law enforcement.

"Let me handle this," I said and walked down the hallway to the door.

It was Sheriff Ohweiler wearing his cowboy hat and Ray-Bans accompanied by a skinny, blue-eyed deputy. "Howdy, ma'am," he said as he handed me the anticipated search warrant.

I took it from his sweaty hand, looked it over and saw it was in order. "Come in," I said.

"You guys are wasting your time. You're not gonna find anything here." That was Juan, who had followed me down the hallway, breaking his promise already. With willpower like that it was no wonder he, tequila and trouble got together.

"I think you want another cup of coffee," said I.

"No, I ..." he tried.

"Yeah you do," I said. "It's in the kitchen." It was the first and maybe the last time he obeyed me.

I followed Ohweiler and his deputy around the house while they conducted their search. It was interesting to observe the places they looked, the things they noticed. If nothing else, it made me see Jayne's place in a new light; we were, in a way, looking at two different houses. I, for example, had been struck by what was absent—the rugs, the furniture, the paintings; they noticed what was there. Their first stop was Jayne's (and now Juan's) bedroom. They pushed aside the weights on the closet floor, then flipped through the clothes in the closet—Juan's Levi's, Jayne's pastel running suits. They were looking, I supposed, for a black leather jacket, a motorcycle helmet. The closest thing they found was a pair of heavy black boots, Juan's with no trace of mud on them. They opened the drawer in the nightstand, picked up a plastic-encased rectangle, looked at the lavender Xanaxes in their plastic bubbles, put them back. Salesman's samples, doctor's freebies. Juan wasn't the kind of guy to go to a liquor store to get his tequila or to a doctor for a prescription either. He'd come by his abusable substances by more creative means. While Ohweiler and his deputy went through the medicine chest in the bathroom making a note of all Jayne's drugs—bioflavonoids and vitamins—I gave some thought to substance abuse.

I'd taken Xanax myself a few times and it relaxed me so well I decided to never take one again; when it comes to abusing substances comatose is not my style. Besides, I had another substance that I could count on—Cuervo Gold. It's a man's drink, I know. You could say that was some kind of reverse macho, you could also say that taking a substance that doesn't come naturally makes it easier to keep a handle on it. The ones that seem to come naturally to women are the ones that knock them out: downers and wine. For men it's the wake-up, aggression inducers: hard liquor, cocaine, beer. Whether that was a biological imperative or social conditioning, I couldn't say. I know I don't want to be a zonked woman; I don't want to be an aggressive man either. There ought to be a middle ground. I'd rather not represent women on medication (or men on alcohol), but I have had some women clients who took Xanax and Valium, too. When one stops working they switch to the other. When the doctor stops prescribing them, they plug into the underground sleepy drug network. Xanax users have a way of finding each other and they look out for each other, too. Women take Xanax when love is on the horizon, when love has taken a hike, when they have to make love to a husband they don't love. I'd never met a man who took Xanax before, but Juan was a man in danger of losing his one true love.

While Ohweiler and his deputy looked under Jayne's bed, I wondered which side of it she slept on. The nightstand side, most likely, where the Xanax was and where a stuffed teddy bear sat on the pillow. The bed was unmade, with a white quilt tossed carelessly over it, the scene of one night's lovemaking that I could verify and who knew how many others? Jayne for one; it was her bed. There was a digital clock next to the bed displaying the red number 2:45. A.M. or P.M.? The clock didn't say. Red numbers were the kind of thing you'd notice if you woke up in the middle of the night, especially if you were clock phobic like me and not used to seeing time staring at you.

"Has the medical examiner established the time of death yet?" I asked Ohweiler.

"As a matter of fact he has, ma'am," he replied. "Midafternoon."

"Midafternoon? Are you sure? That's almost twelve hours before the truck went off the embankment."

"That's what the report says, ma'am."

It's hard to pinpoint the exact time of death, I knew, although an approximate time could be established by body temperature and the degree (or lack) of rigor mortis.

While I pondered this change of events, they moved on to my room, the guest room. I followed. I was staying over again, but I hadn't brought my bag in yet so we didn't have to argue about whether or not they could look through it. Not that I had anything to hide; it was the principle. There was nothing in the room but an empty chest of drawers, an empty bedside table, an empty bed, bare walls, bare floor. It had the look of a nun's cell. They poked through the adjacent bathroom—empty except for one pink towel—and I thought about what had gone on in *this* bed. Not much, when I'd been there. One night had been filled with Juan's wolf howls and cries (Juan wasn't the kind of guy you could ignore, even in the middle of the night—especially in the middle of the night). I hadn't had any dreams that I'd want to remember. Given an ordinary situation, would a nun's room produce more erotic dreams or less? More, I figured. People who are having sex don't have to dream about it.

Having come up empty here, the law marched on to the living room, where the missing paintings were striking by their absence and Frida by her barbed-wire-eyebrowed presence. It's hard not to notice Frida Kahlo. Her eyes found you the minute you entered the room, but what were they saying? *Te acuso?* Whatever you throw at me, I can take it? Tree of hope, keep firm.

Sheriff Ohweiler broke a sweat as he crossed the ballroom-sized floor, but not because he was dancing. He lumbered over to Frida and lifted his Ray-Bans. "Jeez," he said. "What the hell's the matter with her?"

"She was impaled by a stake," I said. "In a bus accident."

"Whew." He took out his handkerchief, wiped the sweat from his chin and then took Frida off the wall and looked behind her. For drugs? A weapon? Frida's eyes were *her* weapon, that and her paintbrush. I was glad Jayne wasn't here to see him take the painting down. I'd seen Juan in action, Jayne in distress; once of each was enough for me.

"That painting is worth more than your house," I said. "I'd be careful of it if I were you."

"Yeah?" Ohweiler hung Frida back on her nail. "Ain't the kind of thing I'd want in *my* house."

One man's artwork goes in another man's garbage bag. People trash priceless treasures and never even know (or care) that they're doing it. I wondered what Ohweiler had on his wall. A tiger on velvet? Elk horns? A mountain lion's head?

He went next to the second most expensive thing in the room, the conquistador credenza. Paying no attention to the quality of the wood or the beauty of the carving, he opened it up. The shelves were stacked with manila legal folders. He flicked quickly through them—what he was looking for wasn't on paper—put the folders back, closed the credenza. Next he went over to the people-sized fireplace, stuck a poker up the chimney, knocked loose some soot. Then he picked up the cushions on the cowboy sofa, felt for lumps, put them back.

There wasn't anything else in the room to search so he went out to the hallway, looked through the closets. Nothing there but running shoes and horse gear. He moved on to the kitchen. Juan, still obeying his lawyer, had taken a cup of coffee and gone out to the portal. Ohweiler went through the refrigerator probably looking for ice cream and cake. He opened a covered pot full of puffy white corn in red chile sauce. "What's that?" he asked.

"Posole," said I.

"Ugh. How can people eat that stuff?" He picked up a loaf of whole grain bread, examined the vegetable bin: lettuce, carrots, jícama. "Rabbit food," he said.

By the look of Ohweiler he didn't consider it food unless it had sugar and fat in it. "There's some sugar in the cupboard," I offered.

He went to the cupboard, looked through the boxes on the shelves, but he didn't find a high-powered rifle, a motorcycle helmet or anything to eat either. He was coming up empty all around. An empty hand for him was a fuller hand for me, but you wouldn't really expect that anyone who would go to the trouble to run Bartel's truck and body off the road nearly twelve hours after he was killed would be careless enough to leave the weapon lying around the house either.

"If they'd known you were coming, they might have put out some cookies and milk," I said.

"Um," replied Ohweiler.

This being an old adobe there was no basement or attic. "We'll check the barns next," he said. He cut across the portal where Juan sat cradling his coffee and for the moment anyway keeping his mouth shut. I stuck to Ohweiler and the deputy like an annoying fly, following them into the horsy-smelling stable. Sunlight filtered through the dust and illuminated hay and horse gear but no horses; they were all outside. This was one place on the property where a motorcycle could be hidden, but it wasn't here. Another place was Juan's van, but I'd already looked and knew it wasn't there either.

"Did your witness see a motorcycle at the crime scene?" I asked.

"No, ma'am. The witness was going sixty-five miles an hour. There's a rest area right near the crime scene and we figure the motorcycle was parked there." His officious politeness was getting on my nerves and being called ma'am made me feel like I was 110.

Ohweiler found no high-powered rifle here either and we left. Just as we stepped into the bright afternoon light Jayne rode up. Coming upon people suddenly on horseback makes an impression, as Cortés and the conquerors knew well. Horseback makes a person more than ten feet tall. The conquistadors heightened the effect by wearing metal helmets and armor that glinted in the sun. Jayne relied on Clairol. She was in riding gear: blue jeans, denim shirt, cowboy boots, but she resembled Lady Godiva with her long blond hair billowing behind her. The sun at her back gave her a golden aura, airbrushed away her wrinkles and made her for the moment movie-star perfect. The sun on the law officers made *them* one skinny man and one fat one who wore shabby uniforms and earned twenty-five thou—or less—a year.

I hadn't seen a horse yet that could stand still and hers danced around, snorted and cast a long-legged jittery shadow. Jayne's nostrils widened when she saw Ohweiler and the deputy step out of the barn. She had a pistol in her holster and a riding whip in her hand, which she tapped against the horse's shoulder. Ohweiler's hand moved involuntarily toward his holster. "What are you doing on my property?" she said.

"We have a search warrant," Ohweiler replied. He had the legal authority but her display was a lot more imposing than his dumpy pose. His hand moved away from the holster.

"It's legal; I saw the warrant," I said.

"You sure?"

"Positive."

"Well, get it over with and get the hell out of here," Jayne snapped, prancing her horse around toward the barn, turning into the light which cross-examined her and found a human being, not a female centaur, one who legally owned her property but was losing the improvements on it. One who dyed her hair and had age lines in her face. One who, even with a lawyer around, couldn't keep pudgy law enforcement with a search warrant away. It's better not to challenge pudgy gray men. They like to bring down the beautiful and the mighty. That's the efficient way democracy works. We destroy those we envy through the courts and the press. It used to take a revolution.

Ohweiler, however, remained cowed. "Yes, ma'am, we're leaving right now," he said.

12

I'd have a chance to depose Bob Bartel's supervisor if Juan was indicted, but why wait till then? I had an uneasiness about this case that made me want to get it resolved, at least in my own mind. My excuse for talking to Boyd was that Sirius was still being held in captivity in the zoo and I wanted to get him out. In the morning I called the USFWS office and asked if Boyd was in. "No ma'am, he sure isn't," a secretary answered, "but he'll be back in about a half an hour. He could see you then."

"How do I get there?" I asked.

"Where are you coming from?"

"Roaring Falls Ranch."

"Oh, that's easy. Come on down the hill, get on I-10 west, get off at the Pomona Road exit, turn right, then go about a quarter of a mile and you'll see a bunch of government-looking buildings on the right. Turn in there, go south to the north-south facing building, then you go to the bottom of the U and turn right. Now the building you want's facing east, next to the chain-link fence, but what you want to do is you want to go to the north side of the building and come in the middle door, but you have to park your car on the west side because only people that work here can park in front of the building. Got it?"

"There will be a sign on the door, won't there?"

"I think so. Now *you* have a nice day."

"You bet," I said.

Pomona Road was a piece of cake, but it took another thirty minutes to find the north-south building, then the building with the north-facing door with no parking for visitors, and I asked directions twice along the way. The government complex was as confusing as the government mind. The FWS office, once I found it, was in a squat cinder-block building that faced either north or south or east or west. Unless the sun was rising or setting I couldn't tell. It had an institutional green interior, gray metal desks and maps all over the walls.

"You didn't have any trouble finding us, did you?" the secretary asked. She was about as old as Anna and about as interested in her job, although not as interested in her appearance. Her hair was unmoussed, unstyled, her makeup absent. It was a country look and she had a country name to go with it—Lynette. I saw it on the nameplate on her desk.

"I think I made a wrong turn at the top of the U."

"I know. Sometimes I have a hard time finding the place myself. Frank's talking on the phone. He'll be with you in a minute." She turned back to her computer and clicked the keys.

I studied the USGS maps on the wall. I'd like to be in a profession where I could hang maps on the wall, although I could do without the metal furniture, the institutional green paint, the cinder blocks and forty years to retirement. All I had on my wall was a UNM law degree. Maps are my favorite form of reading and art. I like looking at the dotted lines that lead to out-of-the-way places and time warps, the red lines that mark the lonesome highways, the high-speed interstates. I like the mountains, the valleys, the blue veins of rivers, the yellow squares of Indian reservations, the green of national forests. I like to think there's all that land out there uninhabited by humans. I was staring at a map of the Soledads trying to get a falcon's fix on them and looking for El Puerto when Lynette told me Boyd had gotten off the phone and pointed the way to his office.

I was expecting a cautious public official. What else would one be when everything they say can be used against them and often is? But that's not the same as being a wary crook or a lawyer. The difference is bureaucrats don't have the right to remain silent. They have to listen to public comment and respond to it, although that doesn't mean they have to say anything. Mealy-mouthed evasion goes with the territory and the longer bureaucrats stay in their jobs, the better they get.

When I saw Frank Boyd I knew I'd be dowsing for water in the desert. His hairline was receding at the same rate as his chin and they had achieved a kind of balance. From straight on he was all nose, eyeglasses and frown. In profile he looked like a Mayan glyph. He was gray, weary, in his late fifties, I'd say, looking longingly at the retirement road, which meant he probably hadn't said anything worth hearing for thirty years, maybe even had forgotten how. The best I could do was keep him talking and hope that something of interest would bubble out. He was having an allergy attack, it being the season when antihistamines are—for some—the drug of choice. There's pollen even in the desert. A box of Kleenex sat on Boyd's desk. His eyes were red and runny and he sniffed when he wasn't sneezing. He wore a white shirt and tie and his overall pallor gave him the look of a man who would prefer to leave the air conditioner on and keep the outdoors out there. His job was to administer the wild, but he could do that by radio from his desk while his field biologists went out and did the studies, took the risks.

"What can I do for you?" he asked. The Kleenex he pulled from the box fluttered like a white bird in his hand.

"I'm Neil Hamel, Juan Sololobo's lawyer."

He blew his nose into the Kleenex and crushed it. "Juan Sololobo," he repeated. That name might be a swear word in Soledad, but Frank Boyd said it like he was saying maybe.

"I'm sorry about Bob Bartel's death," I said. "I spent some time with him and thought he was an exceptional human being."

"Had it all right here," Boyd tapped his forehead. "One of my best people. We care in Soledad. We're all upset by what happened and it's gonna be real hard on Erin and the kids." He threw a Kleenex at the trash basket, reached for another. "What kind of a man would kill Bob Bartel anyway?"

I could have told him that women were on the planet, too, and just as capable of killing as any man, but I didn't. I knew what *kind* of a person would kill Bob Bartel, a person whose interests were threatened, a person who had access to a high-powered rifle, a person whose finger might have already been on the trigger, but as I didn't know which person yet, I replied, "I don't know.

"My client wants to know what will happen to his wolf," I continued. "I'd like to get the charges against him of not securing a vicious animal dismissed because it has been established that the Upward Bound kids cut the chain and set the wolf free. If the charges are dismissed, will you release Siri?" That was a tough question for a bureaucrat because it required a yes or no. The answer I figured would be no but I was interested to see how Boyd would phrase it.

"We haven't quite passed the threshold of coming to a decision about that."

"Can you tell me when you will?"

He squirmed and equivocated until he passed a short, rounded word, painful to him as a kidney stone. "No."

"What grounds do you have for holding the animal?" I knew the answer to that, too, or I thought I did, but I wanted to hear Boyd say it.

"Three calves have been killed on the Phillips ranch. If an animal kills cattle in Soledad County we put it away. We can't release that wolf until we know what's been killing those cattle."

"Three? I thought there were only two."

"Don Phillips came across a third Thursday morning and Bob went out there to check it out. That was the last time I saw him. He radioed in from the ranch and said he'd seen the kill. It was a few days old—old enough for your wolf to have killed it before he went to the zoo. He said he still couldn't say what was doing it, but he'd bring the corpse in for further examination."

"Did he come back?"

"No."

"Was the corpse in the truck?"

"No. I presume it fell out when the truck went off the road."

"Wasn't that unusual for him not to come back to the office?"

"Bob was a field biologist. He said he was picking up some signal with his Yagi antennas that he wanted to check out, then he was going to White Sands and he'd see me tomorrow." Between the allergies and the death of Bob Bartel, Boyd's defenses were slipping.

"Some signal?" It was a trickle and I pounced but too quickly. Boyd darted away.

"Something like that. I think that's what he said."

"Could that signal have been a mountain lion that the FWS had collared?"

"Could. Could also have been a bird the FWS collared."

"Norman Alexander, who's a retired FWS biologist, said …"

"Who said Norman Alexander retired?

"He did."

"That's his version." I should have known everybody in Soledad County would know everything there was to know about everybody else.

"What do you mean?"

"Nothing." I should also have known they weren't going to tell me. "What did Alexander say?"

"That activity-monitored collars can tell you within hours if an animal has died."

"Could."

"Could they also tell you if an animal was being pursued?"

"Might, if you had an experienced operator."

"Bartel was pretty experienced, wasn't he?"

"One of our best." Boyd sneezed, reached for another Kleenex.

"Maybe Bartel picked up Buddy Ohles tracking another FWS-collared mountain lion. Bartel told me he'd had trouble with Buddy and mountain lions before," I said.

"Buddy's got his job to do, we got ours."

"It hasn't been proven that a wolf killed those calves. It could have been a mountain lion."

"It's possible, but they're known to prefer sheep."

"Maybe Bartel came upon Buddy tracking that lion and Buddy panicked and shot him. As Bartel said, you never know what a man's going to do when he's got a weapon in his hand."

"Buddy's a local boy." Juan Sololobo was not.

"He's pretty hotheaded."

"He wouldn't kill anybody. Your client's got a temper and he's got a record, too."

"Did Bob tell you Juan Sololobo threatened him?"

Boyd looked longingly at his watch. We were entering into a new realm of inquiry that made him uncomfortable. "That case is under investigation. It's really not my job to be talking about it. As for your original question, there's nothing I can do about your client's wolf. You know, we're taking care of that wolf because our department has the expertise in caring for it, but when it comes to cattle kills you really ought to talk to Agriculture. That's their department."

"Killing?"

"I didn't say that. If you have any more questions about this matter, you should talk to them." The no action alternative in government is always a viable choice. And if that doesn't work, pass the buck.

"Where are they?"

"They're in the north-south building on the other side of the U. You know where that is?"

"Sure," I said. "Thanks for your time."

"You bet," he answered.

I wasn't in the mood to face more bureaucracy or go looking for north-south buildings either so I borrowed Lynette's phone book, turned to the yellow pages and looked up wrecking yards. Bartel's truck had to go somewhere and Mickey's Salvage was obviously the biggest and the best. He had a half-page ad that said, "Cash for wrecked 4 x 4's and pick-ups. We tow. We also buy junk appliances and water heaters." It was on Green Street, four blocks down Pomona, three blocks left, two blocks right. I knew that because I looked it up in the map in front of the phone book.

"You have a nice day," Lynette said as I handed her back the book.

"You bet," I said.

Mickey's was on the seedy side of town where the cheap motels and the X-rated bookstores hang out. It was sur-

rounded by a chain-link fence so high that even a wolf
wouldn't try to leap over it, but what Mickey was trying to
protect was a mystery to me. If he had anything worth stealing I didn't see it. Mickey inhabited a shack in the middle of
a field that sprouted 4 x 4s, pickups, junked appliances and
broken water heaters, the detritus of home life, road life and
Saturday night drunks. A German shepherd snarled and
flashed its fangs at me from the end of a chain which I hoped
was more dependable than Juan Sololobo's had been. It put
on a fierce display of vicious, neurotic, inbred, human-
trained canine behavior. Dogs ought to have better things to
do than growl at people and guard junk, but that's exactly
what this one seemed to enjoy.

"Woof," I said.

The shepherd barked back, bringing Mickey to the door
with a can of Coors in one hand and a cigarette in the other.
Here was a man who had the courage to be upfront about his
bad habits in a health-obsessed world, but maybe that part of
the world hadn't made its way to Mickey's shack yet. He
wore jeans and a T-shirt with the sleeves rolled up. The
beers had gone to his belly and the cigarettes to his fuzzy
nicotine-yellowed teeth, the sight of which made me run my
tongue quickly over my own. He gave me a what are *you*
doing here stare. I don't suppose a whole lot of women
showed up at Mickey's door alone. The ones that did probably weren't looking for information.

"Shut up, Willie," he said, sipping from the Coors.

"I'm looking for Bob Bartel's truck," said I.

"Why's that?"

Even if you've rehearsed beforehand you never know for
sure what you're going to say until you say it. Everybody has
to lie now and then, if only to stay in touch with their fellow
man, but it's not the kind of thing you'd want to think about
beforehand. I used the old sister routine. Sisters take the

heat for a lot in this world. "I'm Erin Bartel's sister from Albuquerque," I said. "She asked me to stop by and take a look at the truck, see if there were any personal belongings the sheriff might have missed."

"That's not a truck you're gonna want to be looking at."

"I know but she asked me." I did my best to get into pleading, miserable woman voice.

Mickey drew on his cigarette, thought it over. You can still get a conditioned response if you're willing to take the pathetic female road. The trouble is you can never tell whether that response will be pity or attack. I'd found a soft spot in Mickey's plugged-artery heart, however. "Okay. You walk down that aisle there to the left and when you get to the end you'll see it, but you can't take anything out without asking me. So if you see anything you want, you come back here and I'll see what I can do about it."

"All right," I said.

He went back into his shack, shut the door and turned the country music up. Willie's vicious stare told me that he wished it was midnight and it was just him and me alone in the junk.

"Tough break, doggie," I said, circling around the end of his chain. He lifted his lip and bared a fang, one of his favorite expressions. Willie had come a long way from his species-wary wolf beginnings, had become exactly what man had trained him to be—a weapon, no more afraid of me than a speeding bullet would be.

I walked down the junker road past the demolished pickups and 4 x 4s, piles of broken dreams and twisted metal. The broken dream home appliances were at the far end of the lot. Wrecked vehicles had to go somewhere and get dismantled, too, but why would anybody want to use a part from a car that somebody else had died or been maimed in? But if people are willing to put somebody else's heart or lung in their body, you couldn't get too worked up about a used fuel pump. I passed a Blazer whose engine had gotten pushed into the front seat, a Ford pickup that had rolled over, squashed the roof and flattened the metal to the steering wheel. Anyone stuck in that cab would have been dog food. I saw a windshield with a neat hole where a head had poked through. For my next car I planned to buy a tank.

Eventually I found Bob Bartel's truck. It was the only vehicle in the lot with two crushed Yagi antennas on top and a government seal on the door of the cab. The front end was flattened as if it had landed on a boulder and bounced off. The shatterproof glass in the windows was cracked and webbed like the floor of Death Valley in summer. I told myself that Bartel was dead hours before the truck left the road, but it didn't help. I avoided the cab; I wouldn't even want to imagine what it smelled like after days in the sun. What I was looking for wasn't there anyway. I checked the bed of the truck. If Bartel had put the calf remains in here, there should have been blood, hair, bones, something left, even if the carcass had fallen out when the truck went over the embankment. The bed was dented but empty and clean. I looked at the wheels next, noticing the chevron pattern of the tread. Dried mud stuck deep in the cleats of the tires and hung thickly on the casings in grotesque lumps like elephantiasis tumors.

Willie started hyperventilating again as I neared the only way out, the shed. Mickey came to the door, put his fingers to his fuzzy teeth and whistled him quiet. "Find anything?" he asked.

"Maybe," I said.

13

As I headed back to Roaring Falls Ranch on I-10 I passed a car doing the speed limit and then another and one after that. In fact there was a whole series of cars, trucks and motorcycles ahead of me evenly spaced like stepping-stones of GM, Chrysler and Harley. No one goes 65 miles an hour in a 65-m.p.h. zone, not for long anyway, unless a cop is watching or they're in a funeral procession. I took a look at my rearview mirror; the heat made the headlights behind me shimmer like the eyes of a herd. I saw enough vehicles I knew in the procession—Jayne's truck, Ohweiler's police-mobile—to convince me that this was Bob Bartel's funeral. I cut into line, turned my lights on, too, and followed the others to the cemetery, which was at the end of a dirt road on top of a windswept hill planted with white wooden crosses and cement tree-trunk gravestones whose arms had been cut off. It was a desolate place where only plastic flowers bloomed, brighter than real in the August sun.

I parked the Nissan, turned off the lights and followed everybody else up the hill. A sheltering tent had been put up near the grave site with rows of metal chairs facing the coffin. I hadn't been invited but that's never stopped me from going anywhere before. Besides, as this was a religious occasion, I recalled what the sign in the Santa Fe Unitarian Church parking lot says: TRESPASSERS WILL BE FORGIVEN. My instinctive curiosity aside, I had a legitimate reason to be there—to mourn Bob Bartel.

The shade under the tent felt cool as water when I walked into it. As I sat down on one of the metal chairs I thanked God it hadn't been waiting in the hot sun. That was about all I had to say to Him.

I've been to enough funerals where the minister didn't know the deceased well enough to pronounce his or her name so I listened to make sure this one got it right. You'd expect that much in Soledad, where everybody knew everything there was to know about everybody else. After I heard it—Robert Evan Bartel—I tuned out while the minister said the rest of his piece. Was he Baptist? Presbyterian? Congregationalist? Mattered not to me. I thought my own animistic thoughts about Bob Bartel, wondered if his soul was wandering around the Sierra Oscura, whether it was alone or not. Who knows what souls do or whether they communicate with each other? Whenever you think of the dead as having a presence they're always watching over what's left behind, but if they can see, why can't they smell, hear, touch, taste? That's how I thought of Bob Bartel's soul, anyway, following the sensory path, hearing clouds as they passed in the sky, touching stones with the pads of his feet, sniffing scent markers, drinking the taste of fresh, hot blood; following the path with heart, the wary path, the wolf path. Although it's more likely souls—if there are souls—would follow the extrasensory path, using powers about which we haven't a clue. It was something you might ponder if you had a poet's mind, study if you had a scientific mind, dismiss if you had a legal mind.

The service was short and my reverie was interrupted by the clattering of chairs as everybody stood up. The time had come to put the body in the ground. If it had been up to me I would have scattered the ashes to the Sierra Oscura. The family stepped to the grave and Bartel's daughter, a long-legged antelope of a girl, dropped a flower on top of the coffin. His son held onto his mother and tried not to cry. It was an ashes to ashes, dust to dust burial and some might find it comforting but it's not how a child would like to think of a father, in a box in the ground. They'd like even less to think that a murderer had put him there. Most people would want to know, would have to know, who did it, if only so they could have the dubious satisfaction of seeing justice administered.

What I knew, but the children most likely did not, is that in the majority of cases the victim knows the murderer, especially in rural areas. It was a detail well known to law enforcement.

I also knew that if Bartel, a federal employee, had been out in the field doing his job when he was shot, his murder would be a federal crime. If he wasn't doing his job and wasn't on federal land, it would be a state crime. It might cause some quibbling over jurisdiction if the FBI chose to get involved. On the other hand they might just leave it up to local law enforcement. There were probably more than enough federal crimes to keep the feds occupied this close to the border.

In any case, the first suspect everyone always looks to is the spouse. Bartel's wife was a pale, grief-shattered woman who hugged her children and, even to my suspicious eye, didn't look like she'd be capable of murder. Besides, this crime didn't have a domestic MO. Domestic violence is angry and messy and occurs in or near the house. The neighbors hear screaming; there's blood all over the place. A crime of passion is usually a spontaneous gesture and wives tend not to have accomplices. Bartel's murder had been neater and more calcu- lated and Erin Bartel couldn't have called Ohweiler at 8 and gotten the truck off the road at 1:30 without an accomplice. Once she called Ohweiler everybody in Soledad would be on her doorstep wanting to know what was going on. For the moment, anyway, I ruled her out. That only left everyone else I knew in Soledad and a lot of people I didn't.

The ones I knew were all here: Norman Alexander, Buddy Ohles, Frank Boyd, Sheriff Ohweiler, Don and Perla Phillips, Jayne Brown, Charlie Clark. After the ceremony they all hung around comforting each other and talking over what had happened. I started walking down the hill alone but Charlie Clark caught up to me. His unruly mop flopped with every move he made, the gold frames of his granny glasses glittered in the sun. He was wearing jeans, running shoes and a blue T-shirt with piercing yellow eyes that said SAVE THE LOBO. It wasn't exactly funeral attire, but it made the point. "Nice shirt," I said.

"Thanks," Charlie replied. "You know what they're say- ing around Soledad?"

"Probably."

"Juan Sololobo shot Bob Bartel."

"Talk is cheap," said I.

"Not when lawyers are doing the talking."

"That depends on the lawyer. Life seems cheap in Soledad too."

"Especially when it's animal life," Charlie said. He nod- ded toward Buddy Ohles trotting down the hill behind us in hot pursuit of someone. Buddy was wearing a black polyester Western suit with embroidered arrows and silver tips on the collar from Miller's Outpost I'd say, or his big brother. He was scrawny, there was no doubt about it, and the suit sagged on him like skin on a fruit that had had all the juice squeezed out. Maybe he'd been spending too much time in the sun with his cowboy hat off.

"Is that Buddy?" Charlie peered up close when he reached us. "You were camouflaged so good I didn't know it was you."

"You keep out of this, wolf boy, she's the one I want to talk to."

"Shoot," I said.

"You got no right accusing me of killing nobody. I heard you told Frank Boyd that Bob Bartel caught me tracking a mountain lion and that I killed him." News traveled fast in Soledad. In a couple of hours it had flushed Buddy Ohles out of the trees faster than a helicopter spraying malathion.

"I didn't *tell* Frank Boyd anything."

"That's the kind of fool idea a city dweller and a wolf lover would come up with. You know if wolves ate rubber and you got up and found the tires eaten off of your cars in the morning you can bet you city dwellers wouldn't be mouthin' off about bringing 'em back. And there wouldn't be no goddamn lawyers getting paid to represent the wolf lovers either."

"That's the kind of thinking that's made America great," Charlie said. "And just about what I'd expect from the ADC. In addition to the coyotes you guys slaughtered last year, you killed 1,200 bobcats, 7,000 red foxes, 200 black bears, 237 cougars, 80 timber wolves and 4.6 million birds and you spent 38 million of our tax dollars doing it. You know it would only cost half a million dollars a year to reintroduce the lobo, less than one and a half percent of what the ADC spends on killing."

"That critter ain't worth one wooden nickel of my money," said Buddy. "A wolf ain't nothing but a dog on steroids anyway. Who else but you gives a damn if it becomes distinct?"

"You mean extinct?" asked Charlie.

"Extinct, distinct, it all stinks if you ask me." Buddy spat a brown goober at the ground. Having gotten rid of the excess tobacco he went back to expectorating words. "And if you think I killed Bob Bartel, you'd better think again," he barked at me. "I've known him ever since grammar school. I never agreed with him about anything, and if I'da wanted to kill him I woulda done it a long time ago. Your boy Juan whatsits killed Bartel. He's got the antihunt, antikill, anti-American ethnic that's ruining this country and he did it because Bartel took his wolf. Sometimes you have to get down off your horse and tell the people how the cow ate the cabbage so I'm gonna lay it out for ya. A wolf is an outlaw, see, and wolf lovers got no respect for the law either. We don't need wolves down here no more than we needed the dinosaurs or you goddamn lawyers. We spent a lot of money getting rid of lawlessness in this country and now you think you're gonna bring it back. Well, it ain't gonna happen in Soledad County."

"I'll remember that," I said.

"You'd better."

He walked to the bottom of the hill, got into a pickup with a rifle balanced across the back window, put his foot to the pedal, the rubber to the road and drove away. "Asshole," Charlie said. He squinted in the sun, poked the dirt with his running shoe. "What are you doing this afternoon? I'd like to show you some of my Soledad County."

"Could that include the falls?"

"Sure. I used to go up there all the time when I was a kid."

"Okay," I said.

Nobody got on Jayne's property without her permission, or so she'd said. I was a house guest, which entitled me to permission. As for Charlie, well, he'd be my guest. Jayne was leaning on her truck deep in conversation with Norm Alexander when we left, me in the Nissan, Charlie on his motorcycle, no helmet. Either Charlie would be choking on my road dust or I'd be choking on his. I let him go first; he was unprotected. I'd never wondered why (or even if) Charlie rode a motorcycle but it didn't take me long to find out once he roared his engine and took off. The bike was loud and fast. Charlie liked the troublemaker image or maybe he just liked the trouble.

Juan had set up a workbench under the portal and was measuring something when we pulled up. His arms were bare and sweaty and he was wearing one of those belts with hammers hanging out. The carpenter image suited him; it was a more productive way for him to spend his time. There was a plastic gallon jug on the table next to him whose label read OZARKA SPRING WATER.

"Howdy," he said.

"Hi," said I. "You remember Charlie Clark?"

"You're the guy with Wolf Alliance, right?"

"Right," Charlie said. "That was a fine speech you gave for the wolf the other night. Really fine."

"I'm glad somebody dug it. You guys have got your work cut out for you down here. I've never seen such pigheaded opposition."

"Yeah, we've got our John Waynes and our landed aristocracy. The rest of the environmentalists got stalled out, going round and round ordering T-shirts, but we took the initiative, started a lawsuit against the Interior Department and cut through the bullshit. We're going for it with all the gusto we can muster. The lobo will be back."

I've seen a lot of lawsuits get mired in bullshit; I hadn't seen one cut through it yet. But who was I, a cynical lawyer, to disillusion Charlie Clark, who might even be the bright-eyed young environmentalist he pretended to be. I lit a cigarette for the trail and helped myself to a sip of Juan's water, which was not exactly what it pretended to be, although it was water. OZARKA, the label advertised over a picture of a blue mountain stream. The fine print, however, read, "From Ft. Worth Municipal Water Supply, Ft. Worth, Texas."

"This is Texas water," I said.

"Help yourself," said Juan. "So if you guys win what happens to the lobo? It gets reintroduced to White Sands as part of some experimental population, right? Then the FWS can radio-collar 'em, study 'em, drop 'em with tranquilizers and the ADC will shoot 'em whenever they wander off the range."

"Yeah, I know," said Charlie. "But it's a start and we're hoping the younger ones won't get on the radio."

"If they come back on their own like they're doing in Montana then they get classified as an endangered species, not an experimental population. Neil and I got a friend up there who told me that. That means nobody can legally shoot 'em without getting a permit and going to a hell of a lot of trouble, not even if they kill cattle. Why do you think you're seeing all these politicians coming out on behalf of wolf recovery in Yellowstone? Because if the FWS reintroduces them they can manipulate 'em, but if the wolves come back on their own, they can't. The Magic Pack came over from Canada into Glacier and now they're working their way down the Rockies. They'll be in Yellowstone before the ranchers know it. I hear there are lobos left in the Sierra Madres, too."

"Where the wolves and the drug dealers roam," I said.

"They say it's the drug dealers that are keeping them alive. Everybody else is afraid to go in there to kill, trap or even study 'em. There have been sightings in Arizona. Could be some illegal aliens have sneaked over the border into New Mexico. It's not so far away."

"Well, you're never going to get anybody to admit that around here," said Charlie. "The FWS will keep it quiet because they want wolves under their control and anybody else who sees one will shoot, shovel and shut up."

"Soledad ain't my favorite place. As soon as I get Siri back I'm outta here."

Unless, of course, he was indicted and held on charges of murder.

The shadows of the adobe wall crept towards the portal. We were moving from midafternoon to late. It was time for Charlie and me to be out of there. "We're on our way to the falls," I said to Juan. "Want to come?"

"Naah, I want to finish this job up for Jaynie and I've already been there once. That was enough for me. The part of California I'm from water's no big deal."

"Where's the path?" I asked, squinting toward the Soledad Peaks.

"Thataway," replied Juan, pointing at the far side of the parking area.

Juan passed around his bottle of Texas spring water. I thought about asking to take it along, but neither Charlie nor I had a backpack. I didn't feel like carrying it. We each took a hit from the bottle and took off up the path that led to the falls. I never wear a watch myself, but Charlie, like most people, did. "What time is it?" I asked him.

"Five," he said.

The path started out steep and soon got steeper. Started out hot and then got hotter. It was the kind of day when the air feels like an impenetrable thicket and the sun, nourisher of plants, bringer of warmth to other places, is an enemy, a preview of what it will be like everywhere when the next layer of ozone is gone, exposing a raw, angry, scorching sun. Even the birds maintained a stunned silence. What kept me going was curiosity and the belief that sooner or later we'd reach water and could start down.

The back country was about as I'd imagined it—high Sonoran desert, the kind of place you expect a man in huaraches to pop up and tell you that everything matters and nothing, the kind of place rattlesnakes hang out. In all my years in New Mexico I'd always wanted to see a rattlesnake—at a distance—but it hadn't happened yet. I keep my eyes open to the possibility, however. Rattlesnakes like hot, dry places. They have tough skin, too. When the unforgiving sun has turned the rest of us to malignancies, they'll still be here slithering around with the rodents and the roaches.

Although this was desert, it wasn't exactly barren. There was a variety of vegetation which Charlie was happy to tell me all about.

"We got Chihuahua and ponderosa pines, juniper, oak and mountain mahogany; sage, rabbitbrush, chamisa and mesquite; and for cactus cholla, button cacti, yucca and Spanish daggers," he said.

"Botany major?" I asked.

"Yeah. I'm working on my doctorate."

"And then what? The federal government?"

"No way."

After a hard hot mile we came to a tree that was bent over and humped like an old lady who hadn't taken her calcium. It was wider than it was tall, having been twisted and gnarled from the wind and the weather. Its bark was thick, notched, crocodilian. "That alligator juniper is a thousand years old," Charlie said. There was a gouge where someone had taken his little hatchet and had tried to hack it down, a heart that said JH LOVES BJ, slashes where lightning had struck. The tree had survived it all. "A thousand years old," Charlie repeated. "That tree was already ancient at the time of the conquest. It's seen one hell of a lot." He put his arm around the juniper and stared at it.

"I know that people talk to trees, but you're the first person I've seen make eye contact," I said.

"It's a female." Charlie hugged the tree. "In the winter it gets berries, and animals and birds have been eating them for a thousand years. Pretty incredible, huh?"

"*Arbol de la esperanza, mantente firme*," I said.

"What?"

"Nothing."

We continued up the path, one shadow after another, one foot after the other. The sun was on my back, my mouth was dry as dust, my eyes were focused on the path which had been softened by horse plops and chopped up by horseshoe prints, lots of them, some of them recent and sharp, others older and muted. There was also a pair of shoe prints going up and coming down, running shoes a lot bigger than mine, about Juan Sololobo's size. "There's one way Jayne can tell who's been on her property," I thought out loud. "It would be hard to cross here without leaving tracks."

"Did you know a wolf puts its back paws exactly on the spot where the front paws have been?" Charlie said. "It makes it hard to tell how many of them there are. It's hard to tell their number by their howls, too. The sound echoes around and you can't tell if you're hearing one or the whole pack."

"They protect their feet and always pick the best path, too," I said, echoing the Kid.

Charlie had gotten several feet ahead of me and he stopped and waited for me to catch up. He was looking down from a higher place and the sunlight glinted on his glasses. "You really think Bartel caught Buddy tracking a mountain lion?" he asked.

"It wouldn't be the first time." I stopped when I reached

him and wiped the sweat off my face, hoping he'd take the hint and take a long pause.

"Won't be the last either. The ADC and the state Game Commission, which sets the hunting rules, are like that." Charlie squeezed two of his fingers together. "The state approved a regulation that allows Buddy to kill just about anything he wants to. All he needs is a complaining rancher, no evidence required."

"An execution with no investigation, no evidence, no trial, no jury," I said. "Whatever happened to due process?" My mouth was so dry the words stuck to my tongue.

"And ranchers are always complaining that animals have all the rights. There was one rancher in Arizona who had 37 cougars killed to protect 135 head of cattle. And it gets worse. There are people out there, rich Texans for starters, who will pay big bucks to hunt cougars and hang their heads on the wall. The rancher loses a calf or a sheep. Maybe it's killed by a dog, maybe it's killed by a coyote, maybe it dies of natural causes, who knows? Anyways the rancher says he saw cougar prints, calls in Buddy, Buddy finds a cougar miles away probably, tracks it with his dogs until it's terrified and exhausted and climbs a tree. Then he calls in the big bucks hunter on his radio and that guy flies in by helicopter and shoots the cougar out of the tree. They call that sports hunting. The rancher and Buddy split the money and nobody has to worry about hunting seasons or limits or any of that stuff. And if the lion is already collared and Buddy has the frequency, hell, he doesn't even need dogs."

"What do you know about radio-collaring?" I asked.

"The person to talk to about that is Norm Alexander. He was a pioneer. He knows more about wolves than just about anybody else, too, but it's hard to get it out of him. He stays over there in Singing Arrow and keeps to himself."

We started up again, but this time I kept my mouth shut, my eyes focused on the near distance—the path—my thoughts on water, cool water, clear water, wishing I had a backpack with some ice and a water bottle between me and the sun, imagining I was running a race and around the next bend waited a hand holding water, water to drink and pour over your head, water to run down your face and your neck, a shower with an unlimited supply of water, riding a turtle in the sea off Cancún, slapped by the rapids in the Rio Grande Gorge. I thought of Evian, Perrier, Ozarka from the Fort Worth water supply; glasses, bottles, canteens, hands; snow, sleet, hail, ice cubes; springs, wells, puddles, cenotes; fountainheads, watersheds, faucets, hoses. I thought of gentle water, cleansing water, angry water, muddy water, trickles, floods, torrents, drips, flumes, Chinese water tortures, tidal basins, tidal waves, swimming holes, hot springs, water that carved Canyon de Chelly, inundated Glen Canyon, oceans that lap at the foundations of Venice. Water that flows around, under, over, through. Water that follows the path of least resistance. Water that gets where it wants to go no matter what.

When we finally reached them a thirsty mile later, Roaring Falls were a disappointment of hallucinatory proportions, a stream about six inches wide that trickled over the edge of a rock face, fell down about fifty feet and disappeared underground. They whispered but they didn't roar. It was a waterfall only a desert rat would love—or notice. "That's it?" I asked.

"You were expecting Niagara?" Charlie said.

"Well, no, but I've been hearing about these falls ever since I got to Soledad. I was expecting more than this."

"Maybe it's no big deal if you're from California ... or the

Duke City. You guys got wave machines and water slides."

"Ha, ha," I replied.

"This is all we've got and they get cranked up pretty good when it rains."

It wasn't wide but it was tall and it was water, the essence of life and cool, besides. I splashed some over my face, arms and neck, cupped my hands and filled them up.

"I wouldn't do that if I were you," Charlie said as I put my lips to the cup. "Giardia."

I'd lived in Mexico and knew all about giardia and amoebas too. Was one desperately needed sip worth weeks of pills and pain? I looked into my handful of tantalizing, revitalizing, parasite-filled water, opened my hands and let it all spill out.

"You can climb up the rocks to the top of the falls and there's a pool and a rock slide up there. That's where the kids used to go. Come here, I'll show you something." He led me over to the ruins of a building with some scraggly blackberry bushes nearby that had obviously been transplanted from some more congenial place and were struggling to survive. They had berries on them, though, tiny ones. I picked them for the juice. Below the ruins Charlie showed me a ditch lined with stones neatly piled on top of one another and fit together like Lego blocks. "That was a sanitarium for tuberculosis patients in the days people came to the Southwest to get healed and that ..." We looked into the ditch. "... is a diversion channel."

It had a lot more charm than the Duke City's concrete channels, I'll say that for it.

"When we get a good rainstorm," Charlie continued, "it'll fill up and the water will rush through here like the Rio Grande in snowmelt. Water doesn't last very long in the desert, but it's pretty impressive when it's around."

"Where does the trail go?" I asked.

"Thataway." He pointed toward the hoof tracks that circled around the spa ruins and continued on. The running shoe prints, however, headed back toward the way we'd come.

"And then?"

"Up to El Puerto and the top of the Soledads, but I don't go up there anymore. People have been shot at in the peaks."

"By who?"

"Smugglers probably: *marijuanistas, contrabandistas, nar- cotraficantes.* If I'm going to be plugged, I'd like it to happen in a meaningful action. There's nothing like the adrenaline rush of a well-planned action, but one thing I've never been crazy enough to do is confront a hunter with a loaded weapon, or a Mexican smuggler either. There's a path up there that leads right to the border and they smuggle in parrots, bull semen, drugs, you name it. Mexico's twenty miles away, but that's nothing to a Mexican. They used to fly all that stuff in, but now that the DEA has put a surveillance balloon up in Deming they've been catching all the planes and smugglers are back to using their feet and their burros again. That's another reason nobody around here wants the lobo to come back. Ranchers have made their peace with the smugglers and they don't want the government coming around, conducting investigations and screwing things up."

"The horse tracks go that way."

"Anyone who goes on horseback has a four-legged advantage and riders usually go armed anyway. They say they want to be able to shoot their horse if it trips and breaks a leg."

"What time is it?" I asked.

"Six thirty."

An hour and a half up, an hour, maybe, back down. The timing was right, the tracks were right, maybe Juan *had* come here alone the afternoon Bob Bartel was killed. Maybe he and Jayne had made love at 1 A.M. too. His story was holding up so far.

"We ought to start back if we're going to make it by dark," Charlie said.

That was all right with me. If I was going to meet a rattlesnake I'd rather meet one in daylight when I could see it coming. We began walking the three miles back to the ranch. It was a lot easier and faster going down than it had been coming up. The sun matured, mellowed, sank, lost its power to dehydrate and burn. It was a golden orange ball, spreading its radiance across the peach and apricot sky and the solitary plains, throwing some afterglow at the peaks as it went down.

Jayne was standing outside with her arms crossed watching the sunset when we got back to the house. "Nice bike," she said to Charlie.

"I like it, but I don't ride it much anymore. Anybody who cares about wolves and rides a motorcycle these days is suspect."

"Why's that?" Jayne said.

"Because when the lobo pups were stolen, they were stolen by someone wearing motorcycle gear. Any bike-riding environmentalist was a suspect."

"Oh, yeah," Jayne said, looking at the motorcycle and seeing no helmet there. "Well, I see that you don't wear the gear."

"Not any more," Charlie replied. "You've got to be careful when you're radical. They can take you down any time they want."

"How they gonna do that?" Jayne smiled.

"Through the media, by assassination."

Jayne laughed. "You have to be careful not to get too paranoid. You're a wolf activist, not the president, Charlie.

Someday you're going to have to settle down and make a living in the world, too. You don't want to be suspecting your neighbors and everybody else you come into contact with."

"I'll never stop being radical," Charlie said.

"Everybody says that when they're your age," Jayne replied.

14

On the pretext of going out for cigarettes that evening I drove to the 7–11 in Soledad and made some calls from their outdoor phone. One of the advantages of being a smoker is that you have an excuse to get out of the house when you want to. In most houses they're glad to see you go. First I called March.

"Neil," he said in an uneasy voice, not being accustomed to hearing from me in the evening. "Where the hell are you?"

"In Soledad." There was a pause. He knew what that meant—trouble. "You wanted to know what happened," I said.

"You're right. Shoot."

"Remember Bob Bartel, the biologist Juan shook up the last time I was here?"

"Yeah."

"He was murdered and Juan is a prime suspect."

"Oh, God. How did it happen?"

I told him.

"Does he have an alibi?"

"Making love to Jayne is his alibi for the time the body was disposed of. He says he was out hiking alone at the time Bartel was killed. I wouldn't exactly say either one of those was airtight."

"But on the other hand, if he were making them up, wouldn't he come up with something better?"

"Maybe."

"Juan gets a little crazy but he wouldn't murder anyone. You'll find out he didn't do it, I know you will."

"I hope you're right," I said.

My next call was to Norm Alexander, who was listed in the Soledad phone book although he lived in Singing Arrow. Phone books in this part of the world cover several hundred square miles. I told him I wanted to get together with him.

"Why?" he asked in a suspicious voice. Biologists here seemed to be as wary as everyone else.

"I want to talk to you about radio collars," I replied. That didn't make him any less wary, but he said he had to be in Soledad in the morning and would meet me at Hardee's.

By the time I got back to the ranch, Juan and Jayne had gone to bed and, as far as I could tell, to sleep. I spent another restless night in the spare bedroom with no tequila to help either. This time it wasn't the sound of screwing or howling that ruined my sleep, it was the thump of an explosion. "Incoming," I thought when the medium-sized bang woke me up. "Why did you think that?" my lawyer's mind asked once I was fully awake. "Were we at war when you went to bed? With who? Chihuahua?"

Thump. It rattled the glass in the window this time. I got up, went to the window, looked out. The night was bright enough so the yucca cast a pointed shadow and still enough that the shadow didn't waver. No wind warned that a storm was coming. No lightning flashes illuminated the sky. The stars were all in place, the night was smooth as velvet. Bang it went again, unaccompanied by any flare that I could see. Were we resorting to bombs now to stop the drug traffic?

Thump. The thumps weren't advancing or retreating the way thunder would. They stayed in place the way missiles being test-fired at a drone might. I remembered that I was in the shadow of the White Sands Missile Range where things that went thump in the night were missiles and antimissile missiles. Our government was making sure our defense system worked, keeping the volunteer army employed.

It was too noisy and too bright to go back to sleep and what could you hope to dream about after that anyway? Star wars? Refugees? I got up, threw on a T-shirt, jeans and running shoes, walked quietly as a ghost down the hallway and let myself out. It was bright enough to see any incoming rattlesnakes. I raised my arm and waved my hand, my moon shadow following in synchronicity. New Mexico is enchanted at night, so clear that you can follow the moon in all its phases and locate the constellations, so bright you can see where you're going. The thumps in the sky stopped. Either the missiles had hit their drones or they hadn't. The testing appeared to be over. I walked out into the desert until I couldn't see the house anymore, couldn't hear anything but silence, not a cicada, not a boom box, not a coyote, not an owl. I sat down on a rock near a juniper that was a hundred years old or more and looked toward the southern sky. There was one star brighter than all the others that had to be Sirius. I faced the Soledad peaks, silhouettes darker than the sky. "Aaahoooo," I howled softly and then louder, "aaahoooo." There was no answer.

In the morning over granola with a banana and my first cup of coffee, Juan's second or third, I told him that I had to be in Albuquerque tomorrow. The missiles had kept Jayne awake, he said, and she had taken a Xanax and was sleeping in.

Since it was the first time I'd been alone with Juan since I'd talked to Frank Boyd, I also told him that Agriculture or the FWS or whoever chose to take responsibility would not release Sirius until the calf-kill issue was settled even if I were able to get the charges against him dropped.

"I don't care about dropping the charges," he said. "I'm innocent and any jury is going to see that right off."

There are some pervasive fantasies in this country. One, that wars win something. Two, that guns don't kill people. Three, that everyone ought to get rich and star in their own movie. Four, that everyone deserves his or her day in court and when that day comes the case will be presented by a brilliant, committed lawyer, that a lifetime of wrongs will be vindicated by a wise judge and a sympathetic jury. The truth is litigation is largely a boring, time-consuming, expensive crapshoot. Juan had been through the process and had already lost once. What made him think he would win this time? The quality of his legal representation? His belief in his innocence? Ego? Romance?

"What happens if more cattle get killed?" Juan asked. "Then do I get Siri back?"

"I'm working on it," I said. "In the meantime let's just hope you don't get charged with Bob Bartel's murder."

"Is there anything you can do about that?"

"I'm doing what I can. I made an appointment with Norm Alexander this morning."

"Why are you going to see him?" Juan poured himself another cup of coffee, added a lot of sugar, a little cream.

"He could be useful as an expert witness. What you can do is keep quiet, stick around here and don't answer any questions."

"You got it," he said.

* * *

When I got to Hardee's I was grateful for Juan's healthy interest in food. For one thing I got to eat it. The nurturing side of
his character indicated he was either softer than your aver-
age criminal or more complicated. There wasn't anything I'd
want to eat at Hardee's and the coffee had the oily charm of
the fluids you pour in your car. Forget about herb teas. Norm
Alexander had gotten there before me and was eating a
greasy sausage wrapped in a dough parka. I'd eaten at Hardee's once on a long road trip and knew their breakfast
sausage/biscuit combination of slippery fat and sticky dough
was unswallowable. Hardee's had defeated me, I'll admit it.
But Norman Alexander didn't seem to notice that what he
was eating wasn't edible. He didn't seem to notice what he
was eating at all. The breakfast biscuit was disappearing fast.
The fact that he didn't talk much helped. You can always
tell who's been talking during a meal because the talker's
plate is full when everybody else's is empty, only at this
meal Norm started out full and I started out empty. I hoped
to change that in terms of information before the meal was
over, but the odds did not appear to be in my favor.

"Eat here often?" I asked. It could explain his sour expression.

"Only when I come to town and that's only when I have
to." He chewed at his biscuit, sipped at his coffee and didn't
say any more. Hardee's was filled with men older than Norman Alexander, men who were white-haired and bald, men
beyond retirement age, in fact, with nothing to do, who sat
around drinking the coffee, reading the *Soledad Times*,
talking about baseball and the prices cattle were bringing
in. Norm was sitting at a distance, I'd noticed when I
walked in, not a rancher, not retired, not a part of this
crowd. He, apparently, had something to do, but I didn't
know what.

"You had something you wanted to ask me?" he said, finishing his breakfast biscuit, picking up a paper napkin in his left hand and wiping his mouth with it. His scarred right hand, I noticed, remained in his lap. It didn't surprise me that he kept it out of view. It wasn't something you'd want to look at across the breakfast table. Alexander was adept with his left hand, indicating that he was either a natural lefty or he'd made a good adjustment. I've read about the studies that show lefties are more troublesome and accident prone and die younger than right-handers. Alexander, however, seemed to be in control except for the jittery cricket itching to get out of his cheek.

"I'm interested in radio tracking and Charlie Clark told me you're the expert."

"Radio tracking? Why do you want to know about that?" He folded his napkin up into neat little squares.

"As you probably know, my client, Juan Sololobo, is under suspicion for the murder of Bob Bartel. Bartel was out in the field with his radio equipment the day he died. It's possible I may need an expert witness."

"Expert witness? What do I get for that?"

I shrugged. "Whatever the market will bear."

"I don't do that kind of work." Guess he didn't need the money. He tucked the folded-up napkin under his plate.

"Well, since you're here and I'm here could I ask you some questions about the subject?" It's a female trick, open your eyes wide and ask a man to tell you everything he knows. It doesn't work as well as it used to.

"What is it you want to know?"

"Everything."

"It's a big subject." He sipped at his coffee, glanced at the clock ticking on the wall behind me. "And I got started about thirty years ago when radio tracking was in its infancy."

"The early sixties," I said. "A lot of things got started then."

"This was one of the few that actually had merit."

To whom, I wondered, the scientists or the animals?

"I was one of the pioneers as a young biologist in Alaska," Norm said. "The equipment we used back then was primitive. In fact we used to make it ourselves. I remember the first time we put a transmitter on a snowshoe rabbit and the rabbit ran into an electric fence and killed itself. It's gotten more elegant now that the equipment is manufactured commercially, although there is always room for improvement. The electronic components of transmitters are smaller and lighter and biologists have gotten able to track a wide variety of species, everything from whales to crayfish. In fact a fish can be tracked by something as small as a wire under its eye. Frogs, alligators, snakes, as well as wolves, leopards and grizzly bears—they've all been tracked." Like Bob Bartel he got pretty verbal once he warmed to his subject. Enthusiasm for one's work seemed to be a biologist's trait. One not shared by all the professions. "The range has expanded enormously, too. A peregrine falcon was tracked for over 2,000 miles from Wisconsin into Mexico. There was a transmitter on a sea turtle in the Gulf of Mexico that was being tracked by satellite. It came off and washed up in Texas on Padre Island. A tourist saw it on the beach, didn't know what it was, took it home and was using it as a doorstop. He was rather surprised when the FWS knocked on his door and wanted it back."

"I bet. How do you get a transmitter on a large and unenthusiastic mammal like a cougar or a wolf?"

"You drop the animal ..."

"Drop?"

"Shoot it with a tranquilizing dart. Darts take ten or twenty minutes to knock the animal out, and it used to be difficult to locate the darted animal because they'd run off. But now there are radios in the darts so researchers can find them. The darts have barbed tips so they stay in after the drug has been released. They're too expensive to lose."

"Do the tranquilizers hurt the animals?"

"No. I had wolves in Alaska that I hit over one hundred times. Didn't bother them one bit. They forget what happened once the effect of the drug wears off. Once the animal is down and you've got the collar on, you want to take advantage of that to take blood samples and urine samples and do as many studies as you can."

"So this transmitter that you put on the animal sends out a signal that a receiver somewhere picks up."

"Of course. Like a radio station, every animal in a study has its own signal. Researchers in an area use similar frequencies so they can monitor each other's collars."

"How far do signals reach?"

"Ten to twenty miles in the air. No more than three miles on the ground," he said with all the authority a male scientist can muster. "Signals can tell the researcher a lot. They can lead you to the animal, they can help you study migratory patterns, they can tell you how active the animal is."

"Could you tell if an animal were being hunted?"

"Depends. Give me an example."

"A mountain lion, say. The FWS has collared some mountain lions in this area. Say someone were hunting one, could a biologist tell by the signal that it was being hunted?"

"Absolutely," Norm said, speaking with more vehemence than I'd seen yet. The cricket on his cheekbone picked up the beat. "No doubt about it. You know Buddy Ohles tracked and killed an FWS-collared lion about a year ago that a rancher over in Platinum complained about. Bob Bartel was furious and I would have been too, if it were my collar. Bob was a dedicated biologist and I had a great deal of respect for his abilities. His death was a terrible tragedy. He was fighting a futile battle, however. The lobos will not survive at White Sands. For one thing there is insufficient heterozygosity in the zoo population. Wolves can survive in the wild for a long time with fairly close inbreeding and every now and then some outbreeding, but inbreeding is debilitating for captive populations. Even in the best of circumstances, as in North Carolina where there was a receptive citizenry and a much larger and stronger gene pool, half the reintroduced wolves died. And with the kind of animosity the ranchers have here? The lobos will be reintroduced as an experimental population and any wolf that wanders off the White Sands range will be shot. The ranchers will accuse them of killing livestock, a charge that is almost impossible to prove or disprove. The ranchers will complain to the ADC, the Buddy Ohleses of this world will track the wolves and kill them. It is a pity that Bob Bartel died, even more of a pity that his life's work will go for nothing."

"What do you think should happen to the lobo, then?"

"It's not what I think should happen, it's what I know will happen."

"What?"

"If they survive at all it will be as a zoo animal."

"What brought *you* down here to the boot of America?" I asked. "Not ranching."

"Obviously."

"It doesn't seem to be a place that's crazy about science, not the physical sciences anyway."

"America is inhospitable to science. We can't get respect or decent funding, and we've lost our technological edge because of it. It will be the downfall of this country. I came here because I inherited a ranch. I was looking for someplace to settle after I left the FWS, and I'd had enough of Alaska winters."

"So you retired to Singing Arrow?" I asked.

The cricket raised its legs, lowered them again. "Retired? Who told you that?"

"I thought *you* had."

He brought his scarred right hand up and laid it on the table like a badge of service to a lost cause. "The government cut back on my funding and wouldn't give me the support I needed. I quit," he said.

15

I'd seen Norm Alexander for breakfast. I hoped to make it back to Albuquerque for dinner. In between I went out to the Phillips ranch hoping to catch Don and Perla in for lunch, an early lunch, I figured, since ranchers were likely to be out working by daybreak and hungry by noon. Perla, in fact, was making sandwiches on a table under the portal when I got there, baloney and American cheese on white. One blond toddler was sitting in his high chair, the other in her lap.

"Don's about to come in for lunch," Perla said. "You eaten yet?"

"Not since breakfast," I said.

"Well, okay, why don't you join us then?" Although you don't often find water in the desert, you do find hospitality.

"Thanks," I said.

There was a quart-size jar of mayo on the table, another of Gulden's mustard and a big jar of pickles. Something that looked like real butter sat in a plastic refrigerator dish next to a king-sized loaf of white bread from Skagg's Alpha Beta. The gallon container on the table held milk, not Fort Worth tap water; real milk, not skim. Perla dipped a knife in the mayonnaise and began spreading it on a slice of bread. "Mustard? Mayonnaise? Butter?"

"Mayo," I said.

A toddler pounded his plastic cup on his high chair and milk spilled out. "Now, Donny," she said, "you're never gonna live to ninety-five like your great-granddaddy if you don't drink your milk."

Perla took some baloney out of its plastic wrapper, put it on the bread. "Saw you at the funeral," she said to me.

"Saw you, too."

"The Bartels are good folk. We didn't agree with him about everything but we're real unhappy about what happened to Bob and his family, real unhappy."

"So am I."

Perla began peeling the cheese from its plastic slice by slice. The toddler on her lap reached for the mustard. I watched his fingers inching along the table. He smiled and gurgled happily when he got to it and plunged his fist in. I was curious to see what he would do next, throw it at his brother? He brought his hand back to his face, sucked at his fingers, spread Gulden's all over his cheeks. Perla caught on to him. "Oh, Jimmy," she said, "what am I going to do with you?" She wiped the mustard off Jimmy's face and put some cheese on the baloney.

"How was your ride on Chili?" she asked.

"I apologize for taking him like that," I said. "I should have asked you first."

"Heck, he wasn't complaining, he likes to run," she smiled. "Anyways I mighta said no. Didn't you say you didn't like to ride?"

"I got thrown when I was a kid and never wanted to ride again, but I could get to like Chili."

"A bad experience for a kid, that'll do it, all right. Chili's out there in the stable if you want to take him out."

"Thanks anyway," I said. "I have to get back to Albuquerque tonight."

"I don't envy you city dwellers. It's a healthy life we got down here. Don's granddaddy's not the only one living to be ninety-five." And ranchers ate balloon bread, processed cheese and baloney, too. "Don and me, we got a real home for our kids." It was a tough world out there but they'd made an oasis in the desert, snug, settled, comfortable.

I brought the conversation around to the not-so-comfortable subject of predators. "I took Chili because I was afraid Buddy would shoot the wolf."

Perla stopped spreading mustard and looked me in the eye. "You know we ranchers are on the way to becoming extinct ourselves. There's a movement out there to get us off the federal lands, for people to stop eating beef, and now they want to bring the wolves back. It's a well-known and documented fact that wolves will go to cattle. Those calves were expensive losses for us, five or six hundred dollars each. They can keep that varmint locked up and throw away the key for all I care, but it would have been cheaper if Buddy had just shot the thing. Wolves kill just for fun. Did you know that? Don's granddaddy was around when the ranch was loaded with 'em and he told us that. They get into a herd, something snaps in their brains and they start killing."

It was contrary to anything any naturalist had ever observed, but I kept my mouth shut.

"Wolves are prolific, too. They're real stout about that, and they're not gonna stay at White Sands either. They don't belong anywhere near cows and people," said Perla.

Some might say that people and cows don't belong anywhere near wolves, but I didn't say that either. "You don't know for sure that Sirius killed the calves even if he was feeding on them," I said. "Wolves eat carrion."

"Well, we haven't had any kills since that thing was locked up."

"Are you sure? You've got a big ranch. Maybe you just haven't found them yet."

Perla shrugged, looked north where a dust devil was making its way down the road. "You can visit with Don about that. He's comin' now."

Don's Ford truck pulled up and parked. His dust devil, without a slipstream to keep it aloft, settled back onto the road it had risen from. Don's cowboy boots emerged first from the cab followed by jeans, a holster, a plaid shirt and a big hat, all of which were covered by a thin layer of dust. A fat brown dog with short legs came next.

"Dogs kill cattle, too," I said.

"Buster?" Perla laughed. "Are you kidding? Buster couldn't catch a turtle."

Buster did look more arthritic than fierce as he dragged himself over to the portal and fell down in a heap. Maybe he'd made it to ninety-five too.

"Afternoon," Don said.

"Afternoon," I replied.

"What's for lunch?" he asked Perla.

"Same old baloney," she said.

"Hey boys." Jimmy and Donny squirmed with happiness at seeing Daddy again.

Don sat down, poured himself a big glass of milk, bit into his first sandwich. Jimmy's fingers began inching toward the mayonnaise. Perla saw him this time and gave the hand a slap. "Enough, Jimmy," she said.

I started on my baloney and cheese, skipped the milk.

"And to what do we owe this visit from a big-city lawyer?" Don said.

"Now, honey, don't be rude." Perla acted like she was getting fond of me.

"Just asking," said Don. "Keep your hand out of there, Jim."

"Since my client is a suspect in Bob Bartel's murder, I wanted to come out here and see for myself where Bob was the day he got killed, what he was doing."

"Don't trust the wolf man, huh?" Don asked.

"I didn't say that."

"Didn't have to. Heck, I don't blame you. I wouldn't trust that guy either. You want to make sure you're going to get paid."

"That's not what's motivating me," I said.

Don took a look at the aging Nissan, my boring lawyer's clothes, thought it over. "Probably not," he said. "If it was money you were after you wouldn't be driving a Japanese import. Never saw a lawyer drive a car that small, even a Soledad County lawyer. Paul Ohweiler's already been out here and looked at the crime scene."

"I'd hope so. Have the feds been here yet?"

"No. Why would they be? Paul can handle this."

"Bartel was a federal employee. If he was killed in the line of duty it would be a federal crime. If the feds want to get involved, they will."

"Is that right?" Don asked.

"Damn. We don't want them poking around here," said Perla.

"Take care of Jimmy, he's got his hand in the mayonnaise," Don ordered in a dominant male voice, the first time I'd heard him use that tone.

Perla was a homemaker but she was a cowgirl, too, who could ride and shoot better than most men. She got ready to answer back, but something in Don's expression stopped her and she reached for Jimmy's hand and wiped it off. Don chewed slowly at his sandwich, gave the matter considerable thought. "Tell you what. I got a water tank I need to check on near where Bartel was. I'll take you up there after I finish my lunch."

"Thanks," I said.

"No problem," said Don.

Don ate three baloney and cheeses on white, I had one. He had three pickles, I had none. The boys stuffed a couple of pieces of baloney in their faces, a few crumbs of bread. I've never understood how toddlers end up as teenagers when their food ends up on the floor and the table. When Don was finished he leaned back in his chair, stretched, poked the dog in the ribs with his boot. "Buster, you're a lazy cuss," he said. Buster snored back.

"Donny, you want to keep an eye on the kids while I give Granddaddy his lunch," Perla said.

"You betcha," said Don.

"You want to meet Granddaddy Phillips?" Perla asked me. "He's the old West. There aren't many left like him."

Did I? A remnant of the old West, a ninety-five-year-old man?

"He still likes good-looking women," Don said.

"Um," said I, but it seemed rude to refuse, so I followed Perla to Granddaddy Phillips's room.

"Don's mommy and daddy moved into town fifteen years ago," she told me as we walked through the house, which was curtained to keep out the x-ray sun. The rooms were dark and dim but I did notice some elk horns on the living room wall and the wild, beautiful and dead face of a mountain lion. "But there's no way anyone's gonna get Granddaddy off the ranch. He ain't gonna die in a nursing home with the television set on, he says. He sleeps most of the time now, but he knows where he is." Perla knocked on the old man's door.

"That my lunch?" a loud voice answered. The very old are like the very young; the best—if not the only—weapon they have is their voice.

Perla opened the door and we went in. "Baloney today, Granddaddy."

"Again?" he squawked. "We had baloney Tuesday." Granddaddy was sitting in a rocker. He'd probably been a big ole cowboy once, but had shrunk so his cowboy boots didn't reach the floor. His gnarled hands gripped the arms of the creaking rocker. Maybe he slept with the boots on; his hands appeared too bent to remove them. His eyes were bright and he didn't wear glasses. "Who's that?" he squinted in my direction.

"This is Neil Hamel. She's a lawyer from Albuquerque."

"A woman lawyer? Well, hang in there and pray for rain. Come on over where I can get a good look at you." He crooked a wrinkled finger at me. Had he been a day under ninety I never would have gone, but advanced age puts people in some kind of extra human dimension where they get to call the shots. After all, they've made it a hell of a lot further than you're likely to and they know it. I approached the old man's rocker. Perla began setting up his lunch on an adjacent table, tucking a napkin under his chin. His hand grabbed mine like a hawk's talon digging deep into the neck of a doomed rabbit. He pressed it to the arm of his rocker. "Come closer." I leaned forward until I could smell the cavern of his old man's mouth. "You're too pretty to be a lawyer."

"Not that pretty," I said.

"She thinks they ought to bring back the wolves, Granddaddy," Perla said.

"Damn varmints," he snapped.

"I knew he'd have something to say about *that*," Perla said.

"They were a grievous tax in the old days and they would be still. They're smart and they're wily but I killed one hundred of those varmints. I'll tell you something that I bet is gonna surprise you. I agree with you," he squeezed my hand, gave me a wink. "I hope they come back, too. I'd like to hear them howling in the Soledad peaks again."

Perla was startled. "You would? Why's that?"

The old man laughed, kicked his feet against the rungs of his rocker. "So I can kill some more," he said.

Don was talking to someone when we got back to the portal, a small, dark man wearing a large cowboy hat that kept the sun out and the shadows in. Don was explaining in rapid-fire Spanish what he wanted the cowboy to do. His Spanish was better than mine, and all I got out of it was *ganado* (cattle), *agua* (water) and the finale, "*Comprendes?*"

"*Sí*," the ranch hand replied. He straightened his hat, crossed the portal and sauntered behind the house. Perla began gathering the kids up to take them in for their nap. Esperanza, who seemed to materialize at nap time, came around the corner of the house to help. She wore an embroidered *huipil*, her braid hung down her back, her work-hardened bare feet padded the ground. When she passed the ranch hand she lowered her eyes, which could mean she'd never seen him before. Could also mean he was her husband.

"*Buenas tardes, Señorita*," she said to me.

"*Buenas tardes*," I replied.

Don stretched, stood up. "Ready?" he asked me.

"Ready," I said.

"You come back real soon," said Perla, "and we'll visit some more."

"Thanks," I replied.

Don and I got in the pickup with the ubiquitous rifle balanced across the window rack like a carpenter's level. Just like the fuzzy dice you see hanging from low riders' mirrors in Albuquerque, it made a statement. But the dice are there for looks and the gun was not.

The place where Bob Bartel had parked his truck was several miles of sorry land away. We drove over dry land, desiccated land, eroded land, mesquite-studded land, land that had been chomped and hooved and cut by cattle.

"Granddaddy's somethin', ain't he?" Don asked me.

"Yeah," I said.

We kept our silence while we bumped along the ranch road, getting closer and closer to the rocky foothills of the Soledad peaks. Suddenly in the medium distance something ran out from behind one boulder and dashed toward another. It was as quick as a shadow, but obviously from the canid family—a dog, coyote, or wolf.

Don Phillips pressed the brake to the floor—hard—and I slammed forward and smashed my shoulder against the dash. Following his example I hadn't fastened my seat belt. As soon as the truck jounced to a stop, he went for the rifle, yanking it from its window rack. He leapt out of the cab and aimed it at the place where the canid had been. I saw nothing but a boulder and its shadow. The animal had blended into its habitat like dust in a roadbed or water in water.

"Damn," Don muttered, bringing the rifle down from his shoulder.

"What was it?" I asked.

"Don't know," he said. "When it comes to predators I shoot first, ask questions later."

"It might have been a neighbor's dog."

"You're forgetting, aren't you, that we don't have any neighbors out here." He took a long look around before putting the rifle back on its rack. "It doesn't make much difference what it is to the cattle it kills. It doesn't make much difference to me either. I've spent too much time and money breeding my cattle to lose them to somebody else's pet. If it was somebody's dog they can keep it at home."

Don had been calm as a grazing bull before he saw the animal and pulled the gun and it didn't take him long to become that calm again. Getting ready to shoot was no big deal for him, not even worth cranking up the adrenaline for. In the best marriages people are attracted to their mental equals, their temperamental opposites. That's my opinion anyway. In their placidity, however, Don and Perla acted like soul mates, partners in emotion, ranching and what else?

We drove on in silence following the edge of the Soledads. Don didn't drive and talk at the same time. He focused his attention on what he was doing and that was it. We passed a water tank and windmill to the east with some cattle grazing near them. A few miles later, when we reached the place where the north-south fence line was met by an east-west fence line, Don parked the truck and we both got out.

"I've gotten pretty good at cutting sign now that I have smugglers all over my ranch. This is where Bob parked." He showed me the tracks where the truck had stopped.

Having learned a little about reading tracks myself I recognized the chevron pattern from the tires in the wrecking lot.

"You're lucky it hasn't rained since then or these tracks would have washed away. Fortunately Ohweiler came out the next day and took photographs. This," Don showed me some deep dry ruts, "is where he drove in and this," he showed me another set of impressions much less deeply embedded than the first, "is where he drove out."

"How do you know that?" I asked.

"Can tell by the depth of the tread," he said. "When I

called in about ten that morning Bartel told me he'd come out to take a look at the kill and I told him where to find it. He probably got here around eleven when it was still raining."

"Why would he come out here in the rain?"

"Maybe it was the only time he could come, maybe he figured it would stop by the time he got here. Rain doesn't last long in Soledad. Now this was a hard rain. The ground was soft and the tires dug in. If he left here in the morning when the ground was still soft his tracks would have cut in, too, but if he left later in the day the ground would have dried out."

"How much later?" I asked.

"That I can't say, not exactly anyway. The ground dries pretty fast. It could have been afternoon, could have been the middle of the night. We wouldn't hear the truck from the house even in the dead of night."

If he left in the afternoon he could have gone someplace to get killed, someplace not too far away, someplace where no one had seen him on the road, someplace, maybe, where my client happened to be. But if he left then under his own free will why hadn't he taken the calf with him?

Don pointed with the toe of his boot to the lighter track. "I'll tell you one thing. That truck was moving a lot faster going out than it was coming in. Now normally Bob wasn't a fast driver. Either he was excited about something or someone else was driving. Look here." He showed me a set of footprints that vanished once they reached the rocks. "He didn't walk back to the truck or he walked back later in the day when the ground was dry. No return prints."

"What happened to the calf carcass that he came here to look at?" I asked.

"I took it back to the house later and had José bury it."

"You didn't come up here with Bartel?"

"I had a fence to mend and I'd already seen all I wanted to of that calf."

"Why do you think Bartel didn't take it with him like he planned?"

"I'm gettin' to that."

I looked at the fence that continued north beyond the eastern-bound fence. "Is this the end of your property?" I asked.

"One end," he said. "That's the Roaring Falls Ranch north of here. Jayne's property goes up to the top of the Soledad Peaks. I've got 10,000 deeded acres southeast of here, but we don't fence the peaks. Wouldn't be any point. There's nothing up there for the cattle. Besides, that's the smugglers' favorite path. They'd be cutting the fences every day if I tried to fence it."

"How do you get over there?"

"Me? I drive over the pass and through Singing Arrow. It takes close to two hours by truck. Perla and the ranch hands ride their horses over the mountain sometimes. She likes to ride."

I looked across the barbed-wire fence at Jayne's property. There wasn't any sign that anybody had been near here on horseback or on foot. "How far is Jayne's house from here?" I was asking a lot of questions, I knew, but you have to expect that from a lawyer. Don didn't seem to mind answering. "About eight miles as the crow flies."

"Whose property is east of Jayne's?"

"Norm Alexander and the Sanchezes, who go back to the Martinez land grant. Norm's got a little spread about 5,000 acres over there that the Sanchezes originally sold off in the sixties when they needed the cash. You seen what you wanted to see here?"

"Yeah."

"Okay, then, there's something else I want to show you,

something José came across yesterday." He started walking toward the pickup, a sure, solid, Ford truck cowboy. I followed in my running shoes, noticing that my tracks were as light as birds' on the hard, dry ground. We drove a mile or so back to the windmill, passing a bunch of white-faced brown cattle that watched us with placid eyes. High above the water trough a raven beat circles in the sky. Don parked and we walked up to the ashes of a campfire beside the trough. He picked up a plastic water bottle and poked the ashes with his boot. They fluttered briefly like the ghost of a campfire.

"Who do you think camped here and drank my water?" he asked. "Parrot smugglers, bull semen smugglers, marijuana smugglers, wetbacks?"

"Beats me," I said.

"This is what it means to have private property in the boot of America. I'm the sole and the sole has a great big hole in it. I get to share my land with every smuggler and wetback who wants to go from there to here. It used to be the smugglers flew in but now that our federal government has installed their balloon in Deming they've gone back to crossing on foot and burro. And now they've changed the immigration laws so wetbacks can't get real work here, so they've got to feed their families by smuggling. The feds think their war on drugs and illegal aliens is succeeding, but it's me who's paying for it. The Mexicans cut my fences, steal my cattle, bury their drugs on my property, come back at their convenience and dig them up." Don kicked the ground with a dusty boot. "And there's not a damn thing I can do about it. My family's been ranching this land for over a hundred years and there's never been border traffic like this. I feel like I'm in danger on my own land."

"Doesn't this make it dangerous for Perla and the kids?"

"Perla's not gonna leave. Her family's already lost one

ranch to government blundering. Besides, you've only seen Perla with a kid on her lap. She can ride and shoot better than I can. She doesn't think she's got anything to fear and she's grown up with the Mexicans. They're like family to her. I want to just take a look at the far side of the tank while we're here." He began walking around the other side of the trough. The raven squawked, flew away.

"Damn," Don said. He stopped suddenly, staring at a dead calf at his feet. It wasn't pretty—bones with a skin tent stretched over them, the insides eaten out. I didn't look at it for long, but long enough to tell it wasn't fresh. "Looks like one of my visitors got hungry."

"Did they shoot it?"

"Possible. They could also have lassoed it, run it down, stabbed or strangled it."

It could also have been moved here from someplace else by José or Don himself, could even have been the calf that Bob Bartel looked at, but I didn't say that. "Wouldn't someone have heard the shot, if there was a shot?"

"Maybe, maybe not. You know it could well be that Bob came upon some smugglers while he was up here and they thought he was *la migra* or a narc and shot him, drove the truck over to the peaks and pushed it off the embankment in the middle of the night. He kind of looked official in his green outfit, didn't he? I'm gonna call Ohweiler and get him up here to see this. It could be what you're looking for to get your client off the hook."

"If you came across a Mexican while you were out here what would you do?"

"Say *buenas tardes* and drive away. Too many of them have powerful connections across the border that I can't afford to anger, and if they think I called in the feds my problems are going to get a whole lot worse than they are now.

With Mexicans it's better just to pretend they are not there."

"But when an animal gets in your way you shoot it with no questions asked."

"A predator is a predator, but Mexicans are just people trying to make a living. Perla and I are Christians," he said.

16

Either Don and Perla were what they were pretending to be—good Christian ranchers besieged by environmentalists, the weather, the federal government, predators, Mexico and just about everything else—or they weren't. Either he believed unknown smugglers shot Bob Bartel, or he wanted me to think he did. They were in the right location if they wanted to be involved in illegal activities: wildlife poaching, parrot smuggling, bull semen smuggling, human smuggling, drug smuggling. With a lot of temptingly remote acres fronting on the border it could be any, all or none of the above. Don was fluent in the smugglers' language, too. Just how far had he gone to get along with them, anyway? The fact that Don didn't want the federal government on his property might mean something, might not. Nobody wants the federal government around, even those who benefit the most from it.

Don had come up with a tidy solution that could end the investigation: illegal aliens, *narcotraficantes*, *contrabandistas*, *pericobandistas*, one of them thought Bartel was *la migra*, shot him, drove the truck away under the cover of night, left no evidence but a campfire and a water bottle and was never seen again. It wouldn't give Soledad the satisfaction of seeing Juan Sololobo in jail but at least they'd be rid of him. He'd be leaving town with Siri the minute he could anyway. The Mexican smuggler theory would clear Buddy Ohles, Soledad's own, and the Phillipses of any suspicion. As for the feds, it was another border murder of one peripherally their own. If it was clean, how much investigation would they bother to do? And Sheriff Ohweiler? I wondered. Would he buy it? But most of all, what about me? A closed case would send me back to Albuquerque and keep me there. It would get my client off the hook at no one else's expense (the chances of catching a criminal with the smuggler's profile were poor), but was it the truth? It wasn't my job to find out. My job was to represent my client, and these so-called smuggler/murderers were the best thing that could have happened to him. I should forget about the calves with no identifiable cause of death disappearing or getting moved around. Forget that my client had taken a woman's drug, woken up and made love near the time the crime was completed. Not ask whether Norm Alexander quit or retired. Assume the radio signal that Bartel had picked up was a bird, not a radio-collared mountain lion or anything else. Leave it in the capable hands of Don and Perla Phillips and the not so capable hands of Sheriff Ohweiler. Go home and forget.

I stopped at the Galaxy Deli on my way. Ernesto sat in his usual stationary position, chin in hands, ears attuned to every vibration.

"Buenas tardes, Ernesto," I said.

"Es la Señorita Hamel, la mujer de las Papaya Punches?"

"Sí."

"Buenas tardes."

I went to the cooler, picked out a Papaya Punch, took it to

the counter and counted out my fifty cents. "Heard any more wolves?" I asked.

"Someone else was asking me that very same question," Ernesto said.

"Who was that?"

"Bob Bartel."

"When?"

"The night before he died. It was very sad for everyone, his death. And the way it happened," he shook his head. "It was not a good death."

"No, it wasn't. What did you tell him about the wolves?"

"The same thing I told you, that I hear one or more sometimes at night near El Puerto."

"Where do you live?" I asked him.

"On Yolanda's family's ranch on the east side of the Soledad Peaks."

"The Sanchez place?"

"That's it."

"Does she hear them, too?"

"No, she doesn't hear good. She is my eyes, I am her ears."

"How far do you live from El Puerto?"

"About eight miles, I think."

"What did Bob Bartel say when you told him?"

"Thank you," Ernesto said.

"Me, too."

"What?"

"*Mil gracias,*" I said.

It was dark when I got back to Albuquerque, and I could see the city lights from miles away. Heat lightning flashed over Lucero Mesa but it didn't thunder and it didn't rain. A half-moon was hanging on over the Manzanos, illuminating the 328,000-acre Ortiz land grant. The same moon shone on that place when the dinosaurs owned it, when the lobos were king, when the Indians wept and the conquerors conquered. In August the corn grows a foot, they say, under its influence. It wasn't a misty, secretive Eastern moon, it was the kind of clear silver moon that illuminates the truth but still leaves room for the imagination. Under an August moon it takes a long time to fall asleep, even with the windows closed and the air conditioner humming. I spent a couple of hours chasing my thoughts around the bed, wishing I'd told the Kid when I was coming home. Cuervo Gold wasn't doing any good. If I'd had a Xanax I would have taken it, which was one reason why I didn't have any. I got up and started pacing my apartment from the bedroom to the living room and back again, wearing a path through the carpet's deep shag.

The real estate closing I'd come back for took place at the bank the next day at ten. It was close to noon by the time I got to the office and Anna and Brink were making plans for lunch. It was either the Olive Garden or Garduños. Anna handed me a message from Juan Sololobo. "Where do people get names like that?" she asked.

It was a rhetorical question, so I ignored it, went into my office and picked up the phone, but instead of calling Juan back I dialed the Big Sky State, Montana.

"My old buddy, Neil Hamel," March said. "What's happening now?"

"Juan could be getting off the hook."

"I told you you'd do it, didn't I?"

"I didn't do much, except to mention the possibility of federal intervention. As soon as he heard that, Don Phillips, the rancher, came up with the theory that Bartel happened on smugglers who mistook him for *la migra* and shot him. He even produced some evidence to support it."

"It's plausible, isn't it, so close to the border?"

"It's also plausible that Bartel caught Buddy Ohles, the ADC hunter, doing something illegal, he caught Don Phillips doing something illegal, or he caught somebody else doing something illegal. It could be tempting to the Phillipses to get into illegal activities; they can't be making very much money ranching."

"Why not? That ranch was probably paid for one hundred years ago. Ranchers like to cry poor, but they do better than people think, the smart ones anyway."

"The Phillipses aren't dumb."

"There's still no real evidence pointing to Juan, is there?"

"Not that I know of."

"How's he holding up?"

"Staying fluid."

"I know he's been in trouble, but you don't really think he's capable of murder, do you?"

"Maybe not cold-blooded, calculated murder, but emotional, surprised with the weapon in his hand, guilty and frightened murder? Who's not capable under those conditions?"

"But why would Juan have a weapon in his hand unless he was deliberately going after Bartel?"

Why indeed? "I don't know. I also talked to the biologist, Norman Alexander, who was the wolf expert in Alaska. He lives on the other side of the peaks from Jayne. Do you know anything about him? First he says he retired, then he tells me he quit. Frank Boyd, who was Bartel's supervisor, says he didn't retire."

"There was a research biologist in Alaska who got fired five or six years ago when I was still getting paid in sunsets by working for the Interior Department," March said. "The story was he got carried away with his experiments and his high-tech methods. Thought a Yagi antenna made him God."

"That sounds like Alexander. He's into high tech and capable of thinking he's God."

"If he was smart he got a fat settlement like I did when the government fired me."

He'd used part of it to pay my legal fees. "I've been living off it ever since," I said.

"Sure," March laughed. He has the best laugh south of the Yukon and it came wrapped in a thick red beard, too. I remembered all of it well.

"Alexander told me that Bartel could have picked up the signal of a lion that Buddy was tracking and known that it was being tracked," I said.

"I'm not sure you'd be able to tell that from a radio signal. You can track the movement, but to interpret the movement? I don't know."

"How far do those signals reach, anyway?"

"Depends on how good your equipment is, whether you're in the desert or the jungle, whether your transmitter is on a turtle or a giraffe. The more elevated the signal or the receiver, the further the signal will reach. An airplane can track a signal twenty miles away. On the ground you ought to be able to pick up a signal for five miles."

"Suppose a mountain got in the way?"

"You'd still get a signal but it wouldn't be as clear."

"Norm Alexander told me signals reached a maximum of three miles."

"Well, in the years since he's been out of the business, the equipment *has* improved."

"Bartel said that researchers in the same area use similar frequencies so they can keep track of each other's collars."

"That's true, they do."

"Suppose someone didn't want anyone else keeping track of his collars."

"He'd pick a remote location where there weren't a lot of

researchers around. He'd choose signals at the extreme high or low frequency range, and hope nobody went looking for them. They could still be found if someone had a good antenna and took the trouble to go carefully through the dial like he was searching for a hard-to-find radio station, but who would do that? Do you care who did it if Juan is no longer a suspect?"

"Unprofessional of me, I know, but it seems like Bob Bartel deserves that much. You'd care, wouldn't you?"

"Yeah," March said, "but I'm not a lawyer."

Sometimes I felt that I wasn't either.

"You'll let me know what happens?"

"Sure," I said.

The next call was to Juan Sololobo, who answered on the first ring. "Perla Phillips told Jayne that you and Don came across proof that Bartel was killed by drug smugglers," he said.

Stories have a way of getting twisted in the telling. As this one was at least on its fourth round, you'd have to expect some distortion. "We came across evidence that someone was on the Phillips ranch. I'm not sure what it proves, if anything."

"Ohweiler thinks it's leading somewhere."

"How do you know that?"

"I called him."

It was too hot for this. "Juan, I told you not to talk to him," I said in a voice that dripped irritation.

"You didn't call me back and I had to know." Juan was sounding rather petulant himself. "I didn't tell him anything. I just asked if they had another suspect and he said they did but I shouldn't be leaving town just yet."

"You'll let me know if anything new develops, won't you?" I said, dripping sarcasm this time.

"Sure," he answered.

To see just how distorted this story had gotten in the telling, I called Ohweiler next. "I told you not to talk to my client," I said.

"Not a heck of a lot I can do about it when he calls me, ma'am."

"What did you tell him?"

"He's the one who ought to be telling you that."

"He did, but I want to hear your side."

"I told him that I went out to the Phillips ranch and Don showed me the campfire and the dead calf. I told him it looked like Bartel coulda been killed by some wetback crossing the Phillips ranch who mistook him for *la migra*, but that I wouldn't suggest your client leave town just yet."

"Are you going to call the feds in on this? Bartel was probably on duty when he was killed."

"His job was researching wildlife. If he was killed for being *la migra* he wasn't killed for doin' his job so that makes it a gray area. It looks like a pretty simple case to me. I believe I can handle it," Ohweiler said.

I was in the front office giving Anna a tape I'd dictated when the bass on wheels pulled up. "Must be 5 o'clock," I said, glancing at the clock on Anna's desk, which read five minutes to. Brink, who had nothing better to do, looked out the window and was dazzled by the shiny chrome, wire wheels and slick paint job of Stevie's blue and white Impala. Low riders are designed for beauty—not speed, or fuel efficiency either. Around here gawking at them is what they call breaking neck; Brink's neck had been broken. "That car is cherry!" he said to Anna.

"Cherry?" said I. "I've always wondered what that means exactly. Like a ... virgin?"

"It means, you know, something that's been fixed up better than new, doesn't it?" he asked our resident expert,

Anna, raising his eyebrows as he posed the question. "Kind of like Cher or Jane Fonda."

"What would you call it?" Anna asked me. "Neat? Groovy? As in like wow, that's a groovy car? Or primo? How about priiiiimo?"

"I'd call it a waste of money. I suppose Stevie's a member of a car club."

"So?" said Anna.

"Which one? Elvis from Hell? Albuquerque Anarchists? Bernalillo Bandidos?"

"Wrong. Those are Frisbee teams. He's a member of the Vagabonds."

"Are you guys going to the bed-dancing contest?" Brink asked. Lowriders have made a performing art out of raising and lowering their cars with hydraulic lifts. The best displays, however, are the beds of trucks that can be moved up, down and sideways, too, with lightning speed. They get together in parking lots to shimmy and shake. The one with the most action wins, but I couldn't say what.

"We might." Anna looked at the clock and out the window at the waiting Stevie. There was no need for him to beep; his stereo had long ago announced his presence.

"Isn't it time for Blast Off Sound Systems to have their annual stereo throwing contest?" I asked. "Maybe Stevie would like to donate his for charity."

Anna ignored me. Stevie lifted his hand slowly from the chain-link steering wheel, put it back down. It would be an exaggeration to call it anything as committed as a wave. "Are you through?" she asked.

"Sure, take off," said Brink who hadn't, as far as I'd noticed, ever begun.

One of the best ways not to feel like a lawyer on those days when I don't want to feel like a lawyer is to mix up a batch of Jell-O shots and have the Kid over for dinner. I got home late so he brought the dinner, sopapillas from Paco's, not as good as the sopapillas from Arriba Tacos in Santa Fe, but hot enough to remind you that you were in the state where people ask if they need a visa to visit and whether it's safe to drink the water. We sat on my deck slurping cool green Jell-O shots and eating red-hot sopapillas, but it wasn't doing a thing to lower my body's temperature. The blue sky sat on the Sandias' elephant-gray back. Not a cumulonimbus, cirrus or lenticular was in sight. The air was a weight squishing me into my deck chair, embedding the plastic webbing into the back of my thighs. A boom box somewhere played white rapper Vanilla Ice. It would be either Freon hum or boom box beat tonight.

"Well, hang in there and pray for rain," I said.

"That doesn't sound like you, Chiquita," said the Kid.

"It's not," I replied. A ninety-five-year-old rancher had taken temporary possession of my vocal cords.

We finished our dinner and I cleaned up by taking the paper wrappings inside and throwing them away. When it was this hot the only solution is to break a sweat by getting even hotter. I went back out to the deck, rested my cheek against the top of the Kid's thick and curly head. He has curls that you can sink your head or your hand into. They'd be outstanding in piloerection and not bad sprawled across my pillow either.

"Kid, why don't we ..."

"Okay," he said.

Later on when we were lying on the sheets naked, sweaty and cool at last, I watched the lights shine in through the drapes and listened to the Kid's breath sink into sleep. I punched his shoulder. "You awake, Kid?" I said.

"Chiquita, please, I'm tired. I work hard all day."

No one works harder than a Mexican, they say. The Kid wasn't exactly a Mexican. He had grown up there though, which was what I wanted to talk to him about. He never talked about his past, but I'd never asked, not in the middle of the night anyway. "I know but I need to talk to you, Kid."

"Now?"

"It's important."

He groaned. "*Digame.*"

"What were you doing with the Norteños?"

"Why do you want to know that now?"

"You'll see."

"I lived with them for a year before I came here. I was only a boy then, seventeen years old."

"Why did you do it?"

He shrugged his skinny shoulder. "It was an adventure. They own that part of the Sierra Madre and I wanted to cross it."

"Did you ever bring any drugs over?"

"Marijuana sometimes, *cocaina* never. You're illegal if you bring marijuana, you're illegal if you bring nothing. People kill you for drugs, they kill you for your shoes. Why not make some money? You bought and smoked marijuana when you were seventeen, no?"

"Yes."

"I used the money to start my business."

"Do you ever hear from the Norteños?"

"Sometimes when they come to Albuquerque they stay at my house."

"Isn't that dangerous?"

The Kid squirmed, squeezed his pillow. "So many questions, Chiquita, for one night."

"Only a few more, I promise."

"Everything is dangerous. Life is dangerous."

"When you crossed the border did you ever come through Soledad on the old wolf trail?"

"*La vereda del lobo!* Sometimes. Sometimes I went through Arizona, but never Texas. You have to be crazy to cross there."

"Did the Norteños ever make any deals with ranchers, pay them to look the other way?"

The Kid gave me an are-you-kidding look. "The Norteños don't have to pay anybody. Everybody is afraid of them. The Norteños have a—how you say—a reputation on the border. They go where they want."

"Tell me about the wolves in the Sierra Madre. Did you ever see them?"

"There are not many left, Chiquita, maybe fifteen when I was there. You see the *mierda* or the footmarks and you hear them, but you don't see them."

"How far away could you hear them?"

"Eight kilometers maybe in the desert where it is quiet." A little less than five miles.

"That's all? Just eight kilometers?

"That's a long way and you only hear them there because it is quiet. The lobos are very friendly with each other and afraid of people, but the Norteños don't hurt them—they are outlaws, too. The Norteños won't let the *biólogos* in. They won't let them put their radios on the lobos and study them and everybody else is afraid to go there. There was one Norteño, Flaco, who understands lobos. He called them and they came. If you ever see one, you never forget it. The eyes—*los ojos del lobo son el fuego en la noche.*"

"The fire in the night." The fire in his own eyes was flickering out.

"Can I sleep now?"

"*Sí,*" I said.

The wind shifted during the night and the planes started using the north-facing runway at east-west-facing Albuquerque International. It happens sometimes but does it have to happen so early in the morning? The jets sounded and felt like they were twenty-five feet overhead. The glass on the nightstand rattled, the bed shook, the Kid slept on. I looked at his skinny body stretched out naked in my bed and thought about how familiar it was, how unknown and maybe unknowable he was. I thought about the alien population to the south that sneaks across our borders increasing the heterozygosity of our breeding population, expanding the gene pool, adding to our diversity. I woke him with a kiss.

17

I thought it over for a few days, paced the shag carpeting down to pile and on Monday I went back to Soledad. There were some facts I wanted to check at the county clerk's office where the records of real estate transactions are kept, to see if they were facts, that is, and not lies. Most attorneys think the county clerk's office is Siberia where you send somebody else to do your title searches or file your deeds, but I've always found them one of the more interesting places a lawyer might go in the line of duty. A lot of questions can be answered there: who sold a property and when, who bought it, whether the buyer paid cash, who holds the mortgage. You can also find out who inherited the property, who has a life tenancy, how big the property is, who abuts who. If the property has been sold any time recently there should be a survey on file indicating how many acres are, where the houses and barns are located, whether there are any established footpaths, roads, walls, fences, streams. Since people in Soledad got their identities from being property owners, it was time to find out who they really were by searching their titles and looking at their deeds.

When you do a title search you look for any clouds on the title, like liens or encumbrances that would be transferable as debts or limitations on a future owner. You look for poor property descriptions that would make it difficult to establish the boundaries or the size of the property. As you go further and further back you find the descriptions written in spidery ink and then in Spanish and eventually you get to the 1600s when title was granted by the king of Spain. That's where the search ends. You can't search any further than that. The Indians didn't rely on county clerks or deeds or private ownership. It made it easy to steal from them because they thought what they had couldn't be owned. In the old days when land wasn't worth much nobody worried about accuracy of description. A boundary could be described as an alligator juniper or the place where Rosita had her calf. In 1892 an act of Congress was passed to quiet noisy titles with poor descriptions, and at that point deeds were patented by the government if the property owner got around to doing it.

Doing title searches is a little like reading the tombstones in a cemetery, it gives you a sense of the history of a place. I like seeing the old names, the old descriptions, the old deeds. Best of all I like maps, and county clerks' offices are full of them.

I didn't tell Juan and Jayne that I was coming back to Soledad. My plan was to return to the Duke City the same day if I didn't find anything, stay over at a motel if I did. I told the Kid.

"Why you going back to Soledad?" he asked me.

"I want to check the land records and see if anybody has been lying," I said.

"If you don't come back at night, call me and tell me where you are staying," he said.

"Why?"

"Maybe I need to talk to you."

And I'd thought we'd successfully negotiated the transition from almost living together to not. What did he want anyway? He'd never asked me to call before. I didn't think he ought to ask, but I didn't have anything to hide, so I said okay. Brink and Anna didn't seem to care when, or if, I'd be back. They had other things on their minds: Stevie on Anna's, Brink on Brink's.

"I haven't been with somebody in so long I've forgotten how," Brink said in a morose moment. Who would want to be with him, anyway, when all he thought or talked about was himself?

"Use your left hand and pretend it's a stranger," I said.

What I found in the records at the Soledad County Court House on Monday was that March had been right (not that I would have doubted him). I looked up the book and page number of Jayne's deed in the *Direct Index*, located the deed and found that her husband had granted her a life tenancy on Roaring Falls Ranch in 1986 when they got divorced. After she died the property went to the Conservation Committee *in toto*, which effectively kept her from selling it. Who would buy a property with a cloud on it like that? Next I looked in the *Debtor Index* and found there had never been a mortgage on the property; her ex-husband had paid cash. I looked in the *Index to Plats*. There was a survey map on file which I got out, laid on a table and pored over. An old road, marked as a double dotted line, crossed Roaring Falls Ranch, bisecting a single dotted line on the eastern boundary which indicated a footpath. In some places the footpath crossed Jayne's property, in some places it went onto the adjoining property. The adjoining owners were listed as Emilio Sanchez and Javier Rodriguez to the east, Donald and Perla Phillips to the south.

Next I looked up the Sanchezes in the *Reverse Index*, and found they had sold 5,000 acres in the sixties just as Don Phillips had said. Javier Rodriguez was the buyer. He transferred title to Norman Alexander in March of 1987, no mortgage on file. Norm had not inherited his property. Norm had paid cash. Norm had lied at least once. A survey map was on file. I got it out, unfolded it and laid it on the table, too. It showed where Norm's property adjoined Roaring Falls Ranch, where it adjoined the Sanchezes, where it abutted the Phillipses. It showed where Norm's house and barns were located, the curved line of a stream flowing from the Soledad Peaks to Norm's eastern boundary, Route 30, the double dotted line of the old road that went from his property to Jayne's, the single dotted line of the footpath.

The Sanchezes had had a survey done of their remaining land at the time they sold the 5,000 acres to Javier Rodriguez. I laid that map out next to Norm Alexander's. The two maps had been done by the same surveyor, Robert Birdsong, and fortunately they were drawn to the same scale, one-half inch equaled a mile. I'd brought a pocket ruler with me and I got it out and began to measure. It was 8 miles in a straight line from the Sanchez house to El Puerto just as Ernesto had thought, but only 4 miles from the Sanchezes to Norm's house. It was 10 miles from Norm's house to Jayne's by footpath and the old road, and 4.8 miles as the crow files (there was no marked path) from Norm's house to the corner of the Phillips Ranch where Bob Bartel had left his truck—almost 2 miles further than a radio-collar signal would reach if Norm had been telling the truth, about the same distance a signal would reach if March had. I had no reason to doubt March, but Norm's credibility had been strained. He hadn't inherited his property, for one thing. He'd bought it and quite possibly with money he'd gotten from the taxpayers. He said he'd quit and retired from his biologist job. One or both of those statements was also a lie. So why had he bought here in the sole of America where the ranchers were king and the climate was so inhospitable to science?

I folded up the maps, being careful to follow the existing creases, and put them back in their files. Then, just for the hell of it, I searched the Sanchezes' title, wondering if it went back to the act of Congress of 1892 or the act of a king of Spain in the 1600s. The 1600 records are still on file, but they probably wouldn't be kept here. The clerk got me the appropriate 1800s book and lugged it over to the counter. It was bound in faded leather with end papers in the tiny flowers of old wallpaper. The Sanchezes had a patent deed from 1892 that had been written in ink by a scrivener with an elegant style. The capital letters were works of art. The scrivener was obviously someone who enjoyed his work (no doubt it was a he back then) which consisted of writing things out day after day after day. The deed was sealed by the word *seal* wrapped in an ink cloud. "To all whom these present shall come, Greeting," it began. "Given under my hand at the City of Washington, the eleventh day of November in the year of our Lord 1892 and of the independence of the United States the one hundred seventeenth," it ended, signed by the president, Benjamin Harrison. In those days they knew how to pass a title. Deeds were valid, they used to say, as long as grass grows and water flows. This one had stayed in the family for almost a hundred years.

An old Hispanic man with a white mustache, black eyes and a face as wrinkled as a walnut shell stood next to me looking up something himself. He peered over my shoulder. "Look at the beauty of that handwriting," he said.

"It's amazing, isn't it?" said I.

"It sure is. They don't teach writing like that anymore." He had a rather elegant style himself.

"They sure don't. Can you tell me how to get to the library?" That was my next stop. There are a lot of investigatory resources available to the nosy American citizen, if the citizen cares to take advantage of them.

"Right down the street. Turn left when you get outside, you can't miss it."

"*Gracias*," I said.

"*Por nada*," he replied.

The library was another user-friendly stone building. The librarian was a little gray bird with glasses, the kind of woman people forget immediately unless she chirps loudly or finds some other way to make an impression.

"I'd like to use the microfilm," I said.

"Of course." She went back to looking through her card file. The Soledad Public Library hadn't gotten computerized yet.

"Where is it?"

She looked up. "Around the corner to your right, my left, but if you turn around it will also be on your left."

"Thanks," I said.

It had been a long time since I'd looked at a microfilm and I couldn't remember how. The reels were in a file labeled by date. You had your choice of the *Soledad Times* or the *Albuquerque Journal.* I decided on the *Journal* and located the one I was looking for, the second six months of 1987. The hard part was loading the microfilm machine. I got the film on the reels, slid it under the glass and began cranking. It turned all right, but it screeched loudly as it did, loud enough for the librarian to screech back.

"Stop it!" she yelled, hopping out from behind her desk. She could get your attention if she wanted to. "That is not the way to do it."

It was embarrassing to be told how to do something that every school kid knows. "You're not from around here, are you?" she asked, taking the film off and loading it properly.

"Albuquerque," I said.

She shook her firm little head. "I've *never* understood why anyone would live there."

She hopped back to her desk and I cranked the lever through July, and in August I found what I was looking for. On August 14 the wolf pups had been stolen en route from the Rio Grande Zoo. Wolf pups are born in April and by mid to late summer they'd be old enough to take from the mother. The month wasn't too hard to figure, but it was the year I'd had to check—1987, four years ago, five months after Norman Alexander had bought his property in the sole of America.

I rolled the microfilm up, put it in its file drawer and went out the back door. I could have passed this information on to Sheriff Ohweiler; he could also have gotten it himself if he were interested.

I got in the Nissan, drove over the mountain to the east side of the peaks and checked into the Motel 6 in Singing Arrow. I didn't want to run into anybody I knew or do any explaining. The woman who checked me in—Clarice McKean, her nameplate said—had a solid, reassuring presence, an I-can-take-care-of-it aura, but she didn't have that much to take care of. There were about forty units in the Motel 6, but the only occupants so far were a couple of long-distance truckers whose rigs were parked off to the side and me. "Now *you* have a good night," she said as she handed me my key.

The emphasized *you* might have fooled some people, but I knew that no matter how friendly Clarice had been, I was checking into a lonely motel filled with people who'd spent the day alone in their cabs watching the highway and would be spending the night alone in their rooms watching TV. It was a sterile place where glasses came wrapped in wrappers, but sterility isn't so bad if you are in the mood. In fact there can be something kind of anonymous, detached and appealing about highway motels, nobody to argue with, nobody to figure out, nobody to trust or distrust. I drove across the country by myself once on my first and last extended Xanax trip. I took one every night as soon as I got settled in bed. I could have been anywhere, I could have been anybody. Who cared? In about an hour I stopped replaying the highway, my legs stopped twitching and I was out. The next day I had a residual high—not enough to make me careless, but enough to keep me from thinking about anything except getting past the eighteen-wheeler ahead of me and what the next song on the boom box would be (my car radio had been stolen long ago). I was pushing at some kind of solitary-journey envelope. I wondered how long I could have gone on like that, driving the highway, drugged and detached, not happy, not unhappy, not talking to anybody, listening to Bob Marley singing about the shelter of his single bed (reggae makes the best road music). The only thing that broke the meditation was getting hungry and looking for something to eat. It's tough to find edible food on the road in America and my standards aren't very high. After a week of Burger King and McDonald's, the blood was sluggish in my veins and I felt dull as a cow. One week is about all you get on interstate America anyway. By then you've reached one coast or the other and you're faced with a decision north or south, Miami or Boston.

My room at Motel 6 had that familiar, anonymous Sears Roebuck bedspread look and I half-wished I'd be getting up in the morning and getting back on the interstate conveyer belt, but, driven by my professional and personal big three—truth, justice, curiosity—I ripped the wrapper from a bathroom glass, poured in some Cuervo Gold, the hell with ice, picked up the telephone and went to work. My first call was to Norman Alexander.

His throat was like a water pipe full of rust that had to be coughed out before he could say hello. It was the voice of someone who didn't speak much.

"This is Neil Hamel," I said.

He might have preferred a recorded message offering him a box of rattlesnakes. "Yes," he replied.

"I have some more questions about radio telemetry that I need to ask you."

"Is it really necessary for you to be pursuing this?"

"Yes," I said.

"Where are you?" he asked.

"Albuquerque," my first lie of the night. "How about Hardee's for lunch? If I leave early I can make it by noon." My second.

"All right," he sighed.

The next call was to eco-warrior Charlie Clark, who liked the adrenaline rush of a well-planned action. This was a simple action that didn't require much planning, although I could use some help. I wanted to get on Norman Alexander's property and see what he'd been doing there, but I didn't know what kind of fences and obstacles I'd run into on the way.

"Hey," said Charlie when I announced it was me.

"Do you know how to get to Norman Alexander's?" I asked. I could have figured that out myself from all the maps I'd seen, but who better to help me get onto the property than an environmental warrior?

"I know where his place is, but I've never been up there. Norm keeps to himself," Charlie replied.

"How would you like to go over there with me tomorrow?"

Charlie was easy. "Okay," he said. "How did you ever get Norm to invite you? Norm never invites anybody to his place."

"I didn't," I admitted. "He doesn't know I'm coming.

How long do you figure it will take him to get from his place to Hardee's? He thinks I'm meeting him there."

"About forty-five minutes, I guess."

"I'm staying at the Motel 6 in Singing Arrow. Why don't you come here? I'd like to be as close to Norm's at 11:15 as possible, but I don't want him to see us and I don't want him to pass you coming over the mountain either."

The intrigue of it appealed to Charlie's sense of adventure, as I had suspected it would. "I'll wear my helmet and visor," he said, getting into the spirit. "I'll look like anybody then. I can get one for you, too. I know a cottonwood grove where we can hide the motorcycle, wait and watch him go by."

"Okay. What time should we leave here?"

"About 10:30. What's old Norm been up to anyway?"

"That's what we're going to find out."

My next call—one I didn't want to make—was to the Kid. My glass was empty; I filled it. It wasn't that I didn't want to talk to him, I just didn't like the feeling that I had to check in every time I left town. It was setting a bad precedent. I didn't like checking in and I didn't want to know what was going on at his house either. Besides, since we didn't exactly have a verbal relationship, calling long distance was a waste of money.

"It's me," I said when he answered the phone.

"*Bueno*. Where are you, Chiquita?"

"Singing Arrow."

"Where in Singing Arrow?"

"Motel 6. You want the room number?" The snideness in my voice went right by him.

"Yeah."

"201."

"What did you find out today?"

"That someone was lying."

"Who?"

"Norm Alexander."

"The wolf *biólogo*?"

"Right."

"What was he lying about?"

"How he got his 5,000 acres in Singing Arrow. He said he inherited it, but I found out he bought it."

"When?"

"March 1987."

"Where is it?"

"The other side of the peaks from Jayne."

"What are you doing tomorrow?"

"Going over to his place to find out why he lied."

"Did you call the police?"

"No." The Kid didn't ask but I knew my reasons: Ohweiler wouldn't believe me, he couldn't keep his mouth shut, I didn't trust him, I could do it better myself.

"Be careful, Chiquita, and call me tomorrow. Okay?"

"Yeah," I said.

I finished my tequila and went out to look for something to eat. A squashed tarantula was waiting for me on the concrete landing, a life of searching, crawling, looking for something to screw and eat brought to an early end and it could well have been the heel of my running shoe that did it. "Now how could somebody kill something as beautiful as that?" I heard Bob Bartel say.

"By not looking where they're going," I replied.

18

In the morning I called Anna. "Hamel and Harrison," she answered, popping her gum in my ear.

"Hamel," I said.

"She's out of town. You wanna leave a message?"

"This *is* Hamel."

"Oh," she replied, "what's up?"

"I'm going to give you the number of Hardee's in Soledad. Call them at noon, ask to speak to Norman Alexander, tell him I had car trouble on the way down and I am going to be around forty-five minutes late." I was wondering how long Norm would be willing to wait, at least forty-five minutes, I thought. He'd want to eat anyway while he was there. "And then at quarter to one call again and tell him I'm on my way." I gave her the number.

"But I'll be out to lunch then."

"No, you won't."

"But ..."

"Time is of the essence, Anna. This has to be done exactly when I say."

"Oh, all right," she answered. "What'll I say is wrong with your car?"

"Vapor lock."

I had a cup of coffee and a doughnut compliments of Motel 6 in their office while I waited for Charlie Clark. Clarice was as solid, middle-aged, middle American and comfortable in the morning as she'd been at night. No need to ask if she'd slept well. I watched the big sky from her window. It wasn't blue today, it was watercolor gray. There were paintbrush streaks where the clouds met and ran together. In the Soledads it was already raining, closing over the peaks like a gray curtain. It didn't bode well for Charlie's motorcycle. He pulled in promptly at 10:30 by the office clock, giving this the illusion of being a well-planned action and stirring up the gravel in the parking lot. I finished up my coffee and went outside to meet him. He was wearing a black leather jacket, jeans, black motorcycle boots. His helmet kept his blond mop pressed close to his head and the visor hid his face. He could have been any old motorcycle rider on any old motorcycle until he opened the jacket (it was at least 95 degrees) and exposed the yellow eyes of his SAVE THE LOBO T.

"You didn't pass Norm Alexander coming over the mountain, I hope," I said.

"Nope," he replied. "What do you think you're going to find at his place anyway?"

My eyes met the yellow eyes on his T. "You'll see."

He handed me the extra helmet. I fit it over my head and pulled down the visor, which made it look like five o'clock in the morning or nine at night. "How do people see in these things anyway?" I asked. "You'd have to want to hide pretty badly to wear a visor at night."

"You get used to it," he said. "Just like Ray-Bans."

Not exactly. Ray-Bans made me feel mysterious; the

Darth Vader visor made me feel invisible. I could understand how people might be tempted to commit felonies under the cover of the black plastic. The invisibility was just an illusion, however. In fact, you were probably more striking and more visible in this getup, but you weren't you. A raindrop landed splat on my visor.

"Uh oh," said Charlie. "It wasn't supposed to rain until afternoon."

"Blame Granddaddy Phillips. He's been hanging in there and praying for rain."

"Well, let's get over there before it gets any worse."

I climbed on the back of the motorcycle, put my arms around Charlie's waist and hung on. It seemed to me he gunned the engine and spun gravel more than was absolutely necessary, enough to make Clarice come to the window and grimace. We weren't invisible to her. In fact, we looked like the kind of people she wouldn't wish a nice day. The rain held its breath for a while and Route 30 stayed dry. We sped down the road, two black specks camouflaged on the black macadam like a mantis shaking on a leaf. Charlie pulled off at a dirt road that headed straight as an arrow for the backside of the peaks. There was a rocky streambed with a couple of inches of water in it that paralleled the road down the mountain. Cottonwoods grew in a level spot near the intersection. Charlie drove into the grove and we got off and concealed the motorcycle behind a large trunk. I took off the helmet and looked for daylight, but the day had gotten even darker.

"This is a pristine riparian area," Charlie said. "Look how clear the stream is. I bet you could drink from it. I'll tell you one thing you're not going to find at Norm's—cows. If there were cattle grazing up there this little stream would be full of mud and giardia. If the storm continues it'll really get cranked up."

"I hear a car," I said, ducking behind a cottonwood.

Charlie ducked behind another tree and looked at his watch. "Right on time," he said.

"You were expecting Norm Alexander to be late?" I asked.

Norm's brown truck with the covered bed sped down the bumpy dirt road, stopped, flashed a directional signal and turned left on Route 30.

"Let's go," said Charlie, his eyes bright with the rush of a semiplanned action.

"His place is about five miles from here," I said. I'd looked at the map.

"Yeah."

"If it rains hard the road will turn to mud."

"I can make it," Charlie said, "but we'll leave tracks."

"I know."

"How long do we have?"

"Around two hours."

"If we walk, we're gonna leave tracks, too, two of them, and it will cut deep into our time."

By the time Norm got back here he'd probably have figured out what I was up to anyway. I just didn't want him to catch me doing it. "Okay," I said. "Let's go."

About a mile down the road the stream was replaced by a concrete diversion channel that directed the mountain runoff. Several bumpy miles later we came to a fence with a chain-link gate tightly padlocked shut.

"The bike stops here," Charlie said. "I can get *us* over the fence, but not the Harley." He pulled it off the road and laid it down on the ground, half-hiding it in a ditch behind a large yucca. We left our helmets and Charlie's jacket with the bike.

"What now?" I asked.

"We climb over."

"Huh?"

"Trust me." He showed me how to stick one toe then the other into the links and when I got stalled out near the top he gave me a push. Thunder grumbled and lightning danced where the peaks had been before the clouds dropped and covered them up. The wind picked up like it always does when there's a storm coming. Charlie jumped from the top of the gate to the ground, I followed. The rain started to fall, not heavy, but steady and determined.

"Shit," I said.

"Hang in there and pray for sun," said Charlie. He took off his glasses and wiped away the rain. His eyes were bright, his curls were getting plastered to his head. Charlie was in his element, breaking the law and trespassing in what I hoped would be a meaningful action. It only takes a few minutes for dust to turn to mud and before long it was clinging to our treads and we were leaving two sets of running-shoe tracks in the road.

The thunder and lightning skittered along the Soledads' backbone and the rain kept up a steady pace, enough to keep us wet, but not enough to keep us from going where we were headed. The water babbled as it bounced through the diversion channel. Charlie was as alert as a commando, watching, listening. I kept my attention focused on putting one foot ahead of the other, conserving energy. It was a steep, four-wheel-drive, breath-robbing climb. There wasn't much to see but Charlie's bright blue SAVE THE LOBO shirt, the mud at my feet, flashes of lightning and an occasional yucca standing like a wary sentinel beside the road.

As the rain dripped down my neck, I hung in there and prayed for sun: hot sun, dry sun, silent sun, burning sun, the fire around which we dance. I thought about the sun that follows the storm, turns puddles to steam and steam to mist, sun that comes in through the gap in my drapes, plays across the wall and the Kid's skin. Sun that makes the geranium bloom in its pot, that turns your smiles to old leather. Sun that tans your thighs and warms your back, that makes the day Ray-Ban bright and the shadows velvet dark, that turns the sky to peach and mauve and lavender. Sun that warms, burns, sizzles, melts. Sun that ripens corn, grass, tomatoes. Sun that turns red chiles red and green chiles green.

Charlie, who had gotten about fifty feet ahead of me, stopped suddenly at a bend in the road, motioned me forward with one hand and sshhed me with the other. It seemed overly dramatic to me, but if you can't be dramatic in an electrical storm when you're on an eco-mission, when can you? I hurried up to him, but what was the point in being quiet? The runoff rushed through the diversion channel gossiping and bitching all the while. The rain pattered against the rocks and the cactus, the thunder grumbled. We were immersed in a rushing, whooshing environment of water that, no matter what, says what it wants to say and gets where it wants to go. Just as I reached Charlie, I saw a flash of extraterrestrial brilliance and a lightning bolt plunged into the ground not fifty feet away, leaving behind it the spine-tingling smell of ozone. A fraction of a second later—too close to measure—I heard an enormous crack of thunder that jolted us off the ground. There's nothing like the adrenaline rush of a thunder and lightning storm. I started to run—it was an automatic reflex—but Charlie grabbed me by the elbow.

"Wait," he said, "look." Around the bend Norm's house was visible nestled into the rocky foothills. The house wasn't much, a small, dark cabin with a phone line that connected it to the rest of the world. It must have cost a bundle to run a phone line up here and I had to wonder why a man who liked to be alone so much would bother. The house looked buttoned tight. There were no vehicles visible and no sign that anyone was around. Behind the cabin was a medium-sized barn with miles of chain-link fence connected to the far side of it. About a quarter of a mile past the barn, deeper into the foothills, I saw more chain-link fence tucked between some boulders. The diversion channel came off the peaks in a straight line. We climbed up to the barn and saw that the chain-link fence made long runways, fenced over the top so even the most agile animal couldn't leap out or in. The runways led like a kennel into the barn. Paths had been worn from one end of the runways to the other by steady, relentless pacing.

Charlie stopped and the yellow eyes on his T-shirt peered through the chain-link fence. I wondered what the smell of ozone and the sound of thunder would do to a wolf's highly acute sense of smell and hearing. Send it running to its den for shelter? We stood still for a few minutes listening to the rain pouring off the mountain, smelling a ripe animal smell, looking into the dark hole where the runway entered the barn. Yellow eyes appeared at the door, hesitated and were followed by a wolf, a lobo to be exact. I recognized him, having recently seen his compadres at the Rio Grande Zoo. He was coyote brown with white on his face and feet and was shedding his thick fur in large clumps. His neck fur did not piloerect in fear or threat. His ears were alert and pointed. His eyes drew mine like a magnet and bore straight into them in a way that dog or human eyes never did. They were smart, intense, wild animal eyes, but this animal had been imprinted by humans. He was cautious and curious but not frightened. He stepped out of the dark doorway a few feet into the pen and stared at us.

"Holy shit," said Charlie. "That's a lobo. Where the hell did Norm Alexander get a lobo?"

"Stole it from the Rio Grande Zoo," I said.

"It was Norm Alexander?" Charlie was incredulous. "And everybody wanted to blame me. They said I stole the lobos to make a statement, that I took them to Mexico and set them free. Straight-arrow scientist Norm Alexander. Who would have suspected him?" He shook his head, but his curls remained plastered in place.

"It had to be Norm," I said. "The wolves were stolen soon after he bought this property, when they were old enough to take from the mother. Who else outside the government knows how to care for and raise young wolves?" It wasn't entirely a rhetorical question, but Charlie didn't answer it.

"He's keeping this one alive, but I wouldn't say he was caring for it," Charlie said. "What kind of an environment is this for a wolf, chained up in a pen all alone all day? It's an existence, not a life. It can't hunt, it can't run, it can't get close to other wolves." Charlie was looking for an argument, but I wasn't the one to give it to him.

"If we look around here we'll probably find a radio collar with the signal that Bob Bartel followed over the mountain," I said.

Charlie's imagination led him quickly to the next likely step. "Norm killed Bartel? Jesus." The caution of scientists makes people think they're incapable of rash acts. The rashness of radical environmentalists like Charlie makes people think they're incapable of cautious acts. But any lawyer learns quickly how contradictory human nature is. "At least no one tried to blame *that* on me yet. You know wolves howl and make a lot of noise," Charlie said. "It's funny nobody caught on to what he was doing before now."

"Ernesto Sandoval heard something."

"Wait a minute, look at that. See where the fur's been cut away beneath that lobo's neck?" Charlie stepped forward a few feet toward the lobo, the lobo stepped a few feet back. "I bet Norm cut the vocal cords so it couldn't howl. Just another scientific experiment to him." Charlie began making wolf sounds, barking and howling. The wolf stared back and kept his silence. Suddenly Charlie took a pen from his pocket, stuck it between his fingers and jabbed his hand toward the wolf, which quickly jumped away. "See that? He thinks I'm going to hit him with a needle. Norm's probably tranquilized that lobo so often he's turned its brain to mush."

"He claims tranquilizing doesn't hurt them."

"The fuck it doesn't. Would you like to be knocked down and knocked out and come to in a different place not knowing what hit you? That's what I hate about science and technology—it's so intrusive and arrogant. It makes me wish I was studying something else. All the scientist cares about is doing his studies, he doesn't give a damn about the animal. The trouble with scientists is that they can never leave anything alone."

"It's the trouble with humans," I said.

The noise brought two more curious lobos out of the barn. All of them were silent, none of them wore radio collars.

"I bet he's running a breeding farm here, a breeding farm for lobos," Charlie said. "You know what I'd like to do? I'd like to set these guys free."

"Don't," I said. "He's imprinted these wolves to tolerate humans. What do you think their lives will be worth in Soledad County?"

"What do you think their lives are worth now?"

"At least they're alive and they have the possibility of getting a better arrangement. Release them here and they're dead meat. Come on, we've got more things to look at."

"Like what?"

"The other chain-link fence, the cabin." The thunder and lightning were heading south, the rain letting up. Charlie followed me to the cabin. We climbed the steps onto a small, dark porch and tried the door. It wasn't locked. Norm, apparently, hadn't figured anyone would get this far or if anyone did a lock wouldn't do any good. I took one look at the spotless floors and decided we'd better leave our shoes on the doorstep. The tiny cabin consisted of a living room, a kitchen, a bedroom, a bath and another room which appeared to be control central. Five rooms and all of them would have fit into a good-sized one-bedroom apartment. The whole place was anal compulsive, white glove neat, so neat that it made the hair on the back of my neck stand up. Every object in the living room was squared off and free of dust. The books on the shelves were alphabetically arranged by author. There were no overflowing ashtrays or half-full glasses lying around this house. Every dish was put away in the kitchen, the bath towels were folded on their rack, the bed was made up so tight you could have bounced a quarter on the bedspread. Norm's white Jockeys were folded carefully in his bureau, his socks arranged by color: blue, black, brown. In the closet I found jeans, shirts, one suit, hiking boots with no mud in the cleats, a down parka, but no black leather jacket, helmet or high-powered rifle either. In a place as tidy and minimalist as this, hiding places were few. We checked them all, ending up in control central, which had a wall of dials, tapes, graphs. On the worktable we saw an Apple computer, a receiver and a pair of headphones. The unanswered questions were, where was the transmitter and where was the physical evidence?

We traipsed through the living room on our way back out. An Indian throw rug lay in the middle of the floor precisely aligned with the edges of the sofa. It was blood red and pitch black with lightning bolts and swastikas woven into the geometric pattern, and was the only thing that resembled decoration in the spartan cabin. I stopped to look for the black line that leads out of the pattern, the error that Indian weavers put in their rugs so as not to anger the gods by aiming for perfection. The precision with which the rug had been placed, the lack of anything out of place and the total absence of evidence in Norm's house annoyed me. I felt I'd been put in my sloppy place by his aggressive, scientific neatness. It gave me a powerful desire to light a cigarette and drop some ashes on the floor. I didn't, but just for the hell of it I gave the rug a kick. It bunched up and slid across the polished floor, revealing the handle to a trapdoor tucked into the floorboards.

"All right," said Charlie. He yanked the trapdoor up. I peered over the edge and saw a crawlspace with a dirt floor. I didn't see anything down there that would trap or bite so I jumped in. It wasn't quite tall enough to stand up in. I had to hunch over into an old lady hump. A chain dangled from the ceiling and I pulled it, lighting a bare bulb. There wasn't much down here: dirt floor, wooden beams, a hot water heater and a few boxes in the corner. I looked through the boxes. The first three contained books, charts and graphs. In the fourth I found a motorcycle helmet and a black leather jacket but no rifle. By now Charlie had joined me in the crawlspace.

"Look at that," said Charlie, holding up the leather jacket. "Not a bad disguise. Norm can't drive a motorcycle, so who ever would have suspected it was him in motorcycle gear?"

The jacket was severely distressed leather, very chic or very old. Old, I decided, knowing Norm, a remnant of the days when he could still handle a motorcycle, the days before he got bit by the wolf.

"How much time do we have?" I asked Charlie.

He looked at his watch. "Not much. We should get going. I want to get inside the wolf barn before we go."

"Okay, I'm gonna check out the other fence."

I put the motorcycle jacket in its box and turned out the light, and we climbed out of the crawlspace. I pushed the rug back in place, struggling mightily to get it as straight as Norm would. We went outside, closed the cabin door, put our running shoes on.

"I'll meet you back here," I said to Charlie. "Soon."

"You got it," Charlie replied.

He went back to the wolf barn. I climbed the hill next to the churning diversion channel. Whitewater rapids today, tomorrow the water would be gone, leaving an empty, ugly ditch. As I climbed up to the fence I left footprints all over the place but there was no choice. With the evidence we'd found our presence couldn't be kept a secret for long anyway. The chain-link fence made a pen tucked behind the boulder, a long narrow one that led up toward the peaks. There was another lobo in it, but this one hadn't been so imprinted with the people look and smell. It turned and ran when it saw me. I thought it was a female, but it darted away so quickly I couldn't be sure. It had dug itself a den between two boulders and it disappeared inside. Before it vanished I saw that it had a radio collar attached to its neck. There was a trapdoor into the pen like one a house-trained pet uses to let itself in and out. I gave it a push. The door swung in but it couldn't swing back out. It made me wonder if there weren't leg-hold traps around here too.

The rain had stopped, the clouds were blowing away, the peaks reappearing. I started walking downhill slipping and sliding in the mud, steadying myself with a hand against a boulder. Suddenly there was a loud crack behind me and then another, the sound of gunshots and more intimidating even than thunder. Damn Anna, was my first thought, she'd kept her lunch date after all. While she was eating hers I'd become target practice. My second thought was to run. Like a wolf, I can look back and run if I have to. I slid down the slippery slope as I looked up and saw the person standing on a boulder above and behind me aiming a high-powered rifle at my head. I couldn't look long, but long enough to see a medium-sized person, wearing jeans, a black leather jacket and a Darth Vader visor. Could it be Charlie Clark? For a terrifying moment I wondered if he hadn't been what he was pretending to be. But how had he gotten into the uniform and up there? *Crack*, another shot rang out and my right foot slid out from under me. I grabbed a boulder to regain my balance and started running again, focusing all my energy on staying upright.

"Neil," Charlie yelled from down below. "Over here." I looked down and saw his blue shirt sprinting away from the wolf barn. "Someone's shooting at us."

"No shit."

Another crack, another shot and my adrenaline was pumping too hard for me to know whether I'd been hit or not. "There's one way out of here," Charlie yelled, running toward the diversion channel.

I ran after him. The shots were getting closer. The next one hit the ground and splattered mud on my jeans.

Charlie had reached the ditch and was teetering on the edge looking in.

"Don't be crazy," I yelled. "People drown in those things all the time."

"I'll take my chances." Charlie held his nose and jumped.

I looked back, saw the rifle, looked forward and saw Charlie's head bobbing rapidly down the ditch. It's hard to hit a target moving as fast as he was, harder still to hit a target submerged in water. And if you hit one that has already drowned, what difference would it make? You can't get any deader than dead. The next shot nicked the edge of the ditch and broke loose a piece of concrete that landed on my running shoe. I jumped, too.

The water was only knee deep but traveling so fast that it pulled me down and knocked me flat. It was a Class Ten rapid, at least—unnavigable by even the most experienced or insane navigator. The fact that it was shallow didn't make it any slower or less dangerous. You can drown as easily in six inches as you can in the ocean if your face goes under. Fortunately I had fallen backwards so I was bouncing off the concrete walls on my butt instead of my face. It was like riding an Olympic luge course without the sled. There was no telling what had happened to Charlie. I couldn't see him. I couldn't see anything but water and concrete. If more shots rang out, I didn't hear them. All I heard was runoff rush. Considering the two options that had been available to me I began to wish I'd taken the bullet. At least it was neat, dry and quick. Death by drowning and pummeling is a torturous way to go. Water is an elemental, unstoppable force. It's got all the power and it lets you know it. It teases, sucks you down, squishes your breath out, pops you up for another gulp, knocks you down again. I was gasping for breath and traveling a lot faster than the body is meant to move without a vehicle. I fought to keep my feet forward, my face out of the water. At this speed it was impossible to stand. If my feet even touched bottom they were knocked loose immediately. There's only one way for water to go—downhill—and that's where I went, bouncing off the side walls, grateful for every bit of padding I had, lucky this wasn't the Duke City where the diversion channels go on for fifteen miles. This diversion channel's objective was getting the water off the mountain and away from Norm Alexander's buildings. Once it reached a flat place it stopped and dumped the water and me out. I shot through the air and came down with a splat in a pool of mud.

Once I stopped sliding I crawled out of the water's way, sat up, caught my breath, made sure everything was still in place and movable and looked around. Charlie was sitting in front of me happy as a pig in mud. His hair was matted to his head, his glasses were long gone. He squinted at me. "That you, Neil?"

"Yeah."

"Is this heaven or hell?"

"It's mud," I said.

"What a ride," he grinned. "You all right?"

"I think so."

"You look like a drowned rat."

"I feel like one."

"Well, it beats the Albuquerque water slide." Charlie started to laugh and I did, too. What else was there to do? We laughed so hard we shook like dogs and the water sprayed off us. We laughed so hard we could hardly stand up, but we could hardly stand up anyway. We laughed so hard we cried and when we were finished we staggered and helped each other to our feet. There were a lot of places that would hurt like hell tomorrow but for the moment at least were numb to pain. We hiked down to Route 30 and waited for someone to come along so we could hitch a ride. It was 100 degrees. Our muddy clothes began to dry and then to itch.

We looked like Zuni mudheads, clowns and demons at the same time. A rancher came along in a pickup truck, took pity on us and stopped.

"And what have you folks been up to?" he asked before he would let us in.

"We took a ride down Norm Alexander's diversion channel," Charlie said and he started laughing all over again.

The rancher pushed his cowboy hat back on his head and looked at us like we'd been chewing locoweed. He gave us a ride, but he made us sit in the back of the truck.

The rancher dropped us off at the Motel 6 where I had a change of clothes waiting, but Charlie didn't. I showered, changed and left him in the shower while I went out and tried to find someone to wash and dry our clothes. It wasn't just that they looked grungy, they were getting too stiff to sit down in. The Mexican maid, who was pushing around a cart full of dirty linen, agreed to throw our clothes in for a five-dollar tip.

"*Que pasó, Señorita?*" she giggled when I handed her the mud-soaked clothes.

"Don't ask," said I.

When I got back to the room Charlie was in the bed, and, unless he'd gotten into my underwear, naked under the sheet. He patted the space next to him, but I sat down across the room in one of those fake wood chairs that Motel 6 thoughtfully provides. With his skinny chest and nearsighted eyes, Charlie didn't exactly look like a warrior. He squinted in my direction. "I can't see that far without my glasses," he said.

I moved my chair in a little closer. "The maid thought your clothes were pretty amusing but she agreed to wash them."

"Good," he said, "because until I get them back I'm at your mercy. What did you tell her happened?"

"That we were mud wrestling."

"Really?"

"No, I couldn't say it in Spanish."

"What should I do about my motorcycle?"

"Leave it there for the time being and hope Norm doesn't notice. It's too risky to go back there, and besides you can't drive it without your glasses and I don't want to."

"Yeah, you're right." Charlie wanted to rehash the action and keep the adrenaline flowing. "What did you find in the other pen?" he asked.

"A lobo, a female I think, with a radio collar on and much shyer than the others. She hid when I approached."

"Why do you suppose he collared her?"

"Wanted to watch her without being seen himself. What did you find in the barn?"

"Another female and four pups. The pups were getting big, but they were still playful and not shy at all. One of them came up and untied my shoelace. Norm hadn't cut their vocal cords, they barked and growled. I guess that's why he's keeping them inside. He was giving them most of the barn to play in, anyway."

"Did you see any more lobos?"

"Only the ones we saw before."

I did some quick calculations. If Norm had stolen the lobos in '87, by '89 they'd be mature enough to breed. That gave him three breeding years: '89, '90, '91. He should have had a lot more than five adults and four pups by now.

"What do you think he's up to?" Charlie asked.

"Trying to improve the heterozygosity of the breeding population, breeding and selling them," I said.

"To who?"

"Rich people, the kind of people who'd get off on having an endangered species for a pet."

"What do they do with them? Keep them hidden all the time?"

"What do people do with stolen artwork? Look at it themselves? Show it to people who don't know what it's worth? If you said the lobos were wolf hybrids, most people wouldn't know the difference. It's got to be an international market and the kind of people who would buy one probably have enough property that they don't have to worry, anyway." In the heat of discovery I'd moved my chair in closer and placed my hand on the bedside table. Charlie reached out, grabbed hold of it and brought it down to the bed, wanting to prolong the rush of the action, I guessed. It was an awkward gesture, but that didn't make it totally unappealing. I could see through the sheet that the adrenaline was still flowing and he wasn't wearing any underwear either. It would be one way to finish off the adventure. After all, we'd just shared one near-death experience, why not investigate another? I looked into Charlie's myopic eyes, could see he was nervous like a student, not bold like a warrior. I could also tell that I hadn't gotten close enough for him to read my expression. And what was the expression that he couldn't read? Businesslike. There was a time when I would have thrown off my clothes and jumped in, I'll admit it. So what if he was younger, that never stopped me before. For the adventure, I would have said. But that time had gone. There were too many other things to think about: disease, contraception, the Kid, the lobos. Was that maturity? I took my hand back.

Charlie sighed, but continued reliving the action, hoping maybe to bring me back to a fever pitch. "Good thing Norm is such a lousy shot," he said, "or we'd have been long dead by now."

"You may be an eco-warrior," I replied, "but your investigatory skills suck."

Charlie blinked his eyes, which were red and naked as rabbits without the glasses. "What do you mean?"

"That wasn't Norm Alexander."

"How do you know?"

"Because the hand on the trigger was the right hand and Norm is left-handed. His right hand is a club with a useless thumb. He can't even pick up a fork with it. He'd never use it to pull a trigger."

"Who was it then?"

"That's what we're going to find out." I began outlining for him a more carefully planned action. From the way his eyes lit up and the sheet went down I could see this action was at least as exciting as sex, maybe more. We schemed and planned. Charlie sat up in bed, I moved the chair in close. Eventually there was a knock at the door.

The Mexican maid came in giggling at the sight of Charlie naked in my bed. She handed me the clothes pressed and folded in a neat little pile. I can't speak for Charlie but my jeans had never looked so immaculate.

"*Mil gracias*," I said.

"*De nada*," she replied.

19

If the night had been any quieter I would have heard my heart beating and the blood rushing through my veins. It was quiet enough that when I stood still I heard myself breathing—shallower and faster than I like to be. When I moved, my footsteps crunched on the gravel. I was visible, too. There's no place to hide in the desert when there's a full moon, not unless you've got your belly to the ground. Every small step for me was a giant step for my shadow and anybody who happened to be watching. It was two in the morning, however, an hour when everyone ought to be sound asleep. I'd soon find out whether anyone was. The door wasn't locked, the house being lonely enough that locks were irrelevant. Anybody who came that far to break in was not going to be kept out by a lock. I turned the knob quietly and let myself in. I followed the moon's beacon down the hallway, through the door, into the living room where it beamed in the open window. I had a flashlight in my hand and a tape recorder in my pocket, but I hadn't needed to use either yet. I walked up to the pool of moonlight, stepped into the middle of it, spun around on the floor.

I stepped out of the moonlight, turned on the flashlight, walked over to the wall and shone some light on Frida and her monkey, the painting that Jayne hadn't sold because she was attached to it or because it was hot. "Tree of hope, keep firm," Frida said. She was fierce as ever, facing down all comers with her barbed-wire eyebrows. Would she approve of what I was about to do? Disapprove? Give a shit? What did it matter? Bob Bartel had been murdered; Charlie and I had almost been. I had to know by whom and one way to find out about the present is to look into the past, Jayne Brown and Bill Wiley's past to be more precise, and their brushes with the law. I expected to find that information in the legal folders filed in the conquistador credenza, the folders Jayne got through the Freedom of Information Act, which meant that whatever Juan had been involved in, she had been involved in, too.

I opened the credenza and flashed my light across the labels on the stack of manila folders. About what you'd expect to find in any modern woman's valuable papers: a divorce file, a real estate file, a tax file, a car file. Almost everybody has those, but not many have a bulging government file. There it was illuminated by my flashlight's beam, *U.S.A. v. William Wiley, Betty Jo Burnett, et al.* Not quite a foot thick as March had said, but fat enough. I could see why Jayne had changed her name. Who'd want to go through life as Betty Jo Burnett? On the other hand, who'd want to go through life as plain old Jayne Brown, even if she had added a *y*! Why hadn't she chosen something a little more flamboyant? I wondered. She was tough, maybe she thought flamboyancy would get in the way, or maybe after seeing Betty Jo Burnett all over the newspapers, she craved anonymity.

William Wiley and Betty Jo Burnett had been an item in their day, the late '60s, not big enough to go network or national, but big enough to get their names and faces in all the California papers. The articles were in the file. I couldn't tell if the government had clipped them or if someone had added them later. He had put on flab since those days and gotten gray. She had put on silicone and gotten blond. But they were still recognizably Juan and Jayne. Her hair was about as long then as it was now. His was considerably longer then. In fact, he had been another mophead.

I flipped through the file and found the transcript of the bank robbery trial. Some statement was being made then, but these days, when people have gone back to robbing banks out of greed, it's hard to remember what. There probably was some interesting reading in there among the boilerplate, but I didn't have time to look. I turned to the back of the transcript, found that four of the defendants (there were a total of five) had been convicted. Juan, who drove the getaway car, got seven years, just like he'd said. The fifth—Betty Jo Burnett—went free. She was only nineteen at the time and the only female.

I hadn't come here in the middle of the night to find that Jayne hadn't been convicted. There had to be more to it than that. I started looking through the pretrial motions, letters and memos and I found what I had been looking for. One of the tellers at the bank had been shot and killed by an AK-47 during the robbery. An eyewitness—another teller—claimed Betty Jo had fired the shot and identified her in a lineup. Other witnesses had conflicting stories and there wasn't any physical evidence. The bullet was traced to one of the AK-47s, but that gun couldn't be traced to Betty Jo Burnett and there were no fingerprints on it or on any of the guns. The robbers were careful—up to a point—but they screwed up their getaway and got caught. The government was making preparations to try Jayne for murder, basing their case on circumstantial evidence and their star witness, but then that witness recanted his story. Said that he wasn't sure who fired the gun after all, said he wasn't even sure Betty Jo had been there. It blew the government's case, so they went with the conviction they thought they could get—bank robbery. They didn't do so well with Betty Jo. Every prosecutor knows it's hard to convict a good-looking defendant, even harder to convict a young one and, back then anyway, harder still to convict a female. Betty Jo at nineteen was a lot dewier than Jayne at forty-something and she was acquitted. The government never stopped believing Betty Jo had fired the AK-47, but were unable to get enough evidence to take it to trial.

Juan got seven years. He was lucky the robbery took place in the '60s. A few years later the government changed the law, possibly because of people like Juan. Nowadays everyone who participates in a bank robbery that results in murder gets charged with the murder. Whether the defendant drives the getaway car or pulls the trigger makes no difference in the eyes of the law.

The feds kept both Juan and Jayne under surveillance for years, to the point of following Juan's wolf program around the country, which proved that he hadn't been so paranoid after all. The government had a lot of other radical troublemakers to worry about and eventually they forgot about Juan and Jayne and stashed the file away somewhere until she asked for it. The file indicated it had been released in early '87. Why did she ask for it then? I wondered. To find out if she was still under surveillance?

"Find what you're looking for?" A wall switch flicked and the bare bulb overhead filled the living room with stark white inquisition light. The shadows shriveled and ran under the sofa, the moonlight went out the window, the pink velvet drapes came into sharp focus, shifting nervously in place. I remembered the tape recorder I had in my pocket and punched the record button before I turned around and faced Jayne. I was glad I'd hit the button first because one look at her and her hard-nosed Magnum was enough to make me forget everything but the essentials like was the blood still running through my veins?

"It looks like you killed a man," I said.

"Yeah?" She was wearing a low-cut, slinky pink night-gown. The overhead light revealed her muscular arms, her unripe mango breasts, her flat bare feet planted firmly on the ballroom floor, her tousled blond hair, her dark roots, the lines beside her mouth that were hard and determined. "Who?" she asked.

"The bank teller," I said, "for one."

She shrugged. The pink nightgown clung to her breasts, shimmied around her ankles. "I was never tried for that crime."

"The witness recanted his testimony. What did you do? Pay him off?"

She smiled. "In a way."

"You know whether you killed him; you're the one who's had to live with it for over twenty years."

She seemed to be at ease here in her living room even with the harsh spotlight on and the flattering pink lamps off. She was in her nightgown, I was in my jeans, two women together late at night, sharing their slumber party secrets. If only the gun had been a water pistol instead of a Magnum, I might have felt at ease, too. Feeling comfortable got her talking anyway.

"I was just a kid and under Juan's influence," Jayne said. "I didn't mean to kill anybody. The teller reached for a weapon and my gun went off. I was trying to protect us; it was an instinctive reaction. It could have happened to anybody."

Anybody who happened to be robbing a bank and holding an AK-47 in their hand.

"It's kind of like having an abortion," she said, "in the old days when abortion was despicable, illegal and terrifying too. When it's over you can hate yourself forever or you can say you did what you had to do and get on with your life. I was pretty young when I found out what I was capable of."

"How did you feel the second time?" Assuming, of course, that Bob Bartel *was* the second time.

"Believe it or not, that was an accident, too. Bad karma, I guess." She shrugged again.

When someone keeps getting caught committing illegal acts with a gun in her hand it seems kind of a stretch to blame it on karma. On one level criminals want to get caught, and one way they get caught is they talk about their crimes. Like everybody else, they want recognition for their work. Their problem is they don't have anybody to talk to but each other and they know better than to trust each other. The ones that get off have it worse; they don't even have each other. Jayne was only human; she needed to talk.

"Tell me about it," I said like a sympathetic public defender or an expensive shrink. The tape was turning in my pocket, I hoped, recording her every word. Anna would love to transcribe this.

"It wasn't my fault," Jayne said. "Norm had to go into Soledad and I was alone in the barn with the pups. I heard someone coming and I knew it wasn't Norm. He wasn't due back yet and I would have heard his truck anyway. It was someone who'd come on foot, a thief, an investigator, Buddy Ohles? I didn't know, but I knew it was someone who had no business being there. Those are very valuable wolves. There was a hunting rifle in the barn; I picked it up. Bartel pushed the door open, looked all around at the wolves. He was holding his radio receiver, his earphones and his antenna. He must have followed Nepenthe's signal over the mountain. Loki, the mother wolf, was startled and she started fear woofing. I was in the shadows and he hadn't seen me yet. He put down the radio gear, pulled the gun off his back. I'm a mother to those pups, too. I panicked and I fired."

It was a good story, but it wouldn't fly in court. "Bartel never carried a gun," I said.

"It was a dart rifle, but I didn't know that when I fired. He was standing with the light behind him and it blinded me. I told Norm it was stupid to use a radio collar, that someone could track the signal, but no one was doing any studies in the Soledads and he thought the chances of anybody tracking it were infinitesimal—that's his word, infinitesimal."

"Nepenthe was the wolf in the pen by herself?"

"Yeah."

"Why had he collared her?" I asked, even though I thought I already knew.

"To monitor her from the house without being seen himself. He was looking for signs of any unusual excitement or activity."

"Like her reaction to a wild lobo coming over the mountain?"

"That's it," Jayne said, surprised. I guess I was smarter than she'd thought. Smart enough to realize that what Norm Alexander was attempting to do down here in the sole of America was lure an illegal alien, a lonely lobo, over the border to increase the heterozygosity of his breeding population.

"He'd installed physiological sensors so he could monitor her heartbeat," Jayne said. "He knew every timed she peed. If Norm could have gotten inside of Nepenthe he would have done that too. You might say he was obsessed with wolves."

"What brought you two together?" I asked.

"I met Norm years ago at a wolf seminar in California and we'd kept in touch. He'd lost his job, my husband took off and I got nothing but a ranch that I couldn't sell."

"And a hot Frida Kahlo that you couldn't sell either?"

"That, too. I know more about breeding wolves in captivity than Norm does. I was the one who raised and mated Siri's ancestors."

"So you and Norm stole the lobos from the zoo?"

She nodded. "Both of us needed to find some way to make a living. Wolves are what we know."

Wolves and stealing. "I suppose they're worth a lot to the right person."

"A lot. People love wolves and the lobos are one of the rarest mammals in existence. We have customers from all over the world. We breed them every year, and we're making the lobos better than ever. If people ever get smart enough to let the lobos come back to the wild and if a site can be found, our wolves will be the strongest. Private enterprise, you could say. You know the government's going to fuck it up."

I couldn't argue with her about that. "I'm curious as to why you held the meeting here."

"That damn meeting. It was the start of all our problems. If those fucking kids hadn't set Siri free, if Juan hadn't gotten into *your* tequila ..."

If *she* hadn't stolen an endangered species, bred and sold them, I thought. But having a Magnum staring at you helps you keep your thoughts to yourself. It was my wits and a tape recorder against her superior physical conditioning and a gun. At the moment the gun was ahead.

"Juan insisted," Jayne shrugged. "You know how he can be. He chips away at you until he gets what he wants. No one's going to let the lobo come back to White Sands, anyway. It's just an FWS charade to shut up the environmentalists. I thought the meeting would be a lot of hot air and Juan would have been suspicious if I refused to do it. Anything else you want to know?"

"If you shot Bartel before he saw you, how did you know where his truck was?"

"Where else could it have been? There are only three ways onto Norm's property. He hadn't driven through the gate so he either came over the peaks from the Phillipses' or from Roaring Falls Ranch, and he wouldn't have gone on my land without asking me first."

"Bob Bartel was a gentleman."

"I didn't mean to kill him. I told you that. He should have warned me he was coming. You don't go around surprising people in Soledad County."

I replayed the action. "Norm hiked over the mountain and got the truck. He probably wouldn't have had any trouble pushing the gearshift into place even with his bad hand. You came home, gave Juan the Xanax, went out and helped Alexander dispose of the body, set the clock to one when you got back, woke Juan up for an alibi and made love. The Xanax had probably worn off somewhat by then."

"Somewhat. I was pretty wound up and I needed the release. Juan isn't what he used to be when he was Billie, but I was excited enough for us both that night." Her finger was getting itchy on the Magnum's trigger. "You know I'm not going to jail for this. I know what it's like to kill and I know I can live with it. I know enough about jail to know I could never live with that: no outdoors, no animals, no exercise, no men, no freedom. No way."

"It's not going to be so easy to get away with it this time," I said.

"Why not?" she shrugged. "You broke into my house. I thought you were a burglar. That's reason enough in Soledad County."

"What about Charlie Clark? He was at Norm's. He saw the wolves. You fired at him, too."

"Norm and the wolves are well out of Soledad County by

now. And no one can prove it was me that fired. Besides, like Charlie said, he's a radical environmentalist, he could be taken out at any time," she smiled. "Well, I've said all I have to say. I think this little conversation is about to end." It had been a deathbed confession, only she had confessed and I was on death's bed.

"Do I get a last wish?" I asked.

"Why not?"

Now that the talking was over, I didn't have the unnatural calm I usually have when I find myself staring down trouble. A life wish was circulating through my arteries, through my veins. She'd already proven that at any distance she was a lousy shot, but with the Magnum only ten feet away, hitting me would be the equivalent of taking out a house. "I want to hear the wolf howling at Roaring Falls Ranch before I die," I said.

"What?"

"I want to hear the wolf howling at Roaring Falls Ranch before I die." I said it again louder.

The wolf at the window responded with a long, deep howl that made me feel my spinal column was full of Jell-O and startled Jayne so much her silicone shook.

"What the ...?" She turned toward the window, forgetting for an instant that she was holding a weapon in her hand. The pink velvet drapes parted. A two-legged wolf in long scraggly fur and a pointy-eared mask stepped out. Muddy running shoes showed beneath the fur. It whipped off its wolf skin and, with all the gusto it could muster, threw it over Jayne. The gun went off, but its aim was deflected and the bullet sailed into the wall, missing Frida Kahlo, whose karma wasn't so great either, by an inch. Charlie Clark leapt on Jayne, pinned her down with the wolf skin and kneed her wrist until the gun fell out on the bare floor.

"You little shit." She struggled against the skin.

I picked the gun up. It felt warm and sweaty in my palm. It was tempting to turn around and aim it at Jayne, but I didn't. I put the Magnum on the credenza and took my weapon, a lawyer's weapon, out of my pocket.

Charlie straddled Jayne on the floor, high on the excitement of a well-planned and -executed action. "Did you get it?" he yelled.

"Let's see." I rewound, played back the last few minutes. The voices were a little scratchy, but the tape was understandable.

"So I could be taken out at any time, huh?" Charlie said, giving Jayne's arm a twist.

"You know, you're a real bitch," Jayne snapped at me.

Juan had been woken up by the noise and he staggered groggily to the door. He was wearing a pair of blue boxer shorts and his chest was covered all over with soft, fuzzy gray hair. He scratched his belly. "What's happening?" he asked.

"Jayne killed Bob Bartel and tried to kill Charlie and me. I've got it all on tape," I said.

"Jeez, Jaynie, Ohweiler was trying to blame Bartel on me."

"He wouldn't have been able to; I gave you an alibi," Jayne replied.

Actually she'd given herself an alibi, but I'd let the two of them work that one out.

"Why did you do it?" Juan asked. "He just put Siri in the zoo. I would have gotten him back."

Jayne seemed to be all talked out so I answered for her. "She killed him because he caught her and Norm Alexander breeding lobos across the mountain." I'd been wondering if Juan knew anything about it. Probably not, I decided from his sleepy, puzzled look.

"What's wrong with that?" he asked.

"Lobos are an endangered species, Juan. They stole pups from the zoo and started breeding and selling them. It's illegal."

"So? They probably did a better job of it than the government." I wasn't going to argue that point with him. Juan got down on the floor and tried to hug Jayne, but Charlie and the wolf skin were in the way. "Let her go," Juan said. "She's not going anywhere."

Charlie looked at me for approval. "It's okay," I said. I had the Magnum and could shoot at the fleeing legs if I had to.

Jayne sat up straight-backed and dry-eyed and shook the wolf skin off. Juan gave her a hug, but, stiff as she was, it had to feel like hugging cement. I got on the phone, dialed 911 and asked for Sheriff Ohweiler. The dispatcher was reluctant to get him up, but I insisted.

"Oh, Jaynie," Juan said, "it's all my fault. You were just a kid and I got you into trouble." There were tears in his eyes.

Trouble was Juan's middle name. Jayne didn't deny it. She sat stiffly on the floor like her back was in a brace, but she let him hold her.

20

Sheriff Ohweiler and his deputy came over and arrested Jayne, who got dressed, made up and combed her hair before they took her off to jail. No doubt she was already calculating how she'd get off and who would defend her. The kind of help she needed would take more than a lawyer could give, more than a fenced Frida Kahlo.

"By the way," I said to Ohweiler. "You ought to check out the painting; I think she stole that, too."

Ohweiler looked at Frida. Frida looked back. "*That?*" he asked.

"Yeah," I said.

Jayne was wishing she'd shot me hours ago. Ohweiler took the Magnum and the tape with him. Later that morning the state police caught Norm Alexander on I-10 heading into Arizona with a truck full of lobos. They could be tested genetically to see whether any breeding with wild lobos had taken place and no doubt they would be. Charlie Clark went home to sleep, Juan Sololobo went into the kitchen.

I was too wired for sleep or food, so I walked into the desert, sat down on a rock and waited for the sun to come up, which it did eventually, spotlighting the backs of the

Soledads and outlining the jagged shapes of the peaks. In the west I could see a far sierra. As the sun moved up, the morning glow climbed down the sierra and crossed the plains of Soledad step by sangria-colored step. Maybe Bob Bartel's spirit was out there somewhere, drifting easier now that Jayne had been caught. Maybe not. The sun climbed higher, the glow faded, the sierra turned to rock and the plains to dust. I went inside and called the Kid.

He'd played the accordion the night before and hadn't been asleep for very long, but he woke up right away once he knew it was me. "Why you not call me last night, Chiquita?" he asked.

"I was catching a murderer." I told him all about it.

"I want to go to El Puerto," he said when I'd finished. "Can you take me there?"

"I can find it."

"*Bueno*. I am coming down."

"When?"

"Now."

"Why?"

"I tell you when I get there."

I gave him directions to Roaring Falls Ranch and figured he'd arrive in about three and a half hours, around 11.

Then I went into the kitchen where Juan Sololobo, who had gotten dressed and was cradling a mug of coffee in his L-O-V-E hand, was probably exactly what he was pretending to be—depressed. In spite of the name he had adopted, Juan was not a guy who liked to be alone, and he probably never was for long since there are plenty of women out there who don't like to be alone either. He was in a bind this time, however, because Siri was still in the zoo and he wouldn't want to leave Soledad until he got him back. Jayne had asked him to stay in the house and look after it until she was released on bail, but she might not be released on bail, she might never be released again.

"Jaynie's gonna be miserable in prison," he said, feeling sorry for her. "What did she do that was so terrible? She was just breeding wolves."

"She killed at least two men, Juan, and the one that I knew deserved a lot better."

"I know. You're right, but I'm gonna miss her," Juan said, feeling sorry for himself. "You living with someone?" His pale eyes looked me over. Was I mating stock? Not likely.

"No, but I have a friend and he's on his way down here," I said.

"He's a lucky guy," Juan sighed, staring morosely into his coffee. On the other hand, maybe he wasn't as depressed as he was pretending to be. His emotions and affections shifted as quickly as water, placid one minute, whitewater rapids the next. Being around all that emotion made me feel like a kitchen sponge that that sits on the sink pregnant with water. I couldn't wait to get out in the desert to dry out and to see my *solo lobo*, the Kid. He knew what it was like to be alone; being around him made me feel sharp, not soggy. What the Kid held in check was more interesting than all the stuff Juan spilled out. Emotional men have never been my MO. Domestic men either.

"Why don't you call March?" I suggested. "He'll want to know what happened."

"Good idea," Juan said. The call kept him occupied for a little while. At the end of their conversation March asked to speak to me.

"Thanks, Neil, for getting Juan off the hook."

"You're welcome."

"As always, you did a great job."

"Not *that* great," said I.

"It doesn't surprise me much that Jayne was responsible. She's trouble."

"And when are *you* getting married?" I asked.

"Next month."

"Good luck."

"Thanks. You'll keep in touch, won't you?"

"You bet."

"Keep an eye out for Sirius at night. It's in the southern sky. The first star to appear and the brightest."

"I'll keep an eye out for Venus in the daytime too."

He laughed. "Venus moves around a lot. It's trickier."

"You're telling me. Bye March."

"Bye Neil," he said.

It was time for Juan to start getting used to being alone. I left him that way, went into the nun's cell, slept for a few hours and dreamed about nothing. When I woke up he was still sitting at the kitchen table, but he wasn't alone any more. He was talking to the Kid and feeding him huevos rancheros. "Kid," I said. "When did you get here?"

"10:30."

It was now 11:00.

"We've been talking about wolves," Juan said, "and I've been telling your friend here all about Sirius and the lobos over the mountain."

The Kid shook his head. The things people did in America remained incomprehensible to him, but he and Juan both cared about wolves. They had that in common.

"Want some eggs?" Juan asked me.

I could see the Kid was getting restless already, but we had a hike ahead of us and I had to eat something. Juan made the best huevos rancheros in California, so I let him serve me breakfast. The Kid was anxious to be on his way, however. No time for coffee. He looked repeatedly at his watch, tapped his fork against the table and his foot against the floor.

The minute I put down my fork he stood up and shook Juan's hand. "*Mucho gusto*," he said.

"My pleasure," said Juan.

"*Vamos al Puerto*," the Kid said to me.

* * *

I'd never been hiking with him before. He has long, skinny legs that cover the ground a lot faster than mine do. The rain had washed away a lot of the tracks, but it was easy enough to tell where the path went; it had worn through the vegetation. I watched him moving on ahead of me with a quick, fluent motion. He seemed to be hearing everything, smelling everything, seeing everything. He held his head high. His thick curls had the alert springy quality of an antenna. Was he remembering anything? I wondered. What had it been like when he came through here before? Who he had been? He probably hadn't had much more sleep than I'd had, but *he'd* spent yesterday repairing automobiles and playing the accordion. I'd been shot at and diverted down a ditch. I'd caught a murderer and I'd lost my fine edge. I ached, too, in all the places I'd hit the ditch.

He climbed on ahead of me, but when he got to the falls he stopped and waited. The falls were six inches wide again and ended their performance by sinking into the ground. They whispered, they didn't roar. Yesterday's cloudburst had become today's drip. They were falls that only a desert rat could love and the Kid did. He was splashing water all over his face and neck when I got there.

"Be careful; that water could be full of giardia," I said.

He shrugged, filled his hands up and took a sip. Giardia didn't scare him.

"Have you ever been here before?" I asked.

"Not here, no, up there." He pointed toward the peaks.

"I've only gone this far," I said. "There's an old road that comes through El Puerto and connects with this path somewhere."

The Kid nodded, looked at his watch, looked at the sun. "*Andale*, Chiquita, there's not much time."

We followed the path on past the ruins and the stone diversion channel. The Kid stopped and looked in. It was dry as bone today.

"You went down one of *those*?" he asked me.

"Yup."

The Kid shook his head. "*Que cojones*," he said.

"*Que loca*," said I.

There were no footprints on this part of the path, only the partially washed-out prints Jayne's horse had made as she rode back and forth across the mountain. The path twisted like a snake as it climbed around the boulders and eventually met the ghost of the old road, the widest place through the peaks, wide enough for a horse and carriage but not for a highway.

The Kid had gotten ahead again and was waiting for me to catch up. He sat on a rock, but he wasn't exactly resting. He was sniffing the air and for all I knew listening to the clouds as they passed in the sky. I sat down beside him.

"You want to know why I came here, Chiquita?"

"*Digame*," I said, although it could only be one of two reasons, a lobo or a lobo.

"When you tell me about the wolf *biólogo* coming here after the lobos got stolen, I call the Norteños. They tell me one of the lobos in the Sierra Madre is missing. Sometimes when they get big they have to leave the—how you say it?— the family, the friends?"

"The pack."

"They have to leave the pack and look for a lobo to start a new one. It's a problem for them because there *are* no more lobos. So they go away and they live alone or someone kills them. Maybe he came here."

"That's what Norm Alexander was hoping."

"If this *solo lobo* is here, he has to go back to Mexico," the Kid said. "People in this country are crazy. You know, Chiquita, if you want to find a wolf, you don't have to be a *biólogo* with a radio, you have to think like a wolf. You have to be a wolf."

"How do you do that?"

"You remember the time when people lived with lobos, when they hear like a lobo and smell like a lobo. You know why people like lobos? Because they have families, because they are smart, because they are more like people than any other animal, because people and lobos were amigos and they hunted together." He stood up. "*Vamos.*"

I followed him up the road. As we got closer to El Puerto my adrenaline began kicking in and I felt a little less like a limp rag. I took giant steps and landed in his track so we were leaving only one path. I sniffed the air, listened to the wind slice through a yucca's spines and make the joints of an alligator juniper hum. I heard the birds call out. It was hard to move with any grace at the Kid's pace because every muscle rebelled and ached. When we got near El Puerto, the most accessible and crossable spot in the peaks, the watershed where the runoff flowed either east or west and you could see forever in both directions, where Jayne's property met Norm Alexander's, the Kid motioned me to stay low and quiet. He found a sheltered spot behind a gnarled alligator juniper. The prevailing winds, from the west, had bent the tree double. We crawled under it and looked up at El Puerto through the branches.

"Wolves like to be high," he said, "because they can smell more on the wind."

A footpath crossed the road and headed north from old Mexico to New, from starvation to employment, from the heart to the brain, from despair to hope, from citizen to alien. The route was high, narrow, circuitous, exposed. It was the wolf path.

"*La vereda del lobo,*" said the Kid.

"Would a wolf take a path that people use?"

"Many times they won't, but there are people everywhere in Mexico. The wolves in the Sierra Madre know the people smell and maybe this is the only path that went to what the lobo wanted."

"A mate?"

"Maybe."

"How would a lobo know there was another one five hundred miles away?"

"Maybe he didn't, maybe he just went looking or maybe he did know. Wolves are very smart. They know things people don't. Shh."

He motioned me to be quiet, but whatever he'd heard I hadn't. I listened and listened but I heard only the low vibration of the wind. There weren't any human noises up here: no boom boxes, no engines, no air conditioner hum. It felt like the last quiet place in America, a place free of the human need to manipulate, manage, make noise. It was the kind of quiet you could work up a thirst for. The Kid has the patience of the Third World. He could wait all day without moving a muscle, but I ached and twitched. Eventually at some signal that went right by me, the Kid threw his head back and began to howl. "Aaahoooo," he howled and then again deeper and louder, "aaahoooo." There was no answer. He waited and then he howled once more. "Aaahoooo."

This time there was an answering howl, a sound as wild and lonely as the wind. "Aaahoooo." The howls sang back and forth, the Kid's remaining in place, the other's coming from the southeast and moving closer and closer.

"*Mira,*" the Kid whispered. "*Don lobo.*"

"Where?"

"*Allá.*"

He nodded toward the south, toward a dappled place where the path came around a curve and was shadowed by oaks. I looked into it, but all I saw was shade and dry earth bleached by the sun. Then a wolf began to take shape out of the shadows. Part of its fur blended into the path, part of it blended into the shade. Its ears were alert and pointed, its head was hunched forward. The white markings on its face accented its expression. It was the *solo lobo* that hadn't gotten caught in Norm's trap, the one maybe Ernesto had heard howling, not from El Puerto but from somewhere close to Norm's. The lobo stepped forward a few feet on long, stiff legs looking for the source of the howl, staring with curious, intense, yellow eyes, eyes that burned like flames, much brighter than the ones I had seen at Norm's or the zoo. The Kid and I looked back through the branches of the juniper.

"*El fuego en la noche,*" I whispered.

"*Claro,*" said the Kid.

It was a fire that had burned with intelligence and sensory awareness for 20,000 years and was within a flicker, thirty-nine captive lobos and this one, of being extinguished by America forever.

"They have a look that they call *la conversación del muerte,*" the Kid said.

The conversation of death.

"A lobo looks like that at a deer, the deer looks back. If the deer is ready to die, the lobo kills him. If it is not, the lobo goes away and looks for another." The prevailing wind was blowing our words and smell due east across El Puerto, away from the lobo.

He remained still, staring at something, but it didn't appear to be us. Another long, lonely howl sang out from the east side of El Puerto. The lobo turned its head in that direction. The musical calm was shattered by the spine-tingling crack of a shot. The bullet hit the ground in front of the lobo and kicked up the dust. "*Asesino,*" cried the Kid. The lobo turned quickly and with a long loping motion began to run. There was another shot and a cry, a cry of human pain.

It was happening too fast to comprehend and at the same time with all the clarity and brilliance of slow motion. A horse and rider galloped over El Puerto from the east and reined to a stop. The horse was dusty white. The skinny-as-a-cadaver rider wore a black shirt and black cowboy hat. He was a Mexican with the hungry face of a hawk and eyes that looked like they knew all about *la conversación del muerte*. He jumped off the horse and pulled a rifle from his saddle scabbard, which he aimed at some scrub oaks on the far side of El Puerto.

"Kid ..." I began, having no idea what the guy was shooting at.

"*Callate*," said the Kid.

The Mexican fired and a hunter in a camouflage suit scrambled out of the oaks groaning and holding a bleeding arm. He was a ferret of a fellow with sharp features and bright, little eyes, and his jaw was working fast and hard on a tobacco wad. It was the last of the great white professional wolf hunters—Buddy Ohles. I'd know him anywhere. Since he probably wasn't smart enough to figure out what Norm had been up to by himself, Sheriff Ohweiler must have told him.

Buddy kicked his rifle across the path, whimpering and cowering in a submissive gesture, but the Mexican fired again, raising dust at his feet. "No gun," Buddy yelled. "See?" The Mexican was not impressed. He was toying with Buddy and making him dance to his bullets. "*No habla inglés*?" said Buddy. "Goddamn Mexicans," he mumbled. He hopped around in a bowlegged jig while the gunman watched with eyes as hard as obsidian. The horse reared up and whinnied, but it didn't run. The gunman said not a word. *Ping*, and another shot hit the dust. Buddy chewed harder, danced faster, got red in the face and wet in the pants. He probably hated like hell to turn his back on a Mexican but finally he wised up, turned tail and scrambled down the east side of the mountain, stirring up dust as he went. The Mexican reloaded, fired over Buddy's head a couple of times for good measure, picked the rifle off the ground and strapped it across his back.

The Kid climbed out of the juniper and stood up. I followed. "*Que tal, Flaco!*" he said.

The Mexican turned around with no trace of surprise in his flinty eyes at seeing the Kid or me. "*Que tal, Greñas!*" They spoke to each other in rapid Spanish. "Did you see that guy dance?"

"I saw him pee in his pants, too," the Kid said. They both laughed. "Why didn't you kill him?"

Flaco shrugged. "Then everyone would think he had the bad luck to meet a smuggler. Now he will know and they will know better than to shoot at lobos. When will you return to the Sierra Madre?" he asked the Kid. He looked at me and a motion that resembled a smile crossed his skinny lips.

"Who knows?" answered the Kid.

"Till then," Flaco said. He stuck his rifle into the saddle scabbard, climbed on the horse, gave it a kick and headed south.

"'*Ta luego,*" said the Kid.

We watched him ride off and disappear beyond the oak-shadowed bend.

"*Mira,* Chiquita." The Kid pointed toward a place further south where the path curved around the peaks and was exposed. It took a minute to find the lobo, whose fur blended into the dusty background. He was running with a motion that was quick and fluid as the ripples in a river. He turned his head, looked back once and kept on running. The lobo was a symbol, one of the last of his kind in the wild, but also an individual that wanted to eat, live, reproduce, run.

"*Ponte trucha,*" said the Kid, which means be quick, wary, make like a trout.

"Run, lobo," said I, "run, lobo, run."

Here is an excerpt from

THE LIES THAT BIND
Judith Van Gieson

Published by HarperCollins*Publishers*.

I took the high road from Taos, speeding on the straightaways, hugging the curves, dropping a thousand feet from Talpa to Nambe. The low road follows the Rio Grande. El Camino Alto, the high road, is the forest path; I was in the mood for trees and green. The cumulonimbus billowed in the big western sky, the sun reached deep into Carson National Forest and made every pine needle shimmer. A raven landed on the yellow line, flapped its wings and flew away. The tank was full of gas; the radials gripped the road. For the moment me, my Japanese import, and the highway were one. For the moment I could almost believe that nature's laws didn't apply to me, that I'd never grow old, never get fat, never have to stop to buy gas or pee, never wake up in the night and turn on "Love Connection," never drink Cuervo Gold, smoke Marlboros, or mix up a batch of Jell-o shots ever again. I'd been in northern Rio Arriba County, the lawless county, to fight a custody battle and I'd won. The tape that spins messages in the back of my brain spun. "You've got the power," it said.

It was the harvest season, the time of year when red chile ristras drip from the eaves, when you get rid of the old and are dying to make way for the new. I cruised through the high mountain villages of Penasco, Las Trampas, and Truchas, where time stopped a couple of hundred years ago and they still speak Cervantes Spanish, where the air is a cool clear stream, where stone houses mark one edge of the road and mountain dropoffs the other. Take a curve wide here and you'll end up in a living room or the cumulonimbus.

I kept my hands on the wheel, my mind on the road, and turned south on 84 at Nambe. In Pojoaque I passed the Indian restaurant that serves the best chalupa compuesta in Santa Fe County but I didn't pull in; carne adovada burritos were waiting at home. At the Santa Fe Opera the road began to rise again. It was late fall and purple astors and yellow chamisa bloomed in the ditches beside the road. In the far distance the tip of Santa Fe Baldy was covered with snow, its lower elevations streaked with gold. At seventy-five hundred feet, La Villa Real de Santa Fe de San Francisco de Assisi opened up before me like a jewel box spilling precious stones. It was late afternoon and the lights were twinkling on, one by one. I dropped down alongside the white crosses of the National Cemetery, cut across town on St. Francis, and turned south on I-25 which follows the path of El Camino Real, the royal road, that once linked old Mexico to new.

Between Santa Fe and Albuquerque I lost another two thousand feet. Out here in the lower elevations, the land that trees forgot, it's down to basics: sky, rocks, dirt, distance. There are few wildflowers on this stretch of lonesome highway and only two distinct seasons—lots of wind and none. Fall is no wind, when the dirt stays put and tumbleweeds settle down and get an address. It was twilight, the hour, some say, between the dog and the wolf. The sun lit a fire over the Jemez. The southern sky got dark enough that Sirius came out and Venus, too. In fifty miles I'd be home. The Kid would be at my apartment, waiting in the living room or my bed.

I pulled a cassette from the glove compartment and popped it in the tape deck. Van Morrison singing about "The Days Before Rock 'N Roll," the days before America woke up from its sexual, sensual slumber. He named the early rockers: Fats, Ray Charles, Jerry Lee Lewis, Little Richard, Elvis, the guys whose songs come out of the radio at night from places like Harlingen, Texas, and Tulsa, Oklahoma, to stab you with memories. There were women in the early days of rock 'n roll, too, but not often on the radio and not on this tape. Van Morrison's heroes were all men. I remembered a singer I saw a couple of years ago in L.A., a big black woman rocking her way into middle age without missing a beat, but I couldn't remember her name. Two short words and the first one began with an "E." That was it.

The tape played out in Bernalillo. Night fell and Venus and Sirius got lost in Albuquerque's ambient fluorescent glow. I turned off the interstate at Montgomery, got caught at a red light. It happened to be Halloween, el dia del muerto, when children dress up and pretend to be whatever they're not. A bunch of tricksters and clowns crossed the street, carrying their loot and their cap guns in their hands on their way to a party in the Alameda School playground. Some kids playing tag beneath the playground lights cast long shadows. A blindfolded pirate was "it" and was trying to tag someone else by the sound of a voice. "Marco," the kid yelled. "Polo," the other kids answered. It's a game that is usually played in swimming pools in the summer. Marco Polo is the background noise of summer, if you live in a complex with kids and a swimming pool. The pirate lunged at a bunch of grapes, the grapes sidestepped, the pirate fell on his face.

The light turned green, and I stepped on the gas. Three more stoplights and I was home. The Kid, my lover and friend, had let himself in and was sitting on my bed, drinking Tecate and watching football on TV. Realizing recently that in a woman's life TV functioned like romance novels, to induce sleep, I'd recently moved mine to the foot of the bed.

"Hi, Kid," I said, sitting down on the bed beside him.

"Hola, Chiquita." He gave me a kiss.

"You're watching football?"

"Yeah."

"Why?"

"It's Monday night." He shrugged. "Why not?"

The function of TV in a man's life is football. I'd always

thought that one advantage to having a Latin American lover is that they are not as obsessed with brute sports as American men. The Kid's game—soccer—is more delicate and subtle. The players aren't padded like gorillas either, which makes it more fun to watch. The Kid has long, powerful soccer legs that were outstanding in shorts and not bad stretched out in jeans on my bed either. He'd been playing since he was a boy in Argentina and knew how to keep the ball in the air all afternoon if he wanted to. I watched him sometimes on the playing fields at Arroyo del Oso bouncing the ball off his thighs and his head.

I made myself comfortable, picked up the remote and zapped off the TV.

"I was watching the game, Chiquita," the Kid said.

"I hate football," said I.

"I want to see if the Cowboys win."

"It's a replay. The score is in the paper."

"That's not the same as watching."

"I won," I said. So what if it wasn't the Supreme Court—Ramona Chavez would get to keep her daughter and I *had* won. In Rio Arriba County, too, where the law doesn't win that often.

"Good. I'm happy for you. Can I watch the game now?"

"No." I held tight to the remote.

The look he gave me was semi-annoyed, but he was getting my drift. Power, it has been said, is the greatest aphrodisiac and absolute power turns on absolutely. So does only a little bit. "You want to do that?" the Kid asked me.

"Yup."

"Now?"

"Right now."

"Okay," he said.

Later we got up and ate the carne adovada burritos he'd brought. As usual these days there were two extras in the bag with no hot sauce. "For La Bailarina?" I asked, mentioning his favorite lost cause.

"Claro," said the Kid.

While he took them outside to the parking lot I got ready for bed.

"I think it's going to rain soon," he said when he came back in.

"Rain? In October?"

He shrugged. "I think so."

As soon as we got into bed the thunder cracked and drops began to pelt the window. Rainy nights are one of life's great pleasures, especially when you're in your bed. We don't get many of them in the Duke City and hardly ever in October. I thought about the raindrops pounding the tin roof of the car that sheltered La Bailarina in the parking lot, but I didn't feel guilty because I knew that even if the Kid had tried to coax her inside, she wouldn't have come. The parking lot was where she chose to be—on the outside but near enough to be looking in. She'd stay dry, I thought, but the trick-or-treaters would get soaking wet. It would drive them indoors—the tamer ones anyway. The troublemakers would still be out there. The Kid's breathing got slow and regular as he drifted into sleep. I punched his shoulder before he wandered too far down that lonesome highway.

"You awake, Kid."

"Umm," he mumbled.

"I want to ask you something."

"Digame."

"Do you think I'd be any happier if I had a big car? If I went to work for a prestigious firm and made real money?"

"I think you're happy just the way you are."

Lightning flashed exposing one dark peak of the Sandias then another. A large woman rocked her way across a stage in L.A.

"Etta," I said.

"Who?"

"Etta James." It was the name that had gotten lost in the back alleys of my brain, the name of the early woman rock 'n roller.

"Who's that?"

One disadvantage of having a Latino lover, and one who is younger besides, is that you don't know the same music. You can't push a button and call up the past by naming a singer or a song.

"*De nada*," I said. "Forget it."

*   *   *

When the alarm went off at seven thirty, my first thought was that Eddie Chavez had tested the law and I had won. My second thought was that I had the power all over again. "You awake, Kid," I whispered. He wasn't but I kissed his shoulder and woke him. After that we slept again until the sun burst through the drapes and landed on my face. The red numbers on the digital clock flashed eight forty-five. "Shit," I said, sitting upright. "I'll be late for my nine o'clock."

The Kid jumped out of bed, climbed into his jeans and T-shirt and shook his curls into place. I staggered into and out of the shower, put on some boring lawyer's clothes and combed my hair. No time for breakfast sopapaillas or red zinger tea.

He waited in the living room for me. I kissed him goodbye, opened the door, stepped into La Vista's hallway and found myself staring down ninety pounds of disapproving mother.

The sun had crept in through an open archway and was picking out the stains on the indoor/outdoor carpet and highlighting the cracks in the peeling stucco. The woman stood in front of my door with a finger poised to press the buzzer. About five feet two, she balanced carefully on her high-heeled shoes. Her purse was suspended from a gold chain and she clutched it to her side with a pointed elbow. Her sprayed-in-place hairdo was the color of a hard frost. She wore a powder blue suit with gold buttons and navy blue trim. Her eyes behind her contacts were a critical blue. They implied that good grooming and designer clothes gave her the right to decide who was right or wrong. I hadn't even left my apartment yet but I was already in her wrong. While she'd been drinking her morning tea, the Kid and I had been getting laid. Our just-had-sex aura gave us away. She knew we'd been doing it. We knew that she knew and she knew that we knew. She looked at us, we looked back. Disapproval and sex were thick as the dust in La Vista's hallway.

"Are you Neil Hamel?" she asked.

"Yup."

"The . . . attorney?" An attorney, her tone implied, didn't have sex in the morning, or at any time of day or night with someone who is younger, darker, and better looking. Unless, of course, the attorney was a man.

"My office is on Lead," I replied. I was prepared to add but don't bother coming because wills are not my cup of tea and neither are you, but she spoke first.

She took a deep breath, aligned her vertebrae, clutched her purse, cleared her throat. "The police accuse me of killing Justine Virga," she said.

S he'd gotten my attention. The phone started ringing inside my apartment telling me I was late for my appointment. I already knew that so I let it ring. I don't do wills, but I do handle murder cases when I can get them, and she looked like the rare suspect who could afford to pay. "Tell me about it," I said.

She looked around La Vista's hallway at the cracks in the stucco and the closed doors that might be concealing eavesdroppers. Her eyes lingered suspiciously on the Kid like he was a street dog who'd been trying to get into her trash. While she scrutinized him from top to bottom, his uncombed mop of hair, his T-shirt and jeans, she tightened her grip on her purse. My lover and my hallway did not please her, but if she thought I was going to invite her into my apartment and let her disapprove of that, too, she was wrong.

The Kid got her message. "I go now, Chiquita," he said, his grammar clunkier and his accent thicker than it had been in recent memory.

"Bueno." I kissed him again. "See you tonight?"

"Sure. Hasta luego," he said to me. To the woman he added with exaggerated Mexican politeness, "Buenos dias.

Mucho gusto." There's a fine line between politeness and insult and Mexicans know how to walk it. Actually, the Kid's Spanish wasn't Mexican or New Mexican either. It was South American, closer to European Spanish, but the subtleties were wasted on the woman and so was the gusto. She didn't bother to answer the Kid and he didn't waste his time waiting. He tossed his head and walked down the hallway. I watched his long legs turn the corner and listened to the phone ringing. It had become obvious I wasn't going to answer it or ask my visitor in either, but just in case she had any doubts, I inserted my key into the dead bolt and snapped it shut. The woman hesitated and then she said, "Could you give me a ride home? We can talk there."

"Where's your car?" I asked.

"The police took it."

It had the sound of vehicular homicide, a common enough form of murder in New Mexico where a car is a loaded weapon, too.

"How did you get here?" I asked.

"Taxi."

"Why didn't you ask the driver to wait?"

"Because I wanted to talk to you."

"All right," I said, "I'll take you home, but first I need to know who you are and why you came to me."

"I am Martha Conover."

It had a familiar ring, but I couldn't place her.

"You know my daughter," she continued. "Cynthia Reid."

That was it. Cindy and I went to high school together in Ithaca, New York. Martha Conover had been widowed and was the rare single mother back then, I remembered. It gave her full responsibility for Cindy and she took it seriously. She was older than the other mothers—older than mine anyway—and conspicuous by her presence in her daughter's life. She was into real estate investment and seemed to have a need in those days that only real estate could fill. When Cindy got knocked up by Emilio Velasquez, a Spanish exchange student, Martha wouldn't let her marry him. Cindy had the baby. Emilio joined the army and went to Vietnam. A few years later Cindy married Whitney J. Reid, III, a man Martha approved of who was about ten years older and whose political views, even back then, were to the right of Attila the Hun. Whit took on Cindy's child and people thought she was lucky to get him. I wondered if she still thought that, if she'd ever thought that. Last I'd heard they were living in Phoenix. She'd written me once to tell me her mother had moved to Albuquerque and to suggest I look her up, but I didn't. Martha hadn't approved of me when I was in high school—I was Cindy's hippie friend— which made me wonder what she was doing at my doorstep now. Did she think a license to practice law had made me respectable?

I led the way across the parking lot to my yellow Nissan which was loaded with bumper stickers from the previous owner, stickers I'd been meaning to scrape off but hadn't yet. McDonald's recycled brown bags decomposed slowly in the compost heap the floor on the passenger side had become. The files from the Chavez case were sitting on the seat. I put the files in the trunk, picked the litter off the floor, took it to the dumpster and dumped it in. I got in my side, Martha Conover got in the other. She straightened her back, placed her purse square in her lap and fastened her seat belt with a metallic click.

This wasn't exactly my living room, but it was as close as *she* was going to get. Here I was ready to talk and before we went any further there were some things I wanted to know like when, where, how, and who. "When did this supposed homicide take place?" I asked.

"Last night around ten fifteen the police say." Martha peered around her as if the other cars had ears. I continued my line of questioning.

"Where?"

"In the road at Los Cerros, the apartment complex I own and live in."

She was doing all right with her investments; Los Cerros was one of the largest apartment complexes in town. "How?"

"The police say I ran her over."

"What do you say?"

"I hit a speed bump. I was going too fast and I hit a speed bump." Her blue eyes flashed at me. She spun a diamond and sapphire ring around on her finger.

"Were there any witnesses?"

"No."

"The A.P.D. had to have some reason to impound your car."

"There was a dent in the front bumper."

Was there any blood, I wondered, hair, fibers? I'd get a chance to ask the D.A.'s office if and when I took the case. There was another question that always needs to be asked when motor vehicles are involved. "Were you drinking?"

"I had two martinis at the A.A.U.W. meeting," she replied. "That's all."

"Did the police take a Breathalyzer?" I asked.

"I wouldn't let them." Her eyes were defiant and proud of it, but there's a fine line between pride and stupidity and it looked to me like she'd crossed it. Refusing to take a Breathalyzer was a mistake that meant an automatic suspension of her license for a year.

"You're lucky they didn't put you in jail," I said. She shrugged as if to imply she wasn't the kind of woman who got sent to jail. "Didn't the police read you your rights?"

"Yes."

"You should have called me last night before you said anything to them."

"I wanted to discuss it with Whit and Cynthia before I called anybody."

I had one more question. "Who was Justine Virga?"

"She was once my grandson Michael's girlfriend," Martha Conover said.

"You knew her?" When the accused knows the victim (and they do eighty-six percent of the time) it puts a different spin on things.

"Years ago. Can we go now?"

I turned the key in the ignition and backed the Nissan out of its numbered space. "Los Cerros is on . . . ," Martha began.

"I know where Los Cerros is." In the Heights. Those who

have money in Albuquerque escape to the valley or the higher elevations while the rest of us got stuck in the middle.

Martha kept her silence and I thought about what I had to work with, a woman who'd drunk too much and refused to cooperate with the police, a dent in a car, a dead girlfriend. It made me wish I'd kept my nine o'clock.

I found my way to Los Cerros, turned in, and let Martha Conover direct me through a maze of two-story Mediterranean-style stucco buildings with tile roofs and grounds that were carefully landscaped and automatically watered. The speed bumps kept my pace to a boring five miles per hour. A couple of Hispanic guys were trimming the shrubs. The lower part of the complex had ramps leading into the buildings indicating the handicapped lived there, which could well have been a condition for getting a building permit. The middle section allowed children and a couple of them raced their toy cars down the sidewalk screaming. We drove past a swimming pool, a putting green carpeted with green fuzz and an empty tennis court. The road climbed sharply, the apartment buildings turned into town houses and the children disappeared. This was where the more desirable tenants, the singles, childless couples and retirees, lived. A couple of them were hanging around a bank of mailboxes (which also had a tile roof) because they needed their social security checks or because they liked the mailman. The older you get, the bigger the role the mailman plays in your life.

"Go faster here," Martha ordered, "I want to show you what happened." I don't usually obey orders, but I was curious to see how she'd present her case and no one else was in the road so I put the pedal to the floor. The speed bump was painted yellow, about six inches high and hard as a wall. I'd only reached twenty-five by the time we hit it, but that was fast enough. Every bone in my body rattled. The frame on the Nissan shook. A piece of the muffler fell off.

"See," said Martha Conover.

"See what?" I replied.

"A body wouldn't feel hard like that," she said. "What I hit was that speed bump."

She may have convinced herself but she hadn't convinced me. "Over five miles an hour anything you hit feels hard," I replied.

"I was driving a Buick," she said.

"Um," said I.

She directed me to her place at the very top of Los Cerros. It had a hundred-mile view, the kind of view that makes you want to think the big thoughts or earn the big bucks it takes to pay for it. We walked down the sidewalk that led from Martha's parking space to her town house. The grounds were impeccable, the walls of the town houses freshly stained, and there were no cobwebs in the corners. Martha, I figured, didn't do that kind of work herself, but whoever did took pride in it. She turned the key in her lock and let me in. Her town house smelled of Lemon Pledge and was the kind of neat that made me long for La Vista. The carpet was pink pile and didn't have a hair on it. The polished furniture had spindly little legs. The sofa was upholstered in flowered chintz. Ivy in a brass pot sat on the coffee table. The drapes were drawn to keep out the long and dusty view. It was the kind of living room they do well back East where the view is limited to a lawn and the trees at the end of it, ladylike and formal, expensive but comfortable. Martha seemed to be one of those people who take the East with them wherever they go. She offered me a cup of tea.

"Do you have any red zinger?" I asked.

"What's that?"

"Never mind," I said.

While she made her tea I called my office to tell my secretary, Anna, what she already knew, that I'd missed my nine o'clock.

Martha brought the teapot into the living room, sat on the sofa and poured the tea into a china cup translucent enough to see her fingers through. She took one spoon of sugar, one slice of lemon.

I took out my yellow legal pad and put it in my lap. "All right," I said. "Tell me exactly what happened."

"When I left the A.A.U.W. meeting at ten it was pouring rain. It was ten fifteen when I got home. After I hit the speed bump I parked, came inside, and went to bed. I fell asleep and woke up when the police rang the doorbell."

"What time was that?"

"I don't know. I'd been asleep, but I don't know for how long. It seemed like a bad dream. Men in uniform were standing at my door telling me Justine was dead and it was my fault. They made me go outside in the rain and look at the body. I hadn't seen Justine for three years but I recognized her."

"Did you identify her for the police?"

"No. They already knew who she was. They showed me my car with the dents in the fender and the hood." She clutched her hands tight in her lap and looked right at me while she said this. Her eyes didn't wander to the left or the right, the way the eyes of a person who was either guilty or had a guilty conscience might have. "When they left I called Whit and Cindy and they came over."

"They came over here?" Phoenix was five-hundred miles away the last time I'd checked.

"They're living here now in a house I own at Los Verdes Meadows, the golf-course development on—"

"I know where it is. When did they move to Albuquerque?"

"About a month ago. Whit is in real estate and business has not been good in Arizona. They'd been out to dinner. They were in bed when I called but they got up and came over. They suggested I call you, but it was the middle of the night by then. In the morning no one answered at your office and your line was busy at home, so I looked up your address, got a cab and came over."

"Why didn't Cindy come with you?"

"I didn't ask her to." Martha put her teacup down on the coffee table.

"How is she?" I asked.

"All right. It's been difficult since Michael died, but . . ."

"Michael died?"

"Three years ago. He was her only son, my only grandson."

"I'm sorry. I didn't know that." That's what happens when you don't keep up with your friends. "How did it happen?"

"In a car accident. Cynthia and Whit want to get together with you, and I suggested to them that you all come here for dinner tomorrow. Well, are you going to represent me?"

Was I? She was my old friend's mother, but we hadn't liked each other back then and it looked like we weren't going to like each other much now. On the other hand, homicide is more interesting than real estate and divorce and she obviously could afford to pay. "I'll require a retainer," I said.

"I'll pay it."

"All right," I said. "I'll talk to the D.A.'s office. You do realize that refusing to take a Breathalyzer means an automatic suspension of your license for a year?"

"The police told me that."

"I'll be in touch," I said.

"Dinner will be here tomorrow night at seven," she replied. "Why don't you come at six so we'll have a chance to talk."

"I'll check my calendar."

I drove out of Los Cerros in slow motion taking the speed bumps at a pace the Nissan's aging shock absorbers could handle, wondering who the D.A. would assign to this case and why Cindy Reid hadn't called me when she moved to town. I saw a man putting on the green. It was a warm enough day to swim and kids were playing Marco Polo in the pool. "Marco," one kid yelled. "Polo," another one answered. A dark-haired, heavy-set guy in a wheelchair was rolling across the tennis court. He stopped and stared at me as I drove by.